◊◊◊◊◊◊◊◊◊◊◊◊◊◊*THE MAN WITH NO SHADOW*

THE MAN WITH

NO SHADOW

STEPHEN MARLOWE

PRENTICE-HALL, INC., *Englewood Cliffs, N.J.*

10 9 8 7 6 5 4 3 2 1

Library of Congress Cataloging in Publication Data

Marlowe, Stephen
  The man with no shadow.

  1. Franco Bahamonde, Francisco, 1892–   —
Fiction. I. Title.
PZ4.M3495Man [PS3563.A674] 813′.5′4 73–21668
ISBN 0–13–548321–2

For
ROBIN
porque ella quiere ser figura

Only a dead man escapes envy,
for he casts no shadow.
—*Spanish proverb*

Spain and Francisco Franco are, of course, real. But this is a work of fiction, and in these pages they, as well as all other events and characters portrayed, are necessarily drawn not as they exist in life, but as they exist in the author's imagination.

—S. M.

◇◇◇◇◇◇◇◇◇◇◇◇◇*THE MAN WITH NO SHADOW*

1

◇◇

He woke that morning early, a small, potbellied old man in rumpled wool pajamas, disturbed that he had dreamed, in the cold pre-dawn darkness, about Hitler.

A chill November wind blew down from the Guadarrama Mountains to the north, and as he shut the window the palsy started in his right hand. He grasped it hard in his left hand and could still feel the fluttering, as if it wanted to escape the sagging ancient flesh of the arm, the body.

Why should he dream about Hitler?

My God, the old man thought, more than thirty years ago. Hitler long since dead by his own hand in a bunker in Berlin, his opera buffa Italian ally dead, hung from a meathook in a

1

square in Milan. Was the dream a premonition? Nobody lives forever.

Still, he had the stubborn Spaniard's ability to survive. Even Hitler had sensed that, ranting and threatening, in the dream and at their meeting in Hendaye across the French frontier, after France had fallen. They met not in the Führer's railroad car, as the official reports of the meeting had it, but at the Hotel Irritzina, in a small conference room, the best the hotel had to offer, with their interpreters hovering near like the confidential banderilleros of two bullfighters dickering over which bulls should be paired.

"I can't take Gibraltar from the sea," Hitler had said.

No answer necessary. No one could take Gibraltar from the sea, not while the red ensign of the Royal Navy sailed the Mediterranean.

"You have roads. You have rails, General." General, not Generalissimo. "You owe me this. I won your war for you."

"You trained the Condor Legion, a few Stuka pilots. Spain won its own war."

Luncheon had ended. In the dream he remembered the meal. A Basque omelette, some vegetables, orange juice. No meat, no wine. A plate of sweets that Hitler had gobbled in bursts of nervous frustration, crumbs sprinkling his jacket.

The Führer had strange tastes, and no manners. He got up and paced back and forth with that odd twitchy walk of his, in jackboots and dark brown whipcord decorated with the predictable hooked cross.

"Napoleon," the Spaniard droned in his shrill monotone, "wanted to take Portugal from behind. Now you want to take Gibraltar from behind. Napoleon stayed a long time in Spain."

"You will open the frontier," Hitler screamed, in Hendaye and in the dream.

A stretch, an elaborate yawn, while the Führer's dark eyes

2

studied him and then darted this way and that, as if seeking a way out. He looked up at those eyes and stood with a calculated slowness.

"You must forgive me, Herr Hitler. My siesta."

"Your what?"

"A simple Spanish custom. Sensible. We Spaniards are a simple people."

Later, the Führer would tell an aide he would rather have all his teeth yanked than meet again with that simple Spaniard.

A small bow, and then the doors had opened and the Generalissimo went upstairs to his suite. He stayed there two hours. He did not sleep. He did not even undress. He kept Hitler waiting.

When he came down, Hitler said: "I could open the frontier myself."

"What's the hurry? In a hundred years we'll all be bald."

"I could keep you here in occupied France," Hitler threatened in a harsh whisper. "What would happen to your government then?"

The Generalissimo said nothing.

Hitler ranted for nine hours. The destiny of the German people. The corruption of the British. The decadence of the French. He offered to turn Gibraltar over to Spain after the war.

Finally the Generalissimo said: "I have to go back. We'll talk about it another time."

The Führer had other business, and the Generalissimo knew it. A few weeks later Nazi Germany invaded Russia. A few years later Russia repaid the visit, and Hitler shot Eva Braun and took cyanide in the Führerbunker.

The Generalissimo shaved carefully with his left hand. His jaw sagged open. He tried to clamp it shut. It remained slack. His right hand quivered while he dressed. No uniform. A dou-

3

ble-breasted suit and a Basque beret clapped over his head. Lately, the Basque beret had created a stir. The Basque separatists had speculated about it. The cabinet would speculate this morning, when he removed the beret and set it to one side on the green baize of the long table. He wore the beret because his head felt the cold.

In a hundred years we'll all be bald.

He looked at his watch. He would keep them waiting half an hour. He went into Carmen's bedroom across the hall of the second floor of the Pardo Palace, nine miles northeast of Madrid. The drapes were drawn, his wife still sleeping. He did not disturb her. He stood at the window and parted the drapes long enough to see that three black Mercedes limousines were already parked outside, their chauffeurs smoking, shivering in the cold. Frost sparkled on the ground. Winter had come early this year to Europe's highest capital.

The first blow struck him from behind, at the base of the skull. He staggered and clutched the windowsill. Later, weeks later when he began to remember things, he would recall whirling, as if to defend himself against an attacker. There was nobody. The blow to the back of his head, what had seemed a blow, had receded to a dull ache. He looked at Carmen's face, serene in sleep, serene in the One True Faith which he tried to share but did not really share, and shrugged. Another headache. Another one of those damned headaches. Must see Dr. Caballero, he thought. He knew he would not see Dr. Caballero. What had Caballero been able to do for his palsied hand, his sagging mouth? Like most Spaniards, he felt ill at ease with doctors. Or lawyers. Or scientists. They knew more about a thing than you did. You couldn't argue with them. What was the sense of consulting someone you couldn't argue with?

The second blow struck him in the same place, at the base of the skull, as he sat at the head of the conference table and

4

listened to the Foreign Minister's arguments for taking Gibraltar. Hitler thirty years ago and in the dream, and now his own Foreign Minister. Everybody wanted to take Gibraltar.

He wanted to cry out against the terrible pain, but grasped his right hand in his left and made no sound.

"Well then," the Foreign Minister was saying, "we can carve a new province, part of Cádiz, part of Huelva, and call it Gibraltar. Provisional capital, Algeciras. Provisional. See what I mean?"

Admiral Rojas Millan, the President and day-to-day ruler under the eighty-year-old Generalissimo, nodded approvingly, puffy jowls quivering.

Reactionary old goat, as good for Spain as a cold Andalucian winter that would chase all the tourists away and destroy the citrus crops. The Admiral would bear watching, he thought, and that was when the third blow struck, and the fourth. He half rose from his chair. He was all pain then, and a reeling, sinking, everything-going-away feeling.

The chair overturned as he fell sideways, heavily, to the floor, like a bull after a perfect sword thrust.

Francisco Franco had just suffered a massive cerebral hemorrhage.

The bullfighter sat in a café on Calle Larios in Málaga, nursing his fourth Carlos Primero and his fourth cup of what Spaniards call café solo, coffee alone, black as tar, bitter as wormwood, but warming. It was the hour before dawn and, three hundred miles north, in the Pardo Palace outside Madrid, the first blow would shortly strike Francisco Franco from behind.

Heavy in the breast pocket of the bullfighter's jacket was a puntillo, a broad short dagger, the kind used in the bullring to sever the bull's spine when the bull refuses to let the sword or, after the failure of the sword, the descabello, to kill him.

The café should have closed hours ago. The corrugated metal shutter was down, the sweeper had swept the floor three times, the one remaining waiter leaned against the bar, head down on his folded arms. The sweeper was an old man, and wished only for bed. The waiter was younger, and thought about the warmth of his woman's body. Neither one would ask the bullfighter to leave. They admired the bullfighter, and loved him and hated him, and they would remain as long as he did.

The bullfighter thought of death. He had killed three thousand bulls in twenty years, for the love and the hatred of men like the sweeper and the waiter. He would kill no more bulls, except for two next May, the last two bulls of his life.

In half an hour he will kill a man. He will execute a man the way a stubborn bull is executed in the plaza de toros, with the broad-bladed puntillo.

A bull is hide and muscle and bone. A man is skin and muscle and bone. A bull has no soul, but sometimes he has heart, much heart. Perhaps men have souls.

This man he will kill has no soul. He has a gray-green uniform and a machine pistol slung over his shoulder and a shiny black patent leather hat. Or maybe he does have a soul. A patent leather soul.

The bullfighter got up. "Good night," he told the waiter. The waiter had seen him here in the pre-dawn hours before, afflicted with sleeplessness. The waiter would not connect him with the death of the patent leather soul.

"Good morning, maestro," the waiter corrected him, almost smiling.

The bullfighter waited while the shutter was partially raised, and he ducked under it and outside. It was raining. He could smell the sea in the wind-whipped rain. He could feel the weight of the puntillo.

Civil Guards walk in pairs for protection. They rule rural Spain and the provincial cities. A virgin could walk in the middle of the night in safety from one end of Málaga to the other, thanks to the Civil Guards.

Sometimes they are overzealous. Sometimes the marching in pairs with slung machine pistols is not enough. Sometimes they kill people.

He has a woman, the telephone said. He has a woman, matador. Matador: killer. Of bulls, and soon of a man. He has a woman in an apartment on the second alley to the left off Calle Granada after you leave the plaza. He is there most nights, after work. He comes alone. He leaves alone. Not in uniform. Would you recognize him? Oh, I would recognize him, the bullfighter told himself. I would most certainly recognize him. I would recognize him in Málaga or Madrid or Santiago de Compostela, or in hell. The voice on the telephone was no voice he recognized.

He went, at first, just to see, a rehearsal of an act he would never commit. The patent leather soul came out of that alley, all right. He went, and went again. Every Monday, Wednesday, and Friday, at dawn, out of the house on the alley off Calle Granada came the patent leather soul. He never varied the pattern. He fucked by the clock and the calendar.

The bullfighter walked quickly along Larios, away from the sea, jacket collar up against the rain. The street was deserted. The rain hit hard and bounced. He walked faster, reached the broad plaza at the head of Larios, and entered the narrow Calle Granada. Second callejón, second alley on the left. He stepped into a doorway and waited, the puntillo in his hand.

If anyone sees me, then it is over. It is finished and done with. The most famous face in Spain, after the Caudillo.

But no one would see him. He had rehearsed this killing six times already. No one else passed at that hour.

Maybe the Civil Guard would wait out the rain in the woman's apartment, he thought suddenly. He did not like the thought.

Then he heard footsteps. He saw the Civil Guard coming out of the alley, through the silver rain under a streetlight and then closer, a darkness silhouetted against the silver, whistling a paso doble.

A bull dies, well-killed, and the bullfighter circles the ring, a grin on his face, holding high the bloody ear. This was not the same.

Then he saw a face, what was left of a face after three machine pistol slugs have stitched across it, low to the left of the jaw, beside the nose, high on the right side of the forehead.

He took two steps out of the doorway as the Civil Guard walked past, whistling.

A matador does not use the puntillo for killing. A matador uses the downward-tipped sword, or the sword with the cross-bar back of the point, the descabello. A bullring lackey uses the puntillo, one quick thrust behind the great head of the fallen but not yet dead bull to sever the spinal cord. A deft, artful dispatcher of moribund bulls, dressed in white.

"Look, you," the bullfighter said softly. "You know who I am?"

Faintly the bullfighter could see a widening of the eyes in the broad face.

"It was a mistake, matador," said the Civil Guard.

"Yes, of course. A mistake."

The Civil Guard looked to right and left, and behind. He crouched, and a hand darted for the pocket of the raincoat.

You stand watching, using the red serge killing cape to guide the bull, until the forehooves are planted just so in the sand of the arena. Then you go in over the horns, giving the bull a chance to kill you as you kill the bull. It is called the moment of truth. Anything else is cheating.

The hand emerged with a revolver, and the bullfighter heard a click as the empty chamber rotated clear of the firing pin. Then he caught the arm and twisted it, spinning the man and pulling the arm up between his shoulder blades. The Civil Guard gasped and hunched over, head down, back of neck exposed.

When the spine can be severed, half a ton of fighting bull dies like turning off a light.

For an instant he could not do it.

He saw the face again, stitched with bullets.

He put the dagger in, at the back of the neck, and there was a convulsive jerk and the revolver clattered on the pavement as he dropped the dead man.

A blinding light flashed in his face.

A voice, the voice of the telephone, said: "Now, matador. Now we will talk."

2

◇◇

As all good killings should, this one at first looked as if it had been rehearsed.

The boy had wisely led the three-year-old bull into the lee of the semicircular amphitheater, a miniature bullring carved out of the face of the cliff to reduce the effect the Poniente, the west wind blowing in from the Mediterranean, would have on his red serge killing cape. He cited the bull from a distance, calling him with a gutteral "huh-huh, toro." The bull raised his massive head as the boy moved his left wrist to open the cape, and then came at a rushing gallop, tail up, tossing muscle crested with rage, horn tips ivory white under the deep blue sky of a May afternoon in Andalucía. The boy passed him twice, testing passes, and the bull followed the lure obediently.

Then the boy, wearing not a suit of lights but the traje corto, the short dark gray jacket and trousers of the south, fixed the bull in place, studying the position of the forehooves before lowering the killing cape to see that the bull obeyed. The bull did, head going down, eyes fixed on red serge, and the boy rose on his toes and profiled along the length of his arm, the downward-tipped sword an extension of the arm; and then, despite the rehearsal quality of the killing, he spoiled it all by moving too fast, crossing the cape with his left hand almost as an afterthought, driving forward hard, three quick strides and the sword went in at the killing place behind the bull's great skull, disappearing to the hilt as the horns lifted, searching, and the boy hung over them an instant before he cleared them to his own left and the bull bellowed and shuddered and fell dead.

Ricardo Diaz looked at his son, standing over the fallen bull, a smile on his handsome face, somehow not the right kind of smile, a cynical smile, and the boy was all of eighteen years old.

Maybe he had enjoyed Paris too much, Ricardo Diaz thought, maybe Paris had been a mistake. Still, not two hours off the Iberia jet in Málaga, it seemed incredible that the boy could remember the training he had received years ago, could perform as well as he had. He was an athlete, all right. But an athlete and a bullfighter are not the same thing, and Ricardo Diaz could see that on the faces of the matadors who had come to watch his son perform, despite their words of praise as one after another they slipped through the opening in the dark red wooden fence to congratulate José Carlos.

Miguel Márquez and Palomo Linares, both in their prime and fighting seventy and eighty times a year now, were if anything too lavish with their praise. They would soon fight in the same rings with José Carlos Diaz, son of that Ricardo Diaz who, four years ago at San Isidro in Madrid, where ears are awarded grudgingly, had not once but twice during the festival been awarded two ears for his work. It had never happened before and likely never would happen again, and Diaz had shocked the bullfighting world by cutting the pigtail at the end of the season. Thirty-six then and, everyone said, the best, the most complete matador since Manolete or maybe since Belmonte.

The praise of the others was more restrained. Old Antonio Buenavista, thrice retired, balding, built like a tree trunk with a belly, patted the boy's shoulder and turned away to stare down through the umbrella pines and cork trees and across the road to the Mediterranean. The other Antonio, Antonio Ordóñez, said a few words to the boy that Diaz did not hear. Ordóñez was not smiling. Diego Puerta, whose three-year-old bull had been killed for the occasion, solemnly shook José Carlos' hand and turned to make a circle of his thumb and forefinger as Ricardo Diaz came through the opening in the fence. Manuel Benítez, El Cordobés, grinned his magnet of a grin, but that was El Cordobés' style. It would be hard to stop him grinning at a funeral. Buenavista, Ordóñez, Puerta and El Cordobés would never have to enter a ring with José Carlos.

"He's much athlete," said Antonio Buenavista in his deep voice, and Ricardo Diaz accepted the statement as a diplomatic reservation of judgment by the old matador.

"How about a drink?" José Carlos said. Eighteen years old, and too damned much like his father in some ways. And not enough in others.

The drive back from Málaga International Airport had not been pleasant. Diaz had parked the Ferrari in an area reserved for buses. An attendant came over at a quick limping trot, shaking his head until he recognized the great matador, and then of course everything was fine. The limping attendant all but snapped to attention and saluted. Ricardo Diaz was the second most famous man in Spain, and he had known when to quit. The most famous man in Spain, if you could read between the lines of *ABC* or *Vanguardia,* was dying without dignity in Madrid, because he had not known when to quit. Never mind politics, Ricardo Diaz thought. Leave that to Maria Teresa. Leave that to La Quijota, exiled in Paris and, probably, these past two months, putting ideas into José Carlos' head.

Through the crowd of tourists in the international arrivals wing, through the blue-smocked porters and gray-clad customs agents and green-uniformed Civil Guards with their patent leather hats and slung machine pistols, his sharp eyes caught sight of José Carlos, young and blond as his American mother had been blond, waiting at the slowly rotating luggage conveyor.

"How was Paris?"

"I left it more or less the way I found it," said José Carlos as he lifted his leather bag from the conveyor.

They went outside together, father and son, both tall for Spaniards, the younger one fair of skin and hair and looking like a quarterback for the Texas Longhorns, the older one dark and not showing his forty years and looking like a bullfighter. One blue-eyed, the other with yellow-flecked dark brown eyes, one with an open, ingenuous American face, the other dignified but not dour, muy español, very Spanish.

"Still got the old bus, I see," José Carlos said as his father opened the Ferrari's trunk.

"It's got good blood lines," Diaz said. "I think we'll make a stud bull out of it, one of these days."

They were speaking English, as they usually did together, as if in homage to the blond beauty from Dallas who had drunk herself to death because her husband had to fight the bulls. That, among other reasons.

They followed the traffic past the garish billboards that told you how to spend your dollars and pounds and Deutschmarks and guilders in Torremolinos and Marbella. "Expected you yesterday," Ricardo Diaz said.

"You got my telegram, didn't you?"

"A lot of busy people are waiting to see what you can do."

"Let them wait."

Diaz made a right turn on the Carretera de Cádiz, four lanes of new highway that had the added advantage of bypassing the aberration that was Torremolinos, although even from the bypass they caught glimpses of the forest of high-rise hotels and apartment complexes. Traffic thinned out, and Diaz opened up the Ferrari. A BMW with German plates moved into the right lane for them, its red-faced driver staring stonily ahead. The speedometer needle hit a hundred and fifty and stayed there.

After a while José Carlos said: "I was thinking of going back to school."

"Where? The States?"

"No. Madrid."

Ricardo Diaz shut his eyes and then opened them. He saw the face with the three bullets stitched across it. The needle quivered up toward one hundred seventy kilometers an hour.

"I gather you saw Maria Teresa in Paris."

"Sure. What's wrong with that?"

"Nothing. But it would make more sense in the States. Harvard. Yale."

"I guess way down deep I'm a Spic," said José Carlos.

"Cut that out," Ricardo Diaz said. "They shut the university twice already this year. That's no way to get an education."

Lying on the ground at University City in Madrid, dead,

15

your face smashed by three slugs from a machine pistol, was no way to get an education.

"You want an education, go to the States. You want to fight the bulls, stay here."

"Oh, I'll fight the bulls. This season. I promised."

"What did you promise Maria Teresa?"

"Look, Dad. I'm not Al. Al was a different kind of guy."

"What did you promise her?"

"She did most of the talking." José Carlos flashed his quick smile. "She always does. She's coming back, she says."

"They'll throw her in jail."

José Carlos laughed. "First they'll have to find her."

"They'll find her. They'll put her in the cell next to yours."

"Mine? I'm just an apprentice bullfighter about to take his alternativa. José Carlos Diaz, El Americano. On all the pretty posters."

"Tell your Quijota she can shove her politics up her ass. Tell her I said so."

"*My* Quijota?"

Ricardo Diaz made the turn off the bypass to the coast road. He glanced left at the beaches and green shoal waters and the deep blue at the knife-edged horizon. He could see Maria Teresa, with a backpack, descending on Spain from the Pyrenees, the Civil Guards baying at her heels. She'd probably enjoy it. As she'd enjoy turning boys like José Carlos into political activists. She'd done a pretty good job on his brother.

Unless José Carlos learned that, after all, the bulls were in his blood. He'd better learn it in a hurry, Ricardo Diaz thought as they drove up the unpaved road past bark-stripped, ochre-painted cork trees to Rancho Andaluz.

Half a kilometer off the highway, the ranch was a showplace, a low, rambling, whitewashed brick building, hotel-big and usually off-season-hotel-empty, halfway between Puerto Real and Marbella. Tourists would point it out to one another: "That's Ricardo Diaz's place. You know, the great matador?"

The great matador, even before his retirement, had proven himself a disaster of a businessman. Bulls of Navarra crossed with the bigger bulls of Andalucía, and the new strain had inherited the worst traits of each. Even his friends wouldn't fight them. He had sold them for beef. After that came the import-export business, in which a man in Peru made a lot of money while Ricardo Diaz lost a lot of money. Then came the avocado trees, acres of them planted mature at enormous expense. Half of them had died, victim of a blight with a long Latin name. The remaining trees had yielded avocados with flesh as fibrous as sugar cane. The cork trees provided some income, but not much. Spain, like the rest of the world, was going plastic.

The ranch looked pretty good from the road. It looked pretty good from the bullring blasted out of the side of the hill. You couldn't see the crumbling, abandoned outbuildings.

It was only a hobby, Ricardo Diaz's jet-set friends told one another. Good old Rick's held onto his dough. Used to get fifteen, twenty thousand bucks a fight.

Good old Rick was going urbanely into debt. Like a poor hidalgo he hid the fact well. He still had the twin-engined Cessna at the Aero Club in Málaga, and the Dutch-built, teak-decked, twenty-meter motor sailer berthed at the yacht basin in Nueva Andalucía. He had the Ferrari, no longer new but maintained impeccably, and a staff of twenty at the ranch, and he would fly anywhere, any time, when Ari and Jackie or Richard and Elizabeth or anyone else suggested it. They suggested it on the average of twice a month. He had the good life, all right.

After his son had killed the bull, Ricardo Diaz led his guests into the patio between the wings of the ranch house. Bougain-

17

villea fell in purple cascades over the whitewashed brick walls. The servants, still wearing the straw and white colors of the ranch that no longer bred bulls, served Taittinger champagne and lobster and serrano ham and charcoal-grilled skewers of beef heart. Everybody was talking animatedly and nobody listening, as if to prove they were good Spaniards.

Before he saw the car, Ricardo Diaz heard the rattle of its short-stroke engine as it turned off the highway and up the steep unpaved road to the ranch. Then he saw it briefly through the grove of cork trees, an ancient battered Seiscientos dragging its cloud of dust past one wing of the ranch house to the kitchen door. In a little while one of the daughters of the ranch foreman appeared on the patio.

"The left hand," Antonio Buenavista was saying. "Teach José Carlos to use the left hand, and you'll have something."

The girl said: "A man, Don Ricardo. Something about a lottery ticket?"

Ricardo Diaz reached automatically for a cigarette and reminded himself he had given up smoking. Six months had passed since that night in Málaga. They had not contacted him. He had waited with the tension a few weeks and then had put it out of his mind. He had trained himself, as a bullfighter must, to live in the present. Past and future have little meaning for a man who faces death four and five times a week during the long hot temporada, the season of killing. He felt his face stiffen, the same drawing tight of the flesh over the cheekbones and around the mouth he'd experienced in the old days just as the toril gate opened and the bull came exploding out, the only sign of a fear he had almost learned to control.

El Cordobés laughed. "Maybe you won the fat one," he said. "The gordo can keep you in champagne for—"

Diaz cut him short with a gesture, not quite rude, and said: "Excuse me. This won't take long."

18

The man was old. He wore a gray jacket with a black mourning band on the left sleeve, and a small black beret. He doffed the beret.

"Sr. Diaz?" he said. "But yes, forgive me, maestro, the whole world knows Ricardo Diaz." The seamed, leathery face puckered in a toothless smile. Ricardo Diaz had seen that face before, a hundred times, in bullrings from San Sebastián to Valencia, the face of a Spanish peasant, timeworn, sun- and wind-scorched, shy but somehow proud.

"What's this about a lottery ticket?"

"That is what they said, maestro, in Torremolinos. To tell you it was a thing of a lottery ticket. And to give you this." The old man's gnarled hand produced a white envelope. The sad, gentle eyes crinkled. "It is a very rare place now, Torremolinos, is it not?"

Ricardo Diaz agreed that Torremolinos was a very rare place. He took the envelope. The old man's rope-soled shoes scuffed the tile floor in the hallway.

"Who gave you this, viejo?"

The gentle eyes looked away. "I run errands," the old man said. He cleared his throat and then gazed steadily at Ricardo Diaz. "It is wished that you sign for the envelope, maestro."

Ricardo Diaz took the offered paper, and a ballpoint pen, and leaned over a low walnut table to sign his name.

The old man cleared his throat again. Diaz gave him the paper with his signature on it. The old man reached into his pocket and came up with a tattered copy of *El Ruedo* and opened it to the centerfold, where Ricardo Diaz could be seen in full color, in the Las Ventas bullring in Madrid, holding aloft the two ears of the bull he had just killed.

"If I had been there," the old man sighed. "If I had seen it, the giving of two ears twice, in Madrid. Would you write your name again, maestro, for a favor? Would you write, 'To the retired Civil Guard Pedro Ramírez, who has afición'?"

The request was made gravely, and just as gravely Ricardo Diaz autographed the picture. He gave the magazine to the old man, who waited, scuffing his rope-soled shoes on the tiles again.

"Well?" Ricardo Diaz said.

"My pen, maestro."

In spite of himself, Ricardo Diaz smiled. He returned the pen. Ramírez offered his hand, and Diaz shook it.

"I hope you won in the lottery," the old man said.

Oh, I won. I won, all right, Ricardo Diaz thought as the old man left. I won the gordo. The fat one. He watched the small, battered car leave. He opened the envelope.

In it was a glossy photograph of himself. A very good likeness of Ricardo Diaz, killer of bulls, killing a man. The man was falling, having just received the puntillo in the back of his neck, and Diaz was holding the short, broad-bladed dagger at the level his neck would have been an instant before.

Diaz turned the photograph over. On the back someone had written a Madrid telephone number. Diaz took a long slow breath, shut the door and pocketed the photograph. He went back through the house to join his friends on the patio. The late afternoon sun almost blinded him, like the flashbulb on Calle Granada in Málaga, six months ago.

After the others had gone, after José Carlos had taken the Dodge wagon and driven into Torremolinos, Ricardo Diaz had three quick shots of Carlos Primero and went outside to the Ferrari. He didn't want to think, not yet.

Driving fast on the edge of control would keep him from thinking. A woman would keep him from thinking.

Machismo, he told himself wryly. A pointless display of bravery, a pointless gratification of lust. The two keystones of the Spanish male's character, Maria Teresa had once said with amused contempt, cojones in a driver's seat and cojones in bed, Juan Fangio and Don Juan, Santiago and up yours was the way she had put it.

Maybe Maria Teresa was right. He started driving.

Less than twenty minutes later, he pulled into the night-dark driveway of a villa in Benalmádena, the old Moorish town perched a thousand feet above the Mediterranean. It had been an atalaya, a watchtower, for the Moors. On a good day you could see all the way to Gibraltar and across the Med to the Rif Mountains. Now the owners of the big villas watched each other. Foreigners, mostly, but they had discovered Maria Teresa's third keystone of the Spanish character, envy. They envied Simon Beriros, a French Algerian Jew who had arrived in Benalmádena flat broke and built himself a real estate empire in that unlikely place after land values in Torremolinos had risen too high. They envied Dale Wassermann, who made a fortune with *Man of La Mancha* and who, they said, had been lucky and would never have to write again. They envied and lusted after Kate Cameron, that wheat-blond Texas beauty who made Raquel Welch look like a suffragette and who condescended to do a film every year or so, for a million and a half and a percentage of the gross.

In her late twenties, Kate Cameron had never married. And of course they whispered lesbian.

Ricardo Diaz smiled as he got out of the Ferrari. Lesbian. Of course. That was it.

Margarita opened the door for him, her teeth flashing when she recognized him.

"Muy buenas, Margarita," he said. "Is the señorita home?"

"To you, Don Ricardo? Always. And if she weren't, she would fly home like a bird. It is not my right, but you should do yourself a favor, Don Ricardo. You should marry her." Margarita blushed.

"I'll take it under advisement," Ricardo Diaz said in English.

"Don Ricardo?"

"Nothing. Tell her I'm here."

Tell her I'm lonely. Tell her I'm confused. Tell her I don't kill bulls these days, I kill people.

He waited in what Kate Cameron called the museum, fifteen hundred square feet of living room, two stories high, one wall a sweep of glass that looked out over the sea, the other three hung with canvases of Saura, Guerrero, and Joan Miró. Over the huge fireplace was a life-size portrait of Kate Cameron, painted by Picasso when Kate had lived on the Côte d'Azur. Not surrealistic at all, and the old man had been in his eighties when he painted it. He called it Demasiado, Too Much, and he had a point.

"Hello, Rick," Kate said.

He held her arms lightly and kissed her cheek, turning her head when she began to pull back and brushing her other cheek with his lips. "Both sides," he said. "Very continental."

Kate laughed. "Teach me, Rick. I'm a quick study."

She was tall, as tall as he, and as unblatantly sexy as a noble Miura bull is unblatantly brave. She wore a pale blue gold-brocaded Moroccan robe and slippers. The long wheat-blond hair hung to her waist. Her enormous blue eyes looked at him. She was broad-shouldered, even for a girl of her height, but

22

somehow not excessively so. She was long-waisted and had an awesome length of leg between the unexpectedly narrow hips and the Moroccan slippers. Her breasts, pushing against the brocaded silk, were not small, but small for the rest of her. Something subtly wrong in the construction of her, you thought at first glance, as if the bits and pieces had been fashioned for three or four different styles of beauty, but then you looked again and realized she was magnificent.

"Only in Texas," Ricardo Diaz said, and was immediately sorry. She knew his wife had been born a Texan.

"Sure, six-gun Kate, the bane of Bad Man's Gulch." She smiled nervously.

That helped the machismo too, he thought. There wasn't another man, anywhere, who would make her nervous.

"You've eaten?"

"Yes."

"Want a drink?"

"No."

"Joey's back, isn't he? Want to talk about it?" She was the only one who called José Carlos Joey.

"He's back. I don't want to talk about it."

"The generation gap comes to Spain," Kate said. "Along with Coca-Cola, TV, and the naval base at Rota. We export the strangest things."

"You export tall Texas ladies. I kind of need one tonight."

Her fingers played with the tasseled cord of the Moroccan robe. "Tonight," she said, not quite bitterly. Then she managed a smile. "Take me for a drive? I love the way you drive."

"Not now, Kate."

He caught the sadness in her eyes before she glanced in mock exasperation at the high, shadowed ceiling and said: "He doesn't want to eat, he doesn't want to drink, or talk, or drive. Let me guess."

Her bedroom was small, its walls covered with the same gold-brocaded blue as her robe, so that when you entered it, it was like entering her. More brocaded blue for the bedspread, and a single window, wrought-iron barred in Andalucian style, high up, like a monk's cell. She had lighted a candle on the vanity table.

He took her very swiftly, José Carlos gone, Maria Teresa gone, the old man with his lottery ticket gone, all of them safely away with his face in the wheat-blond hair. He hadn't even kissed her.

They lay side by side while she smoked a cigarette.

"I love you, Rick," she said. "And I'm worried about you. You've been so—"

"Let it go, Kate. I came here to get away from me."

She stubbed out the cigarette. "That's honest, but it isn't very Spanish."

"Your eyes," he said quickly in Spanish, using the stylized words of a not very imaginative street-corner flirt, "are bigger than your feet. There's a hole in heaven, so saints can look down on you and wish they were sinners. Like that?"

"Shut up, Ricardo Diaz."

Her fingertips traced the crescent-shaped scar under the right side of his rib cage. A monster of a Pablo Romero bull had done that, in Bilbao. Her fingertips touched the scar across his waist, welted, seven inches long. A Hermanos Núñez bull with a bad left eye did that, in Salamanca. She touched the other scars, the Miura one under his right arm, the second Miura low on his left thigh, the Don Manuel Benítez, high on the inside of his right thigh, when he had fought El Cordobés' lousy bulls as a favor, a horn ripping through and almost severing the femoral artery and damn near killing him.

Then she was on her knees on the bed and kissing the scars she had touched, one by one. He reached up for her, but she

24

pushed against his chest and said, "No, you stay there. Very continental. On both sides."

Later, when she was asleep, he used the phone in her dressing room. He had only been postponing it, after all.

3

◇◇◇

The lowest ranking Spanish law enforcement agency is the policía de tráfico, the traffic police. They wear dark blue uniforms trimmed with white and white pith helmets. When they stop a motorist to write a ticket, they will first salute smartly and offer an apologetic smile. The platforms from which they direct traffic at busy intersections are, in hot weather, shaded by large colorful beach umbrellas, and when the traffic becomes snarled they will often climb down to head for the nearest café and let the motorized anarchists hurl their noisy little cars at one another. They carry sidearms in glossy white leather holsters, the flaps snapped shut so much of the time that many Spaniards say the holsters are stuffed with paper or handkerchiefs, like the athletic supports of certain bullfighters.

A cut above the tráficos are the policía armada, the armed police in their gray, red-trimmed uniforms and visored garrison caps. The policía armada are called out to quiet an obstreperous drunk or break up a barroom brawl or disperse an illegal meeting. They look like ushers in movie theaters or doormen of first-class but not deluxe hotels. They are very good at parades.

The asaltos, the riot police in their black uniforms, are another matter. When they are called out it generally means trouble. They are not called out very often.

The Civil Guards are not called out at all. They are simply there, like sidewalk flirts and blind lottery-ticket sellers and knife-sharpeners with their trilling pipes and camera-toting tourists. They are a quasi-military organization, and because the Spaniards fear them they make jokes about them. They make jokes about Franco too. The most common ornament in a Spanish car is a little Civil Guard doll, dressed in gray-green with a tricorn patent leather hat, smiling as he dangles in the rear window. If you are foolish enough to strike or even insult a Civil Guard, you will probably be hauled before a court-martial. It is a military, not a civil offense, and eight to ten years in a military prison, with no packages from home, is the usual penalty.

The Public Order Police wear no uniforms. They compile dossiers on leftist university students, Basque and Catalán separatists, illegal labor activists, left-wing priests, and troublemakers in general. They are more educated and more prone to corruption than the Civil Guards, who look on them with mild contempt. They are subtle, patient infiltrators of the illegal left, and the Civil Guards prefer a more direct approach.

All Spain's police organizations but one—even, nominally, the Civil Guards—take their orders from the Director General of Security, Colonel Eduardo Santo Domingo. A large stocky man with shaven head, great liquid dark eyes, and a pursed rosebud of a mouth, he is just past fifty and wears dark suits tailored for him on Savile Row in London. A dedicated man, he is frustrated by two challenges to his authority. The first involves a matter of protocol. Colonel Santo Domingo is outranked by the general in command of the Civil Guards. This is no accident. Francisco Franco long ago learned that a confusion of protocol is an effective means of neutralizing two potentially dangerous rivals for power.

Colonel Santo Domingo's second challenge is a private police organization working out of offices on the second story of a red brick building on the Castellana in Madrid, a few doors down from the Plaza de Colón. It is a small, nameless group, and even Santo Domingo is unsure of its exact membership. A good guess, prior to Franco's incapacitating stroke, would have been no more than fifty. A better guess, now, would put the figure as high as a hundred. The organization is growing, and Santo Domingo has been told repeatedly by Admiral Rojas Millan, the President, that its sole purpose is information gathering. Like the Public Order Police, it infiltrates. But whereas the Public Order Police infiltrates illegal groups, the Admiral's private police force infiltrates various Directorates of the government—Information, Economics and Planning, Foreign Affairs. A political moderate, Santo Domingo fears that its ultimate purpose is a right wing coup d'etat.

Six months ago he might have taken his concern to Franco. But now that is no longer possible.

❦

Jesús Quintana walked to the Plaza de Colón at the head of the Castellana and looked at the statue of Columbus. Pigeons were bobbing their heads and cooing in the square. Jesús Quintana never broke stride and the pigeons, at the last moment, reluctantly left the seeds and bread crumbs that tourists had been feeding them, flew off a few feet, and settled again. Quintana played that game with people too. He would walk, eyes straight ahead, through a crowd, and the preoccupied expression on his face would never change as a man or a woman, at the last moment, like the pigeons, would scuttle out of his way. He wondered sometimes if their thoughts, if they had any thoughts, were any more lucid than those of the pigeons. He wondered sometimes if they had any more awareness of their own existence than the statue of Columbus that dominated the square. People were objects to be manipulated, as easily as a rapidly striding man could manipulate the pigeons into flight, and Jesús Quintana took pleasure in manipulating them.

It was a hot Monday late in May. An eye-smarting smog from the petrochemical complex south of Madrid hung heavily in the air. It annoyed Quintana because he had no control over it. He wanted to say, smog, go away, and make it happen. But that would not work. He turned away from the statue of Columbus and made his way up the broad, acacia-bordered Castellana. He walked straight at a fat woman in a black dress and she lumbered to one side, giving him an angry look, and he felt better.

Not yet two o'clock, he told himself, a ridiculously early hour for lunch, except for the tourists. The coffee shop of the Hilton Hotel would be crowded with them, swarms of Americans mostly, whose digestions had rebelled against garlic, olive oil, chorizo sausage and milk-fed lamb, and who would gobble hamburgers and banana splits while telling each other that the bullfights of San Isidro were a barbaric spectacle.

Bullfighters were talented manipulators too, Quintana thought. Parar, templar, mandar. Stop the bull, control the bull, command the bull. But they did not know what they were missing. Playing the same game with human beings was infinitely more satisfying.

Jesús Quintana was a lean, short man in his early forties with dark earnest eyes, a mane of black hair which grew down over his collar, and a carefully trimmed mustache. He rarely conducted business in his office on the second floor of the red brick building a few doors down from the Plaza de Colón. He preferred the anonymity of the streets, the noise of Madrid's crowded cafés, and even the camouflage of the tourists in the Hilton coffee shop.

Colonel Santo Domingo was already waiting in a booth against the far wall of the coffee shop, his bald head bent over the menu, which was illustrated with photographs for the benefit, Quintana supposed, of semiliterate tourists who couldn't even read a bill of fare in their own language. The hostess preceded Quintana to the booth and placed one of the menus for illiterates on the formica tabletop as he slid in facing Colonel Santo Domingo. Quintana did not look at the menu. "I'll have a hamburger and a Coca-Cola," he told the hostess in English.

Santo Domingo looked up, his rosebud of a mouth pursed in a smile. "How can you eat that stuff?"

"When in Rome," Jesús Quintana said. He had a point. Except for the staff, they were the only Spaniards in the place.

A waitress in a yellow dress brought Santo Domingo's lunch. It was the single Spanish specialty of the day, a Sacromonte omelette. With it came a copper-banded oak pitcher of white wine.

When his hamburger came, Quintana opened the soft bun and flooded it with ketchup. The hamburger still tasted like chopped meat and sawdust. He shoved the plate aside. "I do this every once in a while to remind myself how lucky I am to be a Spaniard," he said.

31

"I can give you about fifteen minutes," Santo Domingo told him. "What's on your mind?"

"The Admiral wants to know if you can do a job down in Puerto Real," Quintana said.

Santo Domingo sighed. "It's one of the biggest headaches of the year, Puerto Real. It's almost as bad as Pamplona. We bring in a squad of asaltos and maybe a hundred extra Civil Guards from up and down the coast, and hope for the best. What's the Admiral got in mind?"

"Franco's going."

"You're kidding me."

"No, he's going."

Santo Domingo leaned forward. His shaven skull caught the overhead light. "It's one thing when the Caudillo's up in the president's box at the bullring on his own two feet. It's something else when they've got to carry him there, expose him in public, and still convince him he's Chief of State. Jesus Christ, why don't they tell him the truth and let him die in peace?"

"Is that what you think they should do?" Quintana asked with absolutely no expression on his face.

Santo Domingo shifted in his seat. "How is he?"

Quintana watched a young American girl in tight slacks make her way toward the cash register. "Pretty good ass," he observed. "You can't tell about the legs though."

"I asked, how is he?"

"Don't you know?"

"I'm just a cop."

"Same here," said Quintana, dismissing the state of the Caudillo's health while he drank half the Coca-Cola. "He'll be staying in Puerto Real through Sunday. Open budget for you, Colonel. Put any police elements you need on temporary duty. We want a wall of security ten miles thick."

"Where will he be staying?"

"Private estate. The Salvatierra family has a place in Puerto."

Santo Domingo laughed rumblingly. "I like your sense of humor. Franco's hostess, an anarchist."

"The duchess is in France," Quintana said.

"I know that. It's still her estate."

"Her cousin Alfonso's in residence. He won't give us any trouble."

"Trouble? He'll trip over his noble feet trying to cooperate."

Quintana smiled faintly. "I'll fly down to Puerto as soon as you line things up."

Santo Domingo finished his wine and tapped a knife against his glass to call the waitress.

But Quintana sent her away with a gesture. "There's one more thing," he said. "I got a cousin on my wife's side. A nice kid. A good worker. He did a hitch with the Civil Guards. You'll like him."

"If you mean will I hire him, the answer is no."

"Give him a chance, he speaks three languages."

"Get him a job with Berlitz."

"His wife didn't like raising the family in a barracks. That's reasonable," Quintana said earnestly. "They're both nice kids. You'd be doing me a favor."

"I don't owe you any favors."

The rudeness did not bother Quintana. Santo Domingo had no reason to like him. He was no easy man to like. In the same earnest voice he said: "You could be doing yourself a favor, too."

"The Dirección General de Seguridad," Santo Domingo said, "will survive without your wife's cousin on the payroll." He called for the check a second time, and Quintana did not stop him. As they walked toward the cashier's desk Quintana said:

"At least you'd know who he was. Think about it. One of these days I'm going to get a man in your office."

Santo Domingo gave the check to the cashier and waited for change from his blue five-hundred-peseta note. "Maybe this will surprise you," he said, "but I'm in no hurry. Give my regards to the Admiral, please."

The Director General of Security went up the steps and through the vestibule to the cavernous, tourist-filled lobby of the hotel and outside, his back very straight as a uniformed buttons opened the plate glass door for him with white-gloved hands. Quintana stood in the lobby. He'd had one success and one failure. The one had been as predictable as the other. He lit a Vencedor cigar. During the next week or so half a dozen of his people, all highly qualified, all with less obvious connections, would apply for a job with the Dirección General. Pretty soon he would get a man in there, and Santo Domingo would be another puppet he could play with.

Stop the bull, control the bull, command the bull. It only worked when the bull had never been confronted with a dismounted man before. The bull began to learn, in the twenty minutes of life left to him, that the man was something he could hit with his horns, but by the time he learned it fully he would be dead. For twenty minutes the diversionary cape seemed more solid, more punishable, than the elusive matador.

The Admiral, seventy-year-old *de facto* ruler of Spain while Franco stubbornly refused to die, was Jesús Quintana's cape. Santo Domingo would be his picador, his lance-wielding horseman, whose job it was to protect the matador by giving the bull a false confidence and at the same time weakening the tossing muscle behind the bull's great head. The bullfighter Ricardo Diaz would be Quintana's sword, for the killing of the bull.

Quintana went outside. The smog was worse. He looked at

his watch. The bullfighter would be even easier to manipulate than Colonel Santo Domingo.

🐂

A taxi stopped in front of the main entrance of University City. Two Civil Guards stood in front of the striped sawhorse that blocked the driveway. The younger one dropped a cigarette and ground it under his black leather boot. The driver looked at them uneasily.

"Should I wait, maestro?"

Ricardo Diaz paid him. "No, that's all right. I'll walk back."

The taxi lurched away from the curb and sped off. The younger Civil Guard took two slow, arrogant strides toward Diaz, a thumb hooking the leather strap of his machine pistol. "Turn around and keep moving, man," he said.

"I just wanted to walk inside a few minutes," Diaz said.

"Walk down by the river then. Not here."

The older Civil Guard came over. He had gray hair and a paunch. "You're Ricardo Diaz, aren't you? Why do you want to go inside?"

Diaz shrugged. "No real reason. It's not important. It's a good place to walk."

"It's shut. It's off limits," said the younger Civil Guard.

"Never mind, then." Diaz said, and started to walk away.

The older Civil Guard called him back. "This one," he said contemptuously, "has no use for bullfights. He has afición for football."

"I can't afford the bullfights," said the younger Civil Guard.

"Afford." His companion spat on the ground. "A man affords what he wants to afford. I'll afford a trip to Puerto Real next Sunday, to see Ricardo Diaz give the alternativa to his son. Can he fight, maestro?"

"I hope so," Ricardo Diaz said.

"You want to go inside?"

"It's not important."

"But if you want to."

Diaz watched the older Civil Guard raise one end of the sawhorse that blocked the driveway and move it far enough so that a man could walk through. "Have a pleasant stroll, maestro."

Diaz thanked him and entered the campus. He heard the older Civil Guard saying: "You'd tell the Pope it's off limits, keep moving. Twenty years from now maybe you'll make corporal."

"Mierda," said the younger Civil Guard while his companion replaced the sawhorse.

🐂

Ricardo Diaz stood in front of the three-story Faculty of Philosophy and Letters. He lit a cigarette, his first in months. He drew the smoke deep into his lungs and looked at the broken windows of the red brick building. Shards of glass glinted in the boxwood hedge below them. The acrid tomcat smell of the boxwood was strong. Nobody had repaired the windows smashed in the last riot. Nobody had replaced the bricks chipped and broken by gunfire during the riot before that.

A voice inside Ricardo Diaz's head spoke: *Look, Dad. I'm not Al. Al was a different kind of guy.*

A line of black-uniformed asaltos had cordoned off the Faculty of Philosophy and Letters, a year ago. They carried truncheons and shields and wore helmets with plastic face masks. The students, led by a red-haired American named Davis or David or something like that, came rushing over from the direction of the University Hospital. There were two or three hundred of them. Running at Davis or David's right was Maria Teresa, Duchess of Salvatierra, La Quijota. At his left, sprinting hard, not at all athletic like his brother, came Alberto Diaz, glasses askew on the bridge of his nose. Some of the students began throwing stones. They rattled against the plastic shields of the asaltos. They broke some windows. Then the asaltos moved forward and used their truncheons. A few students screamed. A few of them fell down. They retreated and regrouped outside the hospital. Alberto's glasses were broken. He plucked them off his face and threw them away. Without them his eyes had a vague and confused look.

A few minutes before the first attempt to storm the Faculty of Philosophy and Letters, which had been shut because a professor had made an inflammatory speech against the army, Ricardo Diaz had tried to reason with his older son.

"You're just a kid. You don't understand these things." It had been the wrong thing to say.

"Bullfighting must give you a keen insight into politics," Alberto told him. The words could have been Maria Teresa's.

"It won't get you anything but a cracked skull."

Davis or David had come over. "Who's this joker?"

"My father," said Alberto, embarrassed.

"Well now, the famous bullfighter," said Davis or David. "Friend of the rich and privileged, friend of Franco, friend of —"

"They close down schools in the States too," Ricardo Diaz said.

"Dad, it's something we've got to do," Alberto told him uneasily.

37

"I'm walking out of here. You're coming with me."

A woman's voice said: "Leave him alone, Ricardo," and he was looking at Maria Teresa.

"I'll talk to you later. Al?"

"I'm sorry, Dad," Alberto said, and Davis or David shouted:

"All right, what are we waiting for? Let's go get it!"

The first unsuccessful rush on the Faculty of Philosophy and Letters got them a few bruises and broken bones. A squad of Civil Guards stood watching the competent work of the asaltos as they broke the first attack on the building. The Civil Guards hadn't helped them. Help had not been necessary.

The second rush of the students carried them to the broad white granite staircase. The line of asaltos wavered. A few students climbed the stairs, with Davis or David leading the way. Ricardo Diaz saw the American beat one of the asaltos to his knees with his own truncheon. The hard rubber club rose and fell in the sunlight. The asalto's helmet fell off. Davis or David kept pounding him.

A black van came very fast between the University Hospital and the Faculty of Philosophy and Letters. It jolted to a stop. More asaltos poured out, carrying sawed-off shotguns and wearing gas masks. A whistle blew, and the new asaltos formed a line. When the whistle shrilled again, they fired tear gas grenades at the foot of the granite staircase. The grenades thunked and hissed, spewing thick yellow clouds of gas. Coughing and retching, blinded, the students scattered across the lawn.

Davis or David led an attack on the black asalto van, and even then the Civil Guards stood calmly by, impassively observing the riot but ready for real trouble in the event the asaltos could not handle it. Ricardo Diaz wondered what real trouble was.

The asaltos fired more grenades, Davis or David crumpled choking to the grass, and the students broke.

38

Suddenly, from the thinning cloud of gas at the base of the stairs, Alberto burst out running. He squinted nearsightedly without his glasses. He rubbed his tear-streaming eyes. In one hand he gripped a truncheon. He saw—or possibly, Ricardo Diaz realized afterwards, he did not see—the black van, the gas-mask-wearing asaltos, the Civil Guards standing to one side. He ran toward the Civil Guards, waving the truncheon overhead, shouting:

"No! You've got to stop! Make them stop!"

Maria Teresa saw where he was running, and came after him.

The Civil Guard sergeant pushed the black patent leather hat back on his head, chin strap crossing his lips. The faintest of speculative smiles touched his face as he watched Alberto running awkwardly. He brought his machine pistol up, butt under his right arm, stubby barrel pointing at Alberto. He's enjoying this, Ricardo Diaz thought.

By then Diaz was running too. He called Alberto's name. He heard shouts and coughing. Davis or David sat on the ground, vomiting into his lap. Strands of tear gas hanging in the air made Ricardo Diaz's eyes smart, but he could see Alberto, knees pumping high, left arm flailing, right hand overhead with the truncheon, and he could see the Civil Guard with his machine pistol and his smile. He thought he would reach Alberto in time. He had to reach Alberto in time.

He heard a crumping sound, and a tear gas grenade erupted at his feet, spewing its hissing yellow cloud. He stumbled. He fell and rolled over and got up.

It was a while before he could see, at first not clearly and then with a terrible clarity. The Civil Guard sergeant stood looking down at the ground a few yards in front of him, where Maria Teresa sat on the grass, crying, her white slacks bloody, Alberto's head cradled in her arms, the three machine pistol slugs stitched across his face.

39

It hadn't been much of a riot, really. The asaltos had kept property damage to a minimum. There were a few broken bones. Only one student had died.

※

After the funeral, he saw the Civil Guard commander in his office in Madrid. The general could do nothing beyond what already had been done. The sergeant had been reprimanded, reduced in rank, and posted to the provinces, where it was unlikely he would be confronted with rioting students. The general was respectful but not apologetic.

Colonel Santo Domingo, Director General of Security, was apologetic but not helpful. What can you do with a trigger-happy fool? he asked. You send him to the Pyrenees or the mountains of Ronda, to watch for smugglers. You punish him with the forfeiture of rank and the privileges that go with rank. He was doing his duty, as he saw his duty. I commiserate with you in your loss, Don Ricardo. Was the boy political?

He was an awkward, earnest, budding intellectual who wore thick glasses and, in the months before he died, had followed Maria Teresa around like a puppy. But Ricardo Diaz did not say that. Maria Teresa was then on trial herself.

That summer he took the train to Galicia, the northwest corner of the country, a hilly green misty land that looked more like Scotland than Spain. The train was new and shiny, with low-slung aluminum coaches. The rails spanned gorges and tunnelled through mountains and ended at El Ferrol, now El Ferrol del Caudillo, Franco's birthplace.

Franco, in his prime, went whale-hunting from El Ferrol. It wasn't much of a city. The dun-colored buildings huddled close

40

to the naval shipyard at the head of the inlet, the green hills rolled off to north and east, the weathered old fishing boats bobbed at quayside. The Dirección General de Turismo had built a parador so tourists could visit Franco's birthplace in some comfort. They were usually disappointed with what they saw.

Franco's whale-hunting days were over, but he still sailed aboard the converted minesweeper *Maria de la O,* named for one of his granddaughters.

He invited Ricardo Diaz aboard, and after *Maria de la O* had cruised down the inlet and south toward La Coruña, the two men met alone in the grand saloon. *Maria de la O* plowed through low choppy swells under a leaden sky.

Franco's appearance startled Ricardo Diaz—the scrawny neck, like a rooster's, the right hand shaking uncontrollably with palsy, the slackly hanging jaw. He had dressed nautically for the occasion, in a white yachting cap and navy blue double-breasted blazer.

"You know, Don Ricardo," he said, sipping sherry from a glass held in his left hand, the palsied right hand out of sight below the table, "when I was a boy I wanted to join the navy." His always shrill monotone was high and almost childlike now. "Traditionally, the sons of my family became naval officers. They didn't take me. I was too short, they said. So I joined the army. I wonder where I would be now, had the navy overlooked a few centimeters."

He rambled on, as an old man will. He asked about Diaz's wife, not remembering that she had died more than three years ago. He asked how long it had been since he had last had the pleasure of Diaz's company. It had been two years. Ricardo Diaz had hunted ibex in the Gredos Mountains with the Caudillo. Juan Carlos de Borbón y Borbón, in his mid-thirties then, grandson of Spain's last king, had joined the hunting party.

Juan Carlos would be proclaimed king after Franco's death. He had not been much of an ibex hunter.

When the old man paused in his rambling, Ricardo Diaz leaned forward, both hands flat on the polished surface of the table. "I came here to see you about my son, Excellency."

Franco sighed. He stood slowly, his short legs planted wide against the pitching of *Maria de la O.* "I knew you had come for that, of course. What are we going to do, Don Ricardo?"

"Have the man court-martialed."

"Don Ricardo, I don't know what to tell you. I can't help you. I wish I could."

"He murdered my son."

"I would not have called it murder."

"I was there, Excellency."

"And I have the reports. It was an unfortunate affair. Perhaps the man was overzealous. He has a good record. He was punished, within the structure of his career."

"That's not enough."

"Don Ricardo, listen to me. Try to understand, Spain is a land of many lands. The Catalán hates the Madrileño, the Gallego shepherd doesn't trust the swineherd of Extremadura, the Basques hate everyone, and everyone makes fun of the men of Murcia. The Church complains when I give too much power to the army, the landowners complain because I bring Opus Dei men into my cabinet. The Falange sees its power corrode and thinks I have betrayed the cause. The intellectuals want to jump over the Pyrenees in the blink of an eye and join the rest of Europe. But despite all this confusion, despite all this anarchy, Spain survives, Spain prospers. Do you know why?"

Ricardo Diaz said, more impatiently than he had intended, that he did not know why.

"Certain things can be relied on, Don Ricardo. The sacraments of the Church. The loyalty of the army. The confidence of the Civil Guards."

"I have no confidence in the Civil Guards. They're men, like anyone else."

"I did not say confidence in, Don Ricardo. I said confidence of. They know the government stands behind them. The knowledge makes them incorruptible, and the people know it. They respect the Civil Guards."

"They fear them."

"A little wholesome fear is a good thing, Don Ricardo." Franco smiled suddenly. "As any bullfighter knows."

"I didn't come here to talk about the bulls, Excellency," Ricardo Diaz said.

Franco's eyes narrowed, and Diaz thought he had gone too far. But the old man said: "Let me put it this way, Don Ricardo. The Civil Guards are a few thousand poorly paid men and a mystique. It is the mystique that is important. Their mistakes, their unfortunate mistakes, are dust we must sweep under the carpet. They control a nation of thirty million anarchists, thanks to the mystique. They can do no wrong."

Franco finished his sherry. "No, I wish I could help you, Don Ricardo. But what you ask is impossible."

There was a finality in the statement and in the way Franco sat down again, the concern on his face giving way to amiability. The subject was closed. They could now make small talk, cruising in the choppy gray water south toward La Coruña, the dictator and his privileged guest. "Tell me, will you fight the bulls again? Buenavista came out of retirement twice, Dominguín twice, even El Cordobés. Once the worm gnaws at you there is no escape, eh Don Ricardo? Will you fight again?"

"Excellency," said Ricardo Diaz slowly, "I'm still not ready to change the subject."

The old man's eyes blinked. The left hand clutched the right

43

hand. The Caudillo's face was no longer amiable. "You are not," he said, "but I am."

"I want justice." .

"Yes? What kind of justice do you want? The kind your good friend the Duchess of Salvatierra wanted, or the kind she got? She has been exiled for life, you know, for wanting what she calls justice. I am an old man, Don Ricardo. In eighty years no one could ever tell me what justice truly is. The duchess is a fool. Your son was misguided. I cannot help you."

Ricardo Diaz stood. He felt the flesh over his cheekbones and around his mouth drawing tight. "Then I was a fool too," he said. "For thinking you could."

The two men looked at each other. With his palsied right hand Francisco Franco slowly picked up the phone.

An hour later Ricardo Diaz walked down the gangway of *Maria de la O* and past the red and gold Spanish flag snapping in the wind at the head of the inlet in the town where Franco had been born.

🐂

By late afternoon the wind had changed in Madrid, blowing the smog away from the river and the Casa del Campo, the old royal hunting preserve that bordered University City. Ricardo Diaz walked back across the deserted campus. His son was dead, the Civil Guard was dead, Franco was dying. What had coming here proven?

Even flying to Madrid had settled nothing. Well, he thought, at least that hadn't been his idea. The man he had reached by phone from Kate Cameron's villa had arranged to meet him outside the Gran Corillo Restaurant on Calle Serrano at three in the afternoon.

44

He had called the Aero Club early, so they would have the twin-engined Cessna ready. He'd made the flight in two hours, over the mountains and the flat tableland of La Mancha and into the Castillian smog. A taxi got him from Barajas Airport to Calle Serrano by two-thirty and he walked over to the Veláz-quez Hotel and had a quick drink at the bar, then went back. It was a posh neighborhood. Mitzou sold her leather creations there, Domo sold Bidassoa china, and so did Cartuja around the Corner on Calle Goya. You could buy dolls at Mariquita Pérez, and tile coffee tables and garden furniture at Rohan. Or you could wait on the sidewalk outside the Gran Corillo, where they served the best snacks in Madrid, until a man came up to you and said:

"We better get moving. That's one trouble with a celebrity. They're starting to recognize you."

They were. Ricardo Diaz could see heads turning, could hear his name spoken. The man took his arm lightly and they began to walk along Serrano. He was a trim man conservatively dressed in a lightweight suit. He wore his dark hair down over his collar and had a mustache, but so did half the men loitering on the sidewalk outside the Corillo. He did not avoid passersby on the crowded street. He walked right at them and they got out of his way.

"There's another thing about a celebrity," he said. "They live high, they know the right people, they get the idea they're untouchable. Don't you get that idea, matador. It would be a mistake."

Ricardo Diaz shook free of the hand that held his arm. "You make me wait six months before getting in touch with me," he said, his voice flat with constrained anger. "Then you have to see me on a few hours' notice. All right, I'm here. I didn't fly here to listen to any lectures."

"Do you think waiting six months was my idea? The situation got out of control. I didn't like that any better than you did, believe me."

The trim man stepped off the curb. A car screeched to a stop, the driver shaking his fist and shouting. They crossed the street toward Mitzou's green-framed display window.

"Pretty expensive joint. Thirty thousand pesetas for a leather coat, that's a lot of money. You're not exactly set up for life, are you?"

The man named a figure, an enormous sum, more than Ricardo Diaz had earned in his final successful and disastrous season of fighting the bulls.

"I know what you're thinking, matador. How do you know when an extortionist will stop? We're hoping the money will convince you. It's yours, along with the negative—and no more prints anywhere. How does that sound?"

Without waiting for an answer, the man returned his attention to Mitzou's window. "That's the best window display in Madrid," he said. "Just a few items, carefully arranged. Not a lot of junk cluttering up the display. I admire professionalism, matador. It was a pleasure watching you work in Málaga. But then, you are a professional. How many bulls—three thousand? That's a lot of killing. We even admired your choice of a weapon. A knife. No noise, no chance of missing, and if you use it right the victim's dead before he knows what's happening to him. The trouble with some people, they can't use a knife. A gun's more impersonal. I'm glad a knife doesn't make you squeamish."

Ricardo Diaz stared at the leather coat in Mitzou's window, and at the small bronze plaque that discreetly stated the price. They want me to kill someone, he thought without surprise.

"I imagine you'll be having a busy week down in Puerto. Just don't be hard to find. I'll be getting in touch with you in a few days."

"I'll be there," Ricardo Diaz said. He knew he would probably do what they wanted, knew he had to do it, and that came as no surprise either.

"Don't make any plans for Sunday after the fight. You'll be going to a banquet at Castillo del Moro. That's the Salvatierra estate."

"I know who owns Castillo del Moro."

"Of course. You and the duchess—that wasn't exactly the best kept secret in Spain."

Ricardo Diaz said: "Who do I have to kill?"

"Don't go jumping to conclusions, matador. You waited six months, you can wait a few more days. You'll get a briefing in Puerto before Sunday night." The man glanced at his watch and turned away from the display window.

As far as his companion was concerned, Ricardo Diaz realized suddenly, the meeting was over. "Wait a minute," he said. "Now just wait a goddamn minute. You could have told me that much on the phone."

The man looked at him for a moment impatiently. "I don't like doing business on the phone. I like to see who I'm dealing with." Then his eyes seemed to go out of focus. They looked like glass eyes under the thick mane of dark hair.

"I'll see you down in Puerto. You can count on it."

Ricardo Diaz stood on the crowded sidewalk watching the trim man walk quickly along Serrano, not getting out of anyone's way.

Now at University City he went down the driveway to the gate. The older Civil Guard moved the sawhorse.

"A pleasant walk, matador?"

"Very."

"I'll be in Puerto on Sunday."

"I'll look for you then."

"Good luck, matador." The Civil Guard saluted him as he walked past.

4

◇◇

Antonio Buenavista was waiting for him in the library of Rancho Andaluz. The old bullfighter, a bottle of San Miguel beer in his big right fist, a dead cigar clamped between his teeth, said: "You sure have a lot of books. Ever read any of them?"

"Sometimes," Ricardo Diaz said.

"They teach you anything?"

"That I'm pretty dumb, even for an ex-bullfighter."

"You got a whole damn university in here. This room really gets me," Buenavista said.

Ricardo Diaz did not doubt it. When he visited the ranch, Buenavista sooner or later wound up in the library, as if he had to see it with his own eyes to believe it.

Buenavista finished the beer. He set the bottle in a row with four other empties on the big walnut desk. He put the dead cigar back between his teeth.

"Where were you? Nobody knew where you went."

"I flew up to Madrid for the day."

"In your own plane? You and that crazy Benítez, your own planes," Buenavista said, shaking his head. "In the old days we used to drive all night eating cold chicken and maybe some wine out of a bota, and then with a couple hours sleep we'd fight the bulls and be on the road again the next night. If you fought seventy, eighty bulls a year then, you really knew it. You ached all the way down to the seat of your pants."

Buenavista smiled uneasily. Usually he wasn't so garrulous. He heaved himself to his feet abruptly and stood facing Ricardo Diaz.

"You'd better get into Torremolinos."

Diaz looked at his watch. It was almost midnight.

"What is it?"

"Maybe nothing. Me, I'm an old-fashioned guy." Again the uneasy smile. "I think that kid of yours has a good chance. I'd hate to see him throw it away. You better go and bring him home. I dropped in for a beer. He was drunk three hours ago but holding it. I couldn't pry him loose."

"Where?"

"Try Harry's Bar."

The expatriate American who had once said, "Fuck you, Mr. Ernest Hemingway," to Mr. Ernest Hemingway during the fiesta in Pamplona, was now an habitué of Harry's Bar in

Torremolinos. It was not like Harry's Bar in Paris, which you reached by telling the cab driver "Sank Roo Doe Noo," a clubby place with college pennants decorating the wood-panelled walls, and it was not like Harry's Bar in Venice, just off the Piazza San Marco, where the bartenders knew how to mix a martini that was a work of art. The name was a good idea, though, and the Harry's Bar in Torremolinos, a small place on the Plaza Gamba Alegre, was generally crowded with American and British tourists. The story had got around over the years, and the tourists came to see the man who had said Fuck you, Mr. Ernest Hemingway, either before or after Mr. Ernest Hemingway had thrown a wineskin at his head. The man who had said Fuck you, Mr. Ernest Hemingway, was a permanent fixture at Harry's Bar. He did not contradict the embellishments fifteen years had wrought on the story. It was now accepted that he had offered to take Mr. Ernest Hemingway apart, limb by limb, even though Mr. Ernest Hemingway had considered himself a pretty damn good fighter. Mr. Ernest Hemingway had not taken up the challenge. What the embellished story ignored were the physical conditioning and age of the two antagonists that night in Pamplona. Mr. Ernest Hemingway had been sick and sixty, and the man who had said Fuck you, Mr. Ernest Hemingway, had been neither. A short, wiry man, he had lived off the reputation of his bravery ever since, and off his reputation as an expert on the bullfights, and Torremolinos was a good place to do both. Antonio Ordóñez, who had known Hemingway well, had told Ricardo Diaz that the American writer had been a gentleman, except when drunk. Drunk, he had been a mean, needling son of a bitch. He had been drunk most of the time that year. Ordóñez had no opinion about the habitué of Harry's Bar in Torremolinos.

The man who had said Fuck you, Mr. Ernest Hemingway, was expounding on the decadence of the bullfight for the benefit of half a dozen aging British types when Ricardo Diaz entered Harry's Bar. Dim, smoky and quiet, except for the man's voice, it did not seem the sort of place that José Carlos would try to drink dry. Maybe the clientele changed with the hour, Ricardo Diaz thought.

"I ask you, who do they have these days?" the man who had said Fuck you, Mr. Ernest Hemingway, was saying in a spurious Irish accent. "Linares? He's a bird-boned boy with a few clever tricks and a way of killing so fast you can't tell if he's already out around the horn before he's going in. Miguel Márquez? Show me what he's done in Madrid. Never mind your Málaga or Puerto Real bullfights, it's Madrid that counts. No, I tell you, the bullfight's in a hopeless state of decline."

"You have to consider Ricardo Diaz, don't you?" asked one of the aging British types.

The man who had said Fuck you, Mr. Ernest Hemingway, smiled a quirky, engaging smile. "Do you? Diaz looked so good because the rest of them were so bad."

"He's coming out of retirement."

"Long enough to give the sword to his son, if you call that coming out of retirement. Let me tell you about the son. It so happens he was in here earlier this evening."

Ricardo Diaz said: "You wouldn't happen to know where he went?"

There was a silence, and then one of the aging British types whispered: "Why, I believe it is—it *is*—Ricardo Diaz."

The man who had said Fuck you, Mr. Ernest Hemingway, turned pale. "This is a real pleasure, matador. I was just telling my friends here—"

"Do you know where he went?"

The man looked at his audience, and at Ricardo Diaz. The aging British types seemed to give him courage. "I doubt that he went home," he said with a spiteful smile. "He was here, all right, two, three hours ago and two, three sheets to the wind. Well, he's young. You know what El Gallo, one of the greatest of them all, used to say about training? The bull weighed more than half a ton; he weighed a hundred sixty pounds. Training? He stayed in training by smoking Havana cigars. Buy you a drink, matador?"

"Did he leave alone?"

"In Torremolinos? A good-looking kid like that? He had a blond on each arm. Built, the pair of them."

"Swedes?"

"You Spaniards. If they're two yards tall and blond, they're always Swedes. As a matter of fact, they were American." The man who had said Fuck you, Mr. Ernest Hemingway, looked steadily at Ricardo Diaz. "The other boy with them said he knew a place where they could turn on."

"Where?"

"That's one business I don't fool around with, not in Spain. The kids want it, they can get it. I don't want to know where."

"This one time I guess you do," Ricardo Diaz said in a flat voice, and suddenly the man who had said Fuck you, Mr. Ernest Hemingway, found it difficult to meet his eyes.

"What the hell," he said, "if I were you I'd try The Callejón. The kids call it Sally's Alley. That's the owner's name, Sally. It's on San Miguel."

"I know where it is."

The decor was what Maria Teresa used to call Late Spanish Ugly and it was, Ricardo Diaz observed, pretty ugly even by the honky-tonk standards of Calle San Miguel, which had been the main street of a sleepy Spanish fishing village fifteen years ago and now was the midway of what Maria Teresa called Miami Beach East.

Stained glass chips in a frozen kaleidoscopic pattern decorated the double doors, varicolored globes cast a garish light on the bar, stucco stalactites hung from the low ceiling. Chairs and tables were turn-of-the-century American ice-cream parlor wrought iron, with bright red plastic cushions on the chairs and mosaic-tile tabletops. A few bullfight posters pasted on the wall faced the mounted head of a bull behind the bar. With inward-curving horns, a protruding tongue, and dull hide, it was neither a very good-looking bull nor a very good job of taxidermy. The plaque said the bull had been killed by the British matador Henry Higgins in the bullring of Torremolinos.

The bar was closed, bottles arranged neatly on the backbar, glasses polished, the hardwood surface smelling of a fresh coat of wax. An acne-faced boy was plucking an occasional chord from a reluctant guitar at one of the tables. Three flat-chested girls in black turtlenecks sat with him clapping an ersatz flamenco rhythm without enthusiasm. A fourth had her head down, her dark hair spread like a placemat on the table. Ricardo Diaz rapped his knuckles on the bar.

The hair placemat detached itself from the table, and a flat-chested girl in a black turtleneck came over. The closer she approached, the older she looked. Her lined face was age-puckered around the thin slit of a mouth. She started out looking eighteen at the other end of the room and was pushing a dissipated fifty by the time she reached the bar. Her eyes were bloodshot.

"Say, don't I know you?" she asked.

"I don't think so."

"I swear I know you from somewhere. Wait a minute, you're Antonio Ordóñez, aren't you?"

54

"My name's Diaz."

"That's right, sure. Ricardo Diaz. I knew I'd seen you before." She jerked her mop of dark hair toward a stucco archway at the end of the bar. "Every third word out of their mouths downstairs, it's Diaz. That kid of yours really blows their minds. Sexy looking too. I see where he gets it. There's a definite resemblance."

Ricardo Diaz started to move past her, but she caught his arm. "You want him? I'll go get him."

"Thanks, I'll get him myself."

The bloodshot eyes blinked. "There's a little kind of a problem."

"I know you're selling it and I know they're smoking it," Ricardo Diaz said.

"Well, I got to be careful. Spain."

Diaz brushed past her and went toward the archway.

"Listen," she called after him. "He's a tiny bit spaced out right now. This is none of my business, but something's eating on that kid of yours. If I were you, I'd go easy on him."

The stairs were dark. He had to grope his way down between the stucco walls. He saw dim light below him. He smelled cloying incense and something pungent: attar of roses and hash, the scent of the now generation's church, he thought with the frustration and rage that had been building in him since Madrid. He halted at the bottom of the stairs. At first he thought he would go in there after José Carlos. A little hash was one thing in the States but it could get you five years in jail in Spain, even if you were Ricardo Diaz's son.

But something made him wait while his eyes adjusted to the dimness. Three incense candles lit the small cellar room, their light flickering on the stucco walls. In the center of the floor a coarse blanket had been spread. Two blond girls wearing faded denim jackets and jeans held down opposite corners, both with their heads down staring at their crossed shins. The one wearing granny glasses looked up and said: "Careful, huh? You can't just waltz into any schoolyard and get it around here. That's pretty good stuff."

Carefully, without taking a drag, José Carlos passed a small clay pipe, and the girl with granny glasses took a long pull on it before passing it to the blond boy on her left. He inhaled deeply and gave the pipe to the other girl. She took a drag, coughed, and returned it to José Carlos. He looked at it, made a face, and passed it back to the girl with granny glasses.

"Am I ever spaced out," the second girl said.

They all sat there for a while, saying nothing, doing nothing. The granny glasses caught the candlelight, making the girl look eyeless and alien. She tapped ash from the bowl of the pipe into a platter on the blanket, reached into her pocket and withdrew a metal tin. She thumbed coarse brown hash into the pipe and lit it. She passed it to José Carlos, who shook his head.

"Don't you want any more? That's real Moroccan kif, J.C."

"I guess I don't want any more."

The other girl said: "J.C.'s got other things on his mind. He's waiting to do his thing on Sunday."

"Sure, that's it," José Carlos said. The pipe had come around to him again and he passed it to the second girl and sat there, head down, hands on denim knees.

"I never even saw a bullfight," said the girl without granny glasses. "It must be, you know, scary." Her hand moved in slow motion and touched José Carlos' cheek. She began to caress it. Languidly he pushed the hand away.

"Like wow," said the blond boy in a bored voice.

"No, I mean it. What do you think about when you kill the bull, J.C.?"

José Carlos stared at the pipe, which had reached him again.

At first he said nothing, and then he said: "I have two passports. You know? American passport. Spanish. When I'm twenty-one I get to choose."

"Is that what you think about?" the girl asked.

"Burn the American one," the blond boy said. "My older brother burned his draft card in Harvard Yard."

The girl with granny glasses looked up long enough to say, "Far out, the great big moment in his life," then let her head fall again.

José Carlos said: "I had a brother once." He ran a hand across his face. "He had two passports, same as me. That didn't stop them from killing him. Maybe I don't want either one of them. I guess I don't know what I want."

"My old man knows what I want," the blond boy said. "He sells Pontiacs in Worcester, Mass."

The girl with granny glasses sat up straight. "J.C.'s old man's the greatest bullfighter in Spain. That's a different kind of thing."

"On another fucking planet," said the blond boy.

José Carlos looked at him, and the boy said: "My old man wants me to come home and sell Pontiacs. After college, I mean. Everything comes after college. Diaz's old man wants him to stay home and fight the bulls. There's a difference?"

"I'm too spaced out to argue," said the girl with granny glasses.

"There's a difference," said the other girl. "There's a whole world of difference in, you know, concept."

José Carlos stared at her a long time. The pipe came back to him. He sucked on it and held the smoke in his lungs. "Is there?" he said after a while, and then the four of them passed around the pipe and were silent.

Ricardo Diaz turned and went back upstairs slowly. The same turtlenecks and reluctant guitar held down the table in back. A stylishly dressed woman of about thirty-five was arguing with the woman named Sally.

"—keep away from my husband, you fifty-year-old whore," she was saying.

"I am not fifty," Sally said, and the stylishly dressed woman began to laugh and then changed her mind and began to cry and ran out.

"Well?" Sally asked Ricardo Diaz.

"Don't tell him I was here."

"No, you can't tell them, can you? They make you feel so old, you know what I mean? I was born a goddamn generation too soon, and I opened the wrong can of worms. Those kids'll make mistakes, but they won't be the same kind of mistakes. God. Oh God, I wish I was one of them." She poured herself half a tumbler of brandy and drank it in two gulps.

"I am not fifty," she said.

Ricardo Diaz went outside. Calle San Miguel was still crowded, like the midway of a carnival.

5

◇◇

Francisco Franco studied the image he saw in the gilded mirror, like a man sizing up an antagonist he has met face-to-face for the first time.

Except for a few wisps of clinging white hair, the small head was bald. The nose was aquiline and, he had always liked to think, sensitive. It had a pinched look now. The white mustache was almost invisible against the pallor of his skin, and the thin-lipped mouth sagged even more these days. Only the dark opaque eyes seemed familiar. They stared back at him, trapped in the ravaged face.

It was the face of a very old man who had been close to death and who lived now with the knowledge that he might die at any time, this morning, tomorrow, next week. Of course,

Franco told himself, all men live with that knowledge: only fools pretend an unawareness of it. But this was different. He looked in the mirror and saw his own death.

He turned the wheelchair and rolled across Carmen's bedroom, wheels gliding silently over the Persian carpet. His own spartan bedroom across the hall of the Pardo Palace had been too small for the medical impedimenta that had thus far kept him alive. He felt ill at ease in Carmen's bedroom, uncomfortable in the clutter of rococo furniture, out of place between the gilded walls and Goya and Velázquez tapestries.

It was better than the hospital, though. In the hospital he had been trapped inside the oxygen tent, and the whole world was outside and for a long time he had nothing to do with it. His thoughts had come in odd random snatches, like flipping open the pages of a book and reading a few lines here and there.

His name, for example. Franco y Bahamonde. Father's name, mother's name. Like Colón, who had discovered America and whose statue stood in Madrid, both Franco and Bahamonde were Jewish names. He wondered how many generations back he would have to go to find Jewish ancestors, converts who had accepted Catholicism to avoid exile or the Inquisition. He wondered if that was why he had once opened the French border to refugees fleeing from Hitler's final solution to the Jewish problem.

Or his brother Ramón. Ramón had been the famous Franco when they were young—Ramón the dashing aviator, first to fly solo across the South Atlantic; Ramón the adventurer, participant in abortive coups d'état while his older brother less flamboyantly pursued his military career in Spanish Morocco and became the youngest general in Spain and in all Europe since Napoleon.

Or Prime Minister Casares Quiroga letting the motherland fall into anarchy while he lay dying of tuberculosis, or the

60

politician Calvo Sótelo taken from his own bedroom and shot to death by the asaltos in a police van while the churches burned in Madrid and Barcelona and a man took his life in his hands if he wore a necktie.

Or General Cabanellas, seventy-five years old, a former Republican, reading the decree in the great cathedral of Burgos that gave all power to Francisco Franco. Or the deaths of the others who might have vied for that power—Sanjurjo and Mola, their planes crashing, José Antonio, the Falange leader who had always hated Franco, executed in Alicante by a Republican firing squad.

Or what should have been the most important day of his life, the taking of Madrid in March 1939. And where was Generalissimo Franco? Sick in bed at his military headquarters, suffering from exhaustion and flu while the Army of Africa and the blue-shirted Falangists and the requetés with their red berets paraded along the Castellana. Francisco Franco would arrive later in his tasseled legionnaire forage cap and khaki uniform— Franco, who had borrowed enough of his wife's religion to believe he had saved Spain from the Antichrist.

But what did it all matter? Carmen's rococo bedroom was his world. He slept most of the time. Twice a day a man came to massage his arms and legs and to sponge-bathe him and change the bedding. When they took the oxygen tent away they began to feed him liquids. Or, that is, they raised his head and he sucked at the liquids through a glass tube. That was better than the tube in his nose. Anything was better than the tube in his nose or the bedpan. Silly things, really, but they had taken away his pride.

He had recognized Carmen immediately, even in the hospital. She spoke words, and he understood the words, and inside his head waited words he would say in reply. They would not come out. A scrambling of the intricate circuits between brain

61

and tongue, Dr. Caballero explained later, but he hardly listened. He did not like Dr. Caballero. He never had.

It was better when he could speak a few words, haltingly, in even more of a monotone than usual. It was better when Carmen would sit on the edge of the bed and hold his hand. But he did not really care.

The time of not caring persisted. His thoughts became more coherent, he could think in a straight line for minutes on end, he could sit in his wheelchair and watch his little patch of the outside world: men shoveling snow in the car park, the arrival of Dr. Caballero's Citroën, the guards making their rounds, then less snow and finally no snow, and buds on the trees and rain and sunshine. But he did not care. His time in the world was over. His days consisted of Carmen's visits, the massaging, Dr. Caballero's visits, the medicine which he took obediently, an increasing ability to match words to thoughts, to control the movements of his arms and legs, and not caring about any of it. They had taken his pride. They had not been able to do otherwise, but the fact remained. Even Carmen, with her sympathy. It is very difficult, he told himself, for a vegetable to appreciate sympathy.

And then the not caring went away. It happened suddenly, two months ago, in March, a grim dark day with cold rain sluicing down the windows and the lights on in the room even though it was almost noon. Carmen came, and all at once he wanted to know. Sometimes, then, he made mistakes with words, the brain-to-lips messages confused, and he wanted to say one thing and said another or halted and waited and began to sweat because the word was there inside his head but he could not make it reach his mouth. He was sitting up. He asked, very carefully, like a tape played at too slow a speed:

"Is the Admiral premier? Have they proclaimed Juan Carlos king?"

Carmen looked at his face. She touched his cheek. Tears stood bright in her eyes.

"The succession," he said in his slow tape-recorder voice. "I should have prepared. Forces—this one, that. The Church. Opus Dei. The Army. They could," he stopped. He had the word inside but could not get it out, and then he could. "Destroy Spain. Tear it apart. Forty years. Almost forty years for nothing."

"The Admiral," Carmen said, "is President. Juan Carlos is the heir apparent. They're waiting. Nothing has changed."

"What are they waiting for?"

"You," she said.

And he did not understand, and then because he desperately wanted to, he did understand. He would get well. If he cared. If he tried. He had been Spain. He could be Spain again.

He looked forward after that with impatience to the massaging and the whirlpool baths, and he did whatever they told him except when they told him to stop. Five more minutes, he said. Ten more minutes. His speech improved. One day Dr. Caballero and the male nurse helped him from bed, and he thought it was time to sit in the wheelchair at the window. That was seven weeks ago. He saw the walker, four wheels and aluminum bars on three sides, and a fourth that fastened in back. They positioned him in it. He gripped the bar in front and took a step. His legs almost crumpled. He took another step, and the wheels rolled smoothly. He took three steps and applied pressure with his right hand and turned the walker and came back across the room. His right leg dragged, the foot turned in. Enough for now, Excellency, Dr. Caballero said, but he walked the walker across the room a second time and turned and came back. He used it more every day, and then he used aluminum crutches.

He was frail. He had lost a great deal of weight. His flesh

hung like sagging drapery. He had palsy in both hands, and they shaved him and dressed him until he made them stop. Shaving with a straight razor took a long time, but he could do it. Dressing was an accomplishment, a skill to be learned like hunting whales from the deck of *Maria de la O* with a harpoon gun. He learned it. Soon they allowed him a daily cup of wine, Viña del Perdón, the fruit-smelling, clay-tasting red wine of Navarra that he had always enjoyed. Once a week they allowed him a small portion of centolla, the delicate crabmeat chopped and spiced and served in the shell.

One morning five weeks ago he saw a Mercedes limousine pull into the car park. He saw Admiral Rojas Millan get out of the car. The last time the President visited, he had been bedridden. He smiled a crafty Gallego smile, waiting for the Admiral on the chaise longue near the window.

When Rojas came in, wearing his blue admiral's uniform, he got up and went across the room quickly on his crutches. He supported himself on the brace of the left one and shook Rojas Millan's hand.

"Dios mío," said the Admiral. "You are indestructible." He shook his head, his jowls quivering. His face smiled. His dour eyes studied the Generalissimo.

"I had a little vacation," Francisco Franco said. Rojas waited for him to sit down. He did not sit. He gripped the crutch hard to keep his hand from trembling.

"Later this week," he said. "A Cabinet meeting."

"When, Excellency?"

"As soon as possible. Tomorrow. The day after."

That was the day his pride returned, really returned. The look of amazement in the Admiral's eyes did it.

In a little while it would go away again. The going away of his pride the second time would be worse. To be treated as a vegetable was one thing. To be taken for a fool was another.

He met with the Cabinet once a week in the big, gloomy, wood-panelled Cabinet room downstairs. He structured his whole week around those meetings, studying memoranda, considering options, making decisions. The meetings were short. One hour, Dr. Caballero said. He worked thirty or forty hours preparing for that one hour, so it would be exactly the hour he wanted.

He looked at the members of the Cabinet with new eyes. He had changed, and the change became apparent to him in his fresh evaluation of his subordinates. Rojas Millan had a flaw, not an unforgivable flaw but an unfortunate one. He was not well liked. Even the Chief of Staff of the Army did not like him. He was a martinet to everyone except Franco, over whom he fawned. Eduardo Santo Domingo, the Director General of Security, was a good man. The shaven head made him look like a Prussian general, but the big dark liquid eyes did not lack compassion. Odd, but he had hardly noticed Santo Domingo before. He was a policeman, and he did his job, and that was that. It was more difficult to evaluate the Opus Dei faction. Laymen dedicated to God's Work, whatever God's Work was, and some even took vows of poverty and chastity. They were moderates, and conservatives called Opus Dei "God's Octopus." There were no liberals in the Cabinet. He supposed he had realized that before, but it had never seemed important. Where did you find a real liberal these days? In the universities? Men like Unamuno and Ortega y Gasset had died, had left Spain, had become timid and broken, had gone underground. What would he do with a liberal, anyway? They wanted change, too much change too fast, and Spain was not ready.

He could sense that the Cabinet was watching him, appraising him as he appraised them. His executive functions, suspended for so long, were now limited to one hour a week. They had the rest of the week to administer his decisions or pervert them.

The Minister of Economics and Planning, an Opus Dei man, was the closest thing to a liberal in the Cabinet. Franco allotted him ten minutes at each session, and with proud dry technocratic expertise he reeled off facts. Until recently, he said, Spain exported raw materials, got manufactured goods in return. Living below the poverty level, that had been necessary. But Spain had risen above the poverty level. Per capita income exceeded a thousand dollars a year now. Now, he said, we export shoes, we export cars, we're building buses for the streets of Sofia, Bulgaria. Shipbuilding? We're third in gross tonnage. Only Japan and Sweden sell more ships to the world. Foreign reserves? Six billion dollars. Gross national product up eight percent last year. Have to watch the inflation, though. Twelve percent last year, and twelve the year before.

The figures fascinated the Generalissimo. I did that, he would think. From a have-not nation to the third largest exporter of ships. How far can we go? How far should I go?

A man changes and grows, or he stagnates. A country changes and grows, or it stagnates. That was what the Opus Dei man implied in his dry technocrat voice, and even the implication was enough to draw a sour look from the Admiral.

The changes the Opus Dei man did not quite suggest had to be internal, but had to win approval outside the country. Perhaps Spain had been a pariah long enough.

Relax the police state? Franco wondered. Ease the censorship?

What was he thinking of?

Spain wasn't ready. A nation of thirty million anarchists. He had one hour a week, and all the hours that went into

66

that hour. And how many weeks? He had almost died. Another stroke would kill him.

If the Opus Dei man's ideas brought a sour look to Rojas Millan's face, they brought an expression of tolerant contempt to the face of Jesús Quintana. Before his stroke, Franco had hardly noticed Quintana. A small, lean man with a mane of dark hair and a clipped mustache and a disconcerting way of looking at you, Quintana was second echelon, always sitting behind the Admiral's shoulder, always passing scribbled notes like the other technocrats and experts who came to the Cabinet meetings. And yet there was a difference. Those rare times Rojas Millan broke his dour silence invariably followed the receipt of one of Quintana's notes. Sitting at the long conference table, the President seemed hardly more than a puppet waiting to be manipulated by his deputy.

In late April Franco asked Rojas Millan to stay after the Cabinet had adjourned.

"Quintana," Franco said.

"Quintana?"

"What does he do?"

"Detail work," said the Admiral. "He has a remarkable memory, a logical mind."

"What else?"

"He keeps an eye on things for me."

"What kind of things?"

The Admiral waved a hand vaguely. "You know. Little things that may not seem important to the Public Order Police but could become critical, Excellency, when you . . ."

"When I die?"

The Admiral cleared his throat uncomfortably. "He has a small staff—fifty men, perhaps sixty. It's not much of an operation."

The next question was obvious, and an obvious way of throwing Rojas Millan off balance. It was there inside Franco's head, waiting to be asked. But his mouth could not make the connection. He arranged his features pensively. The words stayed inside. The Admiral looked at him. He hid his desperation. His hands shook. Finally it was all right again, and he said:

"Since they appear to function as police, I assume they report to Colonel Santo Domingo?"

"They function—independently. They don't belong under Security."

"Why not?"

Rojas Millan said nothing, as if the difficulty of speech was something they shared.

"Don't you trust Santo Domingo? Tell me, as an old friend."

"That's it," the Admiral said eagerly. "I'm the oldest friend you have, Excellency. We both want what's best for Spain, after . . ." Another vague hand wave.

"Say it. After I'm dead."

"Well, you did give us a scare. But you'll outlive us all, you'll see," the Admiral said with an anxious smile.

Franco laughed. "Naturally. I'll live forever."

"What I mean," the Admiral said quickly, his dour eyes downcast, "is that after you're gone a struggle for power is inevitable. Jesús Quintana gathers information on potentially dissident elements inside the government."

"Then his small staff of fifty or sixty, would it be reasonable to call them spies?"

"I suppose it could be put that way." It was warm in the conference room, and when the Admiral lifted his hand from the green baize of the table it left a damp print.

Franco remained silent, knowing that desperation would fill the silence.

"You've had complaints? From Santo Domingo? Or some of the others? Opus Dei does its own infiltrating, you know.

God's Octopus. They're everywhere. Quintana's a necessary countermeasure. You have to fight Communists with their own tactics."

"Communists? They're devout Catholics."

"Communists," insisted the Admiral, "reds, anarchists, left-wing agitators, they're all the same."

"And right-wing agitators?"

"I don't understand, Excellency."

"Quintana won't curb dissidence, he'll provoke it. Get rid of him."

Admiral Rojas Millan looked down at his fists, clenched on the green baize. "Yes, Excellency," he said.

Jesús Quintana did not appear at the next Cabinet meeting, or the one after that. One morning early in May, reading the monarchist newspaper *ABC* with his breakfast coffee as he always did, Franco was pleased to see a small article which said that Lieutenant Colonel Jesús Quintana, on detached duty as special assistant to the President, had been promoted to colonel and assigned the command of a small military base in the Asturias. Franco smiled. The coal miners of the north were troublemakers and would keep Jesús Quintana busy.

Franco found more satisfaction in other items in *ABC*. In late April he had issued a directive to reopen the university, and the same edition of *ABC* that carried the news of Quintana's promotion featured an article on University City. Schooling had returned to normal, the campus was quiet, the students had given up rioting in favor of education. A third article told of the Foreign Minister's latest visit to France. He had flown to

Paris on a fact-finding mission. The article did not put it that way, of course. It merely said that the Foreign Minister had gone to Paris to consult on matters of mutual interest to the two countries. Franco had sent him to explore the possibility of a closer tie with the EEC, even the eventuality of full membership should Spain agree to alleviate certain internal situations the French and particularly the Benelux nations found odious. The article in *ABC,* reading between the lines of the article, pleased Franco very much.

The pleasure showed on his face when Carmen Polo de Franco joined him in the upstairs sitting room. It had become a morning routine, and Franco looked forward to it not merely for the company of his wife. Doña Carmen, small, gray-haired, stylishly dressed, was an active figure in Madrid. The Church approved of her. Her total acceptance of the One True Faith set a fine example for the people, and the Archbishop of Toledo was her good friend. The business community approved of her, even if their approval sometimes cost them money. She had acquisitive instincts herself and owned controlling shares of several industrial corporations and department stores. The old grandees, Madrid's high society, approved of her. She attended their galas and charity affairs and felt at ease with the ducal families of Alba, Medinaceli, and Salvatierra. The Army had grown to tolerate her. The technocrats of Opus Dei resented her. Her faith was old-fashioned and unquestioning, and she did not entirely approve of the young priests doing God's Work on the streets of the poorer quarters of Madrid and Barcelona, since it was they and not the archbishop who determined the nature of God's Work.

Franco looked forward to his morning half hour with Doña Carmen because, in a way, she had become his eyes and ears. He was housebound, at Dr. Caballero's orders. His world, for the time being, had been reduced to the Pardo Palace and its walled park. Carmen could, and did, range further—to the

Ministries, to the palaces of the grandees, along the spiderweb strands of the bureaucracy which, God and time willing, he would reduce in size. He came to depend more and more on Carmen for advice, knowing her advice was sound.

His reliance on her disturbed Doña Carmen. "I don't want to do this," she would tell him. "It isn't right that I do this."

"Why?"

"I'm only an old woman, I don't understand these things," she would evade the question.

"I have no one else."

And she would say, with a strange, sad submission: "No, caro. You have no one else. But it does not please me, to do this."

The morning he read of Jesús Quintana's appointment to the military base in the Asturias, she said:

"You're looking well, caro."

"I'm feeling well. Did you see in the paper where that man Quintana—"

"Yes." She nodded quickly, not meeting his eyes. She stood at the window, sipping her coffee.

"Today," he said, "I think. The Foreign Minister . . . he's been in Paris three days now. I want details. I have a feeling he's making progress, real progress."

She turned away from the window. She looked at him for a long time. "No," she said.

He did not understand. He thought she was disputing his evaluation of the Foreign Minister's mission.

"I'm going nowhere for you today," she said.

"We've been all through that. I know you don't like to. It won't be forever. Caballero says—"

"I know what Caballero says."

"In a few weeks I'll be able to—"

Again she cut him off: "No."

"Carmen," he said. "What is it?"

71

She turned away from him again. Her voice was so low he hardly heard it. "I brought you a visitor."

She crossed the sitting room to the inlaid rosewood desk and stood before the telephone console. She pressed a button but held her hand for several seconds on the cradled receiver before lifting it. "Send him up," she said finally. She went to the window and stared out at nothing.

In a little while there was a knock at the door and Carmen, her back still turned, called: "Please come in, Dr. Vega."

A young man with a round face and round glasses and the dry, earnest voice of someone totally competent within his small sphere of activity entered the room, bowed and said, as if Carmen had coached him: "You're looking very well, Excellency."

Franco stood, using his aluminum canes. Vega. It was a name he should have known. But names troubled him these days. Sometimes he could not make the connection. "Dr. Vega," he said, and speaking the name triggered something and he remembered. Dr. Anselmo Vega was rector of the University of Madrid. An Opus Dei man? He thought so, but wasn't sure.

"The Chief of State tires easily," Carmen said in a flat voice. "You will have three minutes to present your case, Dr. Vega."

The dry, earnest voice used the three minutes competently, even brilliantly. Franco listened, at first not understanding, and then not willing to understand, and then hoping desperately that the shock of understanding did not show on his face, and then finally not caring. It was as if the roof of the Pardo Palace had fallen on him.

He managed to mumble something encouraging. The round eyes behind the round glasses in the round face smiled at him. Anselmo Vega bowed again. Carmen ushered him to the door.

"He wants," Franco said, and stopped. The words would not come. The words would not and would not come. "He wants."

The brain waited with the words formed. The mouth could not speak them. The body trembled.

Carmen guided him to a leather chair. The cushion sighed under his weight. She hovered over him.

"He wants me to open the university."

Carmen did not speak.

"I don't," he said, and the words again eluded him. He stared up at her. "Newspaper," he said. "Bedroom."

Carmen was gone. He waited through a small terrible segment of forever.

Carmen returned with the newspaper. He held it and tried to open it. He wet his fingers, but that did not help. His hands were trembling too much.

"It's there," Carmen said. "Happy students attending their classes at University City. You didn't imagine it." She began to cry.

The newspaper slid off his lap. "The university is still closed," he said.

"And Jesús Quintana still works for the Admiral," she told him. "If I went to the Foreign Ministry for you, I'd find the Minister at his desk."

"But the newspaper."

"Special. Printed every day. For you."

He went deep inside himself and distantly heard her words.

Once a week the Cabinet convened and let him play at being Chief of State. A deception, a small deception so that he might die in peace.

Her words went away. She went away.

He burrowed deeper into himself. Instead of Carmen he saw Dr. Caballero. He was surprised to find himself in bed.

It was as if he had already been laid to rest in the Valley of the Fallen.

73

6

$\diamond$

The big, gray, swaybacked steers waited patiently while a ranch hand from the ganadería, the bull-breeding ranch, of Concha y Sierra slid the bolt and opened the front compartment of the truck. At first there was nothing but the black opening in the side of the Pegaso truck and the ramp down which the bulls would come. It was a hot clear morning. A wind from the mountains lifted dust from the bare red earth of the corrals where the bulls would wait out the final days of their lives.

The mayoral—the foreman of the ranch hands who had delivered the bulls to Puerto Real from the Concha y Sierra ranch south of Sevilla—climbed the ramp and swatted at the side of the opening with his flat-brimmed hat, then leaped down.

A massive black head with wide, upward-curving horns appeared in the opening. The steers pawed the earth, their nostrils quivering. The bull came suddenly in a spurting slide down the wooden ramp, forelegs buckling at the bottom. Not as big as a Pablo Romero or a Miura, it was a compact, powerful beast with rage-crested tossing muscle and glossy black hide.

"Much animal," said Antonio Buenavista.

Miguel Márquez nodded. "He'll go five hundred kilos anyway." Márquez would fight in the plaza along with Ricardo Diaz and José Carlos on Sunday, the last day of the fiesta.

Two steers trotted into position and led the bull between the fences into the corral. The truck moved a few feet, aligning the next compartment with the ramp, and a second bull emerged and slid down. The truck moved again, and a third bull came out. The steers led them off.

The fourth bull scrambled very quickly away from the bottom of the ramp, hooking at air with his horns. Like confetti tossed into the wind, the two dozen men who had come to see the unloading scattered in all directions. The bull galloped downslope through an olive grove toward electrified barbed wire, two steers trotting in pursuit. The horns hooked at one of them, missing, and the second steer leaned its flank against the bull to calm him. As the first steer came back from the other side, the bull turned in his own length and hooked again, horns missing again in the bull's eagerness, but the strength and weight of the upward tossing head was enough to throw the steer. Thrusting and hooking, the bull attacked, horns gouging deep furrows in the red earth. The fallen steer did not move. Soon the second steer came into place alongside the bull, and the bull lifted his head slowly, feeling the weight against him. A few moments later he went trotting off obediently between the steers. The final two bulls were conveyed to the corral without incident.

Miguel Márquez smiled bleakly. "That one," he said. "I

wouldn't like to draw that one for Sunday." Márquez was short and built squarely, his head squarish too with wide cheekbones and a wide jaw. The horns of the Concha y Sierra bulls, when he fought them, would reach almost to his armpits.

Ricardo Diaz had watched the unloading in silence, feeling the skin of his face drawing tight.

"The one that got away?" Buenavista asked.

"Sure," Márquez said. "That bicho of a number 48." The number was branded on the bull's glossy black flank.

Buenavista considered. "I don't know. It was an accident. I like the way he moved."

"The steer didn't," Márquez said.

"You could fight a good faena with him," Buenavista said. "He would charge straight, that one."

"That he charges Ricardo instead of me," said Márquez in mock solemnity. "Or José Carlos."

Buenavista shrugged and then laughed, patting his broad belly. "Well, it's certain he won't charge me."

"What do you think of them?" Ricardo Diaz asked. He trusted Buenavista's judgment. Buenavista probably knew more about the bulls than any man living.

"Good," said Buenavista. "A good lot. The number 15 might be manso. He might be cowardly, Ricardo. The way he pawed the ground at the bottom of the ramp. The 38 could have a bad left eye. He never even saw the steer moving in on him. The 15 and 38 you'll have to watch. The 48 I like. You could win two ears and the tail with the 48."

"Look, Antonio," Ricardo Diaz said suddenly, the impulse coming while Buenavista had spoken. "Would you fight on Sunday, as a favor to me?"

Buenavista smiled. He thought it was a joke. But then he looked at Diaz's face and said: "With this belly? My fighting days are over."

"I meant as José Carlos' confidential banderillero."

77

"Man, I couldn't plant the sticks. Too much beer. My legs are gone."

"Plant them any way at all. Just be there. You could help José Carlos."

"So could you."

"I will. You could help him more."

Buenavista looked at Diaz and then into the corral, where the Concha y Sierra bulls, calm and confident now that the unloading was over, stood patiently close together in the sunlight. All except the number 48. The 48 stood at the fence, studying the men with a deadly interest. Buenavista scratched his grizzled head. "Well," he said, "I'll have to search around for a suit of lights to fit this beer belly."

The mayoral of the Concha y Sierra ranch came over. He was a tall spare man, part gypsy, with hooded eyes and a tobacco-brown complexion. "Matador," he said three times, ducking his head in a slight bow to each of the bullfighters. The word came out ma-a-aw in his thick Andalucian accent. "You like the bulls?"

They all agreed that they were very fine bulls.

The mayoral rolled a cigarette with one hand. "Drinks," he said. "To lay the dust. Courtesy of Concha y Sierra."

The two dozen men who had come to see the unloading, mostly nonprofessionals who had paid a small admission fee that would go to the bullfighters' pension fund, gathered outside the barn behind the corral. A makeshift bar had been set up, two wide planks supported by brandy casks. One of the ranch hands served as bartender, dispensing brandy, manzanilla, and anís. On a cast-iron stove an old woman was brewing coffee and frying churros in deep olive oil.

Ricardo Diaz had drunk his morning coffee and brandy a thousand times like this, with the heavy hot olive-oil-tasting fried batter of the churros, the sun warm on his back, the good cameraderie of the professionals and their expert talk about the bulls, the eager-to-be-there, anxious-to-please conversation of the aficionados, the feeling that this was the life he had wanted to live, and he had lived it. But now he drank but did not taste the brandy, he heard but did not heed the conversation, he spoke and it could have been someone else speaking. In five days it will be Sunday, he thought. Five successive days the bulls would die in the plaza de toros of Puerto Real, the customary Pablo Romeros to open the fiesta tomorrow, then Miuras on Thursday, for those foolish enough or desperate enough or down on their luck enough to enter the ring with the big, nervous, deadly bulls of Don Eduardo Miura, then on Friday the tame, pleasing, bred-to-specifications Conde de la Corte animals, and on Saturday the bulls of his friend Diego Puerta, and finally on Sunday these Concha y Sierra bulls.

And what else, on Sunday?

He had another brandy, feeling it in his throat smooth and mellow and this time tasting the good caramel taste of it. He would not let himself dwell on the problem of Sunday. Sunday was, Sunday must be, a lifetime away.

Someone was talking to him in English. He saw the dark, black-Irish dark, handsome face of the man who had said Fuck you, Mr. Ernest Hemingway.

"What's the matter with that kid of yours, matador? He should have been here, you know."

"For the unloading? Some of us consider it bad luck."

"You don't. Neither does Márquez."

Ricardo Diaz said nothing.

"Did you find him last night?" The question was asked with faintly anticipatory malice.

"He was there."

"Well, glad to've been helpful."

"Sure," Ricardo Diaz said. "Thanks."

79

"He drank a lot, you know, at Harry's Bar. That and hash is one lousy combination. I'm telling you this for your own benefit."

"All right," Ricardo Diaz said. He turned his back and walked past the corral to where he'd parked the Ferrari. The Concha y Sierra number 48, still at the fence, followed him with his eyes.

The jets would arrive now, every half hour, at Málaga airport, and the buses and taxis and hired cars would bring the tourists along the coast road past Torremolinos and Fuengirola to Puerto Real. They would come from all over Spain, all over Europe, from as far away as San Francisco, California, which had its own Club Taurino that flew a chartered jet to Málaga every year for the fiesta.

Some small number of the very rich would come in deepwater yachts to Banus' moorings in Marbella. Ricardo Diaz was one of the reasons they came. In the old days it had pleased him to be collected by them, the way they collected this year's best-selling novelist or a new rock star who, they said for one season, could reach as high as Yma Sumac.

The hippies, whatever they were called now, would come with guitars and bedrolls and air mattresses, and at night they would sleep on the beach or in the plaza near the old church.

Fifty thousand people, all told, would descend on Puerto Real for the five-day fiesta. The plaza de toros, packed tight, could hold ten thousand spectators. Extra waiters and shoeshine boys by the hundreds would arrive from Madrid and Barcelona and Sevilla. Pickpockets would flourish. The tráficos and armed police, reinforcements brought in from all over the province, would look the other way when they could. Prostitutes from Cannes and Nice would compete with the ready and willing Suecas, the blond casual lovers from northern Europe. There would be the predictable number of fights, the predictable number of knifings, the predictable quantity of pot and hash smoked, the predictable profit made by scalpers who bought up whole blocks of tickets and sold them at far more than the twenty percent markup the law allowed. Every night there would be fireworks, and there would be dancing in the streets and bad flamenco guitarists and worse flamenco singers, and later, before the dawn, the fiesta game of musical beds that would lead to the predictable number of broken marriages.

A few, a very few of the fifty thousand visitors to Puerto Real, would actually know something about the bullfights.

The man who had said Fuck you, Mr. Ernest Hemingway, would hold court every day at the Café Central under the orange trees across from the church, expounding at length on the deficiencies of this particular fiesta and the decadence of bullfighting in general. You should have seen Dominguín, he would say. You should have seen Ordóñez in his prime. You should have seen that Mexican kid Arruza that got killed in a car crash. You should have seen Ricardo Diaz before the cynicism got to him.

Ricardo Diaz, feeling only a little cynical now, was walking along Avenida Generalissimo Franco. It was early afternoon, and the unloading of the Concha y Sierra bulls five hours behind him. It was early afternoon, and Sunday five hours closer.

He walked with the crowd, alone in the crowd, tight-packed between the shopfronts, the sun hot overhead now, the mosaic-tile sidewalk littered, the cafés mobbed with tourists reading newspapers in a dozen languages.

—I'm telling you, Sam, I saw it a hundred pesetas cheaper in Torremolinos, the crowd said.

—Cigarette butts on the floor and the seats, for crying out loud, I'm gonna write a letter to Iberia, the crowd said.

—Je m'en fiche, the crowd said angrily.

—That pair of boobs on her, the crowd said.

—Ven acá, ven acá, the crowd said anxiously. Donde está tu hermana?

—I'm telling you, they always call him the Chief of State in the papers, I can read Spanish, he'll be right here in Puerto Real for the weekend, he always comes, the crowd said.

—Liebling, du solltest ihn nicht glauben! the crowd said.

—Isn't that Ricardo Diaz? I swear it's Ricardo Diaz, the crowd said.

—No, he's too young. Diaz is an older man.

—I still think, the crowd said.

—And poor dear Bertie went down three times before he stayed down. Later we learned the other fellow was middle-weight champion of, the crowd said.

"Hello, Ricky," the crowd said.

He saw Kate Cameron seated alone at a front row table of the Café Central. She was wearing a large straw sunhat, and dark glasses hid her blue eyes. She folded a copy of yesterday's *International Herald Tribune*. She brushed at a strand of her long wheat-blond hair that had escaped the hat and said: "You never know who you're going to run into in Puerto Real on a Tuesday afternoon."

He found a chair and brought it over to the little table. Kate was drinking campari-soda. He ordered a Carlos Primero, and put it back in one swallow and ordered another before the waiter left with the bottle.

"It's good to see you, Kate," he said, and meant it.

"Then smile? Just a little bit? I thought Scots were dour."

"It's one of those days."

"Bulls come?"

"Right on schedule."

"Well?"

"They're bulls. José Carlos ought to do all right."

"I was thinking about you. It's been four years, Rick."

"Diego's bringing some three-year-olds over to the ranch. I'll be okay."

"Richard and Elizabeth got in last night," Kate said. "They're together again. I tried to get in touch with you. We're having lunch at the Hacienda. Join us?"

"I don't think so, Kate."

"Wait a minute, let me finish. They've celebrated this current reconciliation by buying a screenplay about Goya. Could you imagine a better Goya than Richard or a better Duchess of Alba than Elizabeth?" Kate leaned forward. "Remember *Around the World in Eighty Days,* when Dominguín did those bullfighting sequences?"

"Luis Miguel was pretty damn good," he said. "Why?"

"There's a supporting role for a bullfighter in this Goya script, and I mentioned you. They're interested."

"I guess I'm not."

"They'll be on location right here in Spain. Why don't you at least think about it?"

"Kate, I'm not broke yet."

"I didn't mean it that way. It's just that you, well, since you are at loose ends, I thought . . ."

"Oiga," he called, and the waiter came with the bottle again. "When do they start filming?" he asked Kate.

"Late next month. In Madrid and Sanlúcar and Zaragoza." She was smiling. "Oh, Rick, you'll do it, won't you? You'll really do it."

"I'll have lunch with them. I'll think about it."

83

"There's a part for me, too. Sort of a cameo but a good one. Wouldn't it be fun working together?"

"What kind of part?" he asked, surprised. Kate Cameron did not take small roles.

She removed her sunglasses and looked at him. "The bullfighter's mistress. Maybe they could change the script. Maybe he could make an honest woman of her."

The food at the Hacienda, which stood on a hill less than two miles from Rancho Andaluz, was superb. The maître d' knew Ricardo Diaz and Kate Cameron, and of course he recognized Richard and Elizabeth. They had a table in an alcove with a window that looked along a lane of umbrella pines to the sea. The maître d' insisted on ordering for them. They had coquinas, the tiny clams steamed in white wine, and then a small succulent leg of milk-fed lamb each, and a salad with aged manchego cheese. They drank a bottle of Martínez Lacuesta and two of Riscal.

Richard used his deep voice persuasively. They hadn't really done a big one, he said, since *The Borgias*. Really big, with the sweep of a *Lawrence of Arabia* or a *Dr. Zhivago*. The Goya script was just right. It had everything—the alienated artist, the court intrigues, the country in revolution, the Napoleonic invasion. They'd try to bring it in at twenty million, but twenty-five wouldn't give the backers apoplexy.

"Who's the bullfighter?" Ricardo Diaz asked.

"Pepe Hillo," Richard told him.

"Hillo? He'd turn over in his grave if he knew I was going to play him."

"The hell he would," said Elizabeth, with the sort of smile that almost, but not quite, overshadowed Kate's.

"Look," Richard said. "We'll set up a screen test in Madrid next week. You come through and the part's yours. You don't, and you could still do the bullfighting sequences."

"He'll come through," Elizabeth said. "He's beautiful. Isn't he beautiful, Kate?"

"There's a pretty good death scene in there, you know," Richard said. "Hillo was killed by a bull."

7

◇◇

The Moorish watchtowers were strung along the coast from north of Valencia all the way to Gibraltar like beads on the Mediterranean necklace of Spain. A thousand years ago a signal fire could be lit on Jebel Tariq, and another one up the line, and another, and in a few short hours the Moorish garrisons could be alerted and the caliph in Córdoba or Granada ready for trouble. It was as good an early-warning system as any devised until the advent of electricity, and the Moors had made good use of it.

Now most of the watchtowers along the rugged coast had crumbled into ruin. A few had been restored. An eccentric Englishman summered in one near Alicante. An abstract painter from Belgium married a Spanish heiress who bought him one on the coast south of Granada, and he used it for a studio.

The old noble family of Salvatierra had restored the big Puerto Real watchtower and incorporated it into their estate. It stood on a promontory over the sea, and from it the grounds of the estate fanned inland toward the highway. There was a high stone fence with barbed wire on top where the wide frontage of the property dropped to the vega on the seaward side of the road. A crushed-shell driveway climbed from the massive gates and past the gatehouse between rows of dusty eucalyptus trees. The gatehouse itself would have satisfied most people's dream of a castle in Spain, but beyond it in a date palm and jacaranda park stood the mansion itself, the roof of blue tile, the windows and doors blue-tile trimmed, the building stone quarried and cut to match the watchtower itself. There were fifty rooms in the main house and four large guest cottages hidden in the park. A swimming pool, a row of cabanas, two clay tennis courts, and stables dotted the property. A flight of stone steps climbed steeply from the pool area to the watchtower itself, where the resident Salvatierra, Don Alfonso, cousin of the exiled Duchess Maria Teresa, kept under lock and key the collection of whips and high leather boots and eighteenth century feminine costumes necessary for the sexual stimulation of the boys and jaded women, always foreigners, who visited him, and of Don Alfonso himself.

Don Alfonso, crisply turned out in white Lacoste shorts and shirt, was playing tennis with a tall young woman named Miss Kitchen. Don Alfonso was a handsome man of thirty with the sloping shoulders and flat smooth muscles of a gentleman athlete. Miss Kitchen, who would be catching the seven o'clock BEA Trident from Málaga to London, could not match Don Alfonso's skill at tennis, and he was now in the process of demolishing her in straight sets. Miss Kitchen had been something else in the medieval tower last night. A product of the partner-switching car clubs in Paris and the audience-participation circuses in London, she had been, with no coaxing from Don Alfonso, magnificent. He had worn his Marie Antoinette costume with its frills and ruffles and she the high black boots. For a while she had stood, whip in hand, watching him undress, and then she had flung the whip aside and said, "You silly man, you're all thumbs," and undressed him herself. Then, looking quite demure through it all, she had, with an expertise learned in the London circuses, used her fingertips on nerve endings at the back of his neck, under his arms, and in his groin, reducing him swiftly to a state of ecstatic pain before they coupled. Her talents were amazing, and he would invite her back to Castillo del Moro, paying her way from London any time she wanted him. He wanted her again already, but there was the guest he expected any minute now.

"Match point," he called across the net, and sent an ace whistling past Miss Kitchen's tardy backhand swing.

They changed into bathing suits, they swam in the pool, they showered and dressed and were sipping orange juice and sherry over crushed ice at the poolside verandah when Jesús Quintana arrived.

Handsome, inbred, effete, and, except for the location of his estate, Quintana decided after the first five minutes, quite useless. But the estate was a fortress and Don Alfonso de Salvatierra was only too glad to turn it over, for a few days, to the government. Ingratiating himself with the government by moving into one of the guesthouses and opening his gates to a small army of security people was the least Don Alfonso could do, and he was eager to do it. He could even dare hope that in time the government might take the title from his exiled cousin and confer it on him. In rare instances such things had happened before. Quintana knew that, and knew that Don Alfonso knew it, and saw no reason to dash Don Alfonso's hopes. But the title would not benefit from being conferred on this inbred aristocrat and, probably, they would let La Quijota keep it.

"A security force of a hundred men," Quintana said. "You have room?"

"No problem, Colonel."

"We'll want to block the stairs going down from the cliff to the beach, and install floodlights. Is there another way up?"

"Not unless you happen to be a rock climber." Don Alfonso smiled.

"Could a helicopter land here?"

"You *are* taking precautions, Colonel."

The polished urbane effeteness of the man made him seem even more unreal than most, a clever mannequin set on earth for Jesús Quintana's amusement.

"I'm not worried about a helicopter landing here. I want one to."

"The Generalissimo's coming by helicopter?"

"We could remove the fence between the tennis courts," Quintana said.

"No problem, Colonel."

"And give your staff a holiday."

That too was no problem.

"Who's the woman?"

"Miss Kitchen?" Miss Kitchen had retired to one of the guest cottages. "A friend."

"Get her out of here."

"She's leaving on the seven o'clock for London."

"Your cousin in Paris?" said Quintana.

"Yes, that's right. The duchess is in Paris."

"You don't know that. I didn't say that."

The mannequin's left eyelid twitched.

"Your cousin rented a small apartment on the rue des Quatre-Vents in the septième. It has not been occupied since last Thursday."

"We have family friends," Don Alfonso said. "In the Charente, in the Tarn, on the Côte d'Azur."

"We know that," Quintana said.

"She could be anywhere in France. Or in England. In England we have—"

"The duchess left Paris for Narbonne last Friday in a private plane owned by a nephew of the Count of Paris. Or, that is, the flight was logged to Narbonne. She piloted herself. The plane did not land there. We have reason to believe your cousin is in Spain."

The mannequin's left eyelid twitched again. "Dear me," Don Alfonso said.

"Her return at this time," Quintana said dryly, "is a coincidence. She could have had no knowledge of the Chief of State's pending visit to Puerto Real. Nevertheless, Maria Teresa de Salvatierra is a rallying point for certain dissident elements, particularly among the university students and the young priesthood, as you're aware. Has she contacted you?"

"Of course not!" Don Alfonso cried indignantly.

"We are aware," Quintana said smoothly, "that no love is lost between you and the duchess. Still, Castillo del Moro is her home."

"She'd be insane to come here."

"Who knows what she'll do? She's unpredictable. We want no—unseemly disturbances during the Chief of State's visit. We would be disposed most favorably toward anyone informing us of the duchess' whereabouts. Most favorably, Don Alfonso."

Don Alfonso's teeth gleamed white against the tan of his face. "If I learn anything, you'll hear of it immediately, Colonel."

The two men spent an hour exploring the grounds of Castillo del Moro. Quintana asked questions, jotted notes in a small leather-covered notebook. Castillo del Moro, he congratulated himself, had been a fine choice. It would be a simple matter to turn the estate into a maximum-security fortress. Don Alfonso would see how well Quintana had done his job, and remember. Quintana would also visit the Civil Guard commandant in Puerto Real, and his thoroughness would again be evident. He would confer with the commander of the army base south of Málaga airport. There too he would leave the memory of his thoroughness. He would dine with the director of Radio Peninsular at the station between the Golf Parador and the army base, to discuss setting up a communications center. The same meticulous attention to detail would leave the same memory of a security officer going about his work skillfully and with undeniable zeal. Jesús Quintana was a man who knew his work, and who cared.

Like the rest of Spain on Sunday, he would be numb with shock and grief when the unforeseeable happened. Thorough security measures, meticulously planned and admirably executed, could protect the Chief of State from an organized attempt against his life. They could not protect him from the impulsive act of a half-crazed assassin.

"I was beginning to think you didn't live here any more," the woman said.

Barefoot, wearing white duck bell-bottoms and a crimson

blouse, she was perched on the desk in the library of Rancho Andaluz. Glossy black braids hung down over her full breasts and she sat hunched forward with her legs crossed Indian style. Her face was heart-shaped, with a small nose and short upper lip that left her mouth parted slightly in repose, giving her an expectant, and expectantly sensuous, look. There was a doll-like quality to her, accentuated by the way she sat hunched over the book in her lap. Standing, the top of her head would barely reach Ricardo Diaz's shoulder. She was thirty-two years old and looked ten years younger.

"What the hell are you doing here?" Diaz asked.

She held the book out for his inspection and then tossed it across the room, where it landed, pages fanning, on an easy chair. "Reading Unamuno's *The Tragic Sense of Life,*" she said. "Like most Spaniards, Unamuno alternates between taking himself too seriously and not seriously enough. Which is more than you can say for the French, or maybe less."

She spoke, as she always did, in a breathless rush of words, as if she had to clear her mind of one idea before plunging on to the next.

Diaz strode to the desk, grasped her arm and yanked her to her feet. She looked up at his face. "Are you going to sock me or kiss me?"

Her eyes bothered him. They always had. Cats had eyes like that, he thought, wide and depthless with a beautiful mocking savagery.

"I asked, what the hell are you doing here?"

"In general? Or specifically? In Spain or at Rancho Andaluz? I got a little tired of Paris. The Left Bank, with all the sidewalk cafés full of sidewalk café existentialists. Mais oui, mademoiselle, one must make a leap from despair to a commitment to the unknowable. One can make this leap most easily by leaping into my bed, mademoiselle. I was propositioned three hundred and twenty-seven times, philosophically of course, on the Boulevard St.-Germain and in the Luxembourg Gardens. I'm starving, and I need a bath."

"Who knows you're here?"

"Only the cook. Conchita?"

"You can't stay here," Ricardo Diaz said. "You were crazy to come back."

She went to the window. The last blue light of dusk looked in through the glass. "Then I'll leave," she said gravely. "Barefoot, carrying a phony French passport that says I'm Marie Pongerville from Clermont-Ferrand, nothing to eat, nowhere to go, a price on my head. . . . Can I take the Unamuno? Times like that, there's nothing like a good book."

There was a soft knock at the door. Conchita, fat and smiling and bearing a tray, came into the room. She dropped the smile when she saw Ricardo Diaz.

"It's all right, Conchita," he said.

"You are a good man, Don Ricardo," Conchita told him.

Maria Teresa nodded. "I always said if you have to work for the rich, pick a man who grew up in poverty."

Conchita did not know whether she was supposed to smile. She smiled tentatively and busied herself at the desk, placing a linen napkin and silverware on a straw placemat. "Gazpacho and a grilled swordfish steak, Doña Maria Teresa," she said. "As you were in a hurry."

Conchita bowed and left. "She'd join my anarchist party if I asked," Maria Teresa said. "Couldn't you see her exhorting handsome coal miners and stalwart truck drivers and clear-eyed peasants, like La Pasionaria in Madrid? If Conchita joined, she'd get card number two. You could have number three, Ricardo."

"You weren't even born when La Pasionaria left Spain."

"And you were what, three years old? Two? She's still

around, you know, in Russia somewhere, last anybody heard. That's her mistake. I mean going there. If you ever have to choose between fascism and communism, better settle for fascism. The power-to-the-people types are dangerous fanatics. Are you still fanatically in love with me, Ricardo?"

"Do yourself a favor and get out of here."

"Myself a favor?"

Ricardo Diaz shrugged wearily. He knew she wouldn't leave, and knew he wouldn't throw her out.

She turned, the braids swinging, and as much as they ever could look anything, the depthless cat's eyes looked grave. "I'll say this fast, Ricardo. Or I'll try. About Al."

He remembered her sitting on the ground at University City, Alberto's smashed head on her lap, crying. "You don't have to say anything."

"Maybe you don't have to listen. But I have to say it. I haven't had a real night's sleep since then, not once. I dream about it. If I could do anything to bring him back, including dying in his place, I'd do it. I swear I would."

"All right. It's done. Leave it alone."

"You blame me for what happened."

"I don't blame anyone. Go on and eat."

He lit a 1X2 and inhaled the smoke of the harsh tobacco while he watched her eat. She became totally engrossed in the bowl of gazpacho, the swordfish steak and the jar of white wine. It was as if her body rebelled against the darting quality of her mind, attending to its necessities with an animal's directness. She patted her lips with the napkin and sighed.

"How long will you stay?"

"I need a rest. I need to sort things out."

"Then what?"

"Then I don't know. I guess I was a pretty effective agitator before they exiled me. Rich duchess believes in democracy, if

95

not worse. But now I'd have to stay in hiding, and I just don't know. There's a priest I have to see, in Málaga, for starters. Young. Pink-faced and scrubbed-looking like a schoolboy, but he's ready to kick his bishop in the ass. They'll come from inside, you know. The changes. They'll have to. Now about that bath. Six layers of French grime and three of Spanish. Then I'd like to sleep about twenty-four hours, with an occasional interruption not only permitted but encouraged, muy señor mío."

He managed a half-smile as she came stretching up against him, flinging her arms around his neck in an exaggerated gesture of a passion that was nevertheless real.

"Give me half an hour for that bath," she said against his mouth. "Well, make it fifteen minutes. Those French, they're pretty lousy lovers. Yammer, yammer, yammer, all the time."

He laughed and, doing it, realized he hadn't in days.

8

◇◇◇

Sitting near the window of Carmen's bedroom in the Pardo Palace, the old man could hear the sounds of activity downstairs: footsteps going back and forth, voices, the occasional ringing of a telephone. He was dressed for outdoors, in a khaki uniform that had been taken in here and there to fit him despite his loss of weight.

The helicopter hadn't arrived yet. Through the window Francisco Franco saw half a dozen air force noncoms in the car park. The sky was clear. It would be a good day for the flight to Puerto Real.

Admiral Rojas Millan had proposed the trip, without warning, a few days ago. "There's talk," he had said. "There was bound to be. You haven't made a public appearance since your illness. We think it would be beneficial if you did."

The day before, he had been given a thorough examination by Dr. Caballero.

"We?" he asked the Admiral.

"The Cabinet."

"Why wasn't I consulted?"

"We didn't want to disappoint you. There was the necessity of the physical examination first. Dr. Caballero is very pleased with your vital signs."

Vital signs, he thought now, waiting for the helicopter. What an odd way of putting it. That the stubborn heart pumps sufficient blood. That the bellows of the lungs bring enough oxygen into the bloodstream. That the viscera function properly. That the wires taped to greased spots on the temples record adequate electric activity in the brain.

There had been no talk of vital signs before another trip, by air, almost forty years ago. There had been no talk of a public appearance. Far from it.

Three generals had waited in Spain to rise against the crumbling government of Prime Minister Casares Quiroga. Sanjurjo, Goded, Mola, his fellow-conspirators—it was so long ago he hardly remembered what they looked like. Two of them dying in the first months of the revolution. Sanjurjo taking off in an overloaded ancient biplane and crashing. Goded executed by a Republican firing squad in Barcelona. Mola sharing the convictions of the others but not their ambition. That left Francisco Franco, youngest general in the Spanish Army. A national hero after he had put down the rising of the Rifs in Morocco, he had been exiled by Casares Quiroga to the command of an insignificant garrison in the Canary Islands.

That meant Sanjurjo, Goded and Mola would have to wait. No one could overthrow the government in Madrid without the Foreign Legion and the Army of Africa, and neither Sanjurjo nor Goded nor Mola commanded their loyalty.

It was ironic that, in those early days, no Spanish plane could fly fast enough to elude the government patrols; ironic that no Spanish pilot could be trusted to attempt the mission.

The plane was French, the pilot an Englishman named Bebb with a big insolent mustache and laughing eyes. Plane and pilot had been recruited by the London correspondent of the monarchist newspaper *ABC,* and ever since *ABC* was the newspaper Francisco Franco read.

A Dragon Rapide, the plane could fly faster than any then used by the Spanish Air Force. It left London with a few British passengers as window-dressing and refueled in Lisbon. Captain Bebb lacked a flight plan and the necessary papers. He had charm, Franco remembered, and he must have used it on the Portuguese officials. The twin-engined biplane refueled and took off for Las Palmas in the Canary Islands.

Francisco Franco had come by ferry to Las Palmas from the out-island garrison. The plane took off, and the window-dressing passengers and Captain Bebb gaped while the new passenger opened a briefcase and changed his khaki uniform for Arab robes and turban. The Dragon Rapide would land in Casablanca that night, where the window-dressing passengers would have a well-earned holiday.

The final leg of the Dragon Rapide's flight was Casablanca to Spanish Morocco. Captain Bebb, shortly before landing in Tetuán, saw the pudgy, high-voiced Spaniard again open his briefcase. He pulled out the rumpled khaki uniform. In a few minutes he was a soldier again.

"What are you," Bebb asked, "some kind of a bloody quick-change artist?"

Franco understood the pilot's English, but was unaccustomed to speaking it. He replied in French: "I am General Franco."

They soared low over the minarets of Tetuán and landed at

the military airport, where units of the Foreign Legion and the Army of Africa waited.

The revolution began that day.

At least this uniform is pressed, Franco thought now in the Pardo Palace in Madrid. He supposed he ought to wear some medals.

He did not know why the Admiral had proposed the trip to Puerto Real. His reasons were convincing only up to a point.

"A public appearance in Madrid is one thing," he had said. "But even a sick man could make a brief show of himself. It would prove nothing."

"I *am* a sick man."

"You're getting better every day, Excellency." Rojas Millan rarely called him Excellency. Usually it meant the Admiral was unsure of his ground. "But the people don't know that. Tell me, have you ever missed the fiesta in Puerto Real?"

Like the Cruz Roja in Madrid, the Puerto Real bullfights were a charity affair. The bullfighters took nothing for their work. Even the impresario of the plaza de toros donated the gate receipts to half a dozen charities approved and sponsored by the Señora de Franco.

"I missed them once or twice."

"Almost never, Excellency, in thirty years. If you go now, the talk of your—incapacity to govern will be only that, talk."

The timing, quite accidentally, had been perfect. Had the Admiral suggested the trip a few days earlier, he might have refused. He might have said, have the decency to let me die in peace.

Quintana still whispering in the Admiral's ear, Paris unvisited by the Foreign Minister, University City a pile of red brick buildings standing empty on the hill over the Manzanares River. The awareness of the deception had almost destroyed him. He had stopped caring and, he supposed, Caballero then would have had a different report to make on his vital signs.

But he began to think. Very well, he told himself. They are deceiving you. They might have gone on deceiving you in whatever months or weeks or days you had left.

Or worse. If they knew you were aware of the deception, they could keep you a prisoner in the Pardo Palace, the jailer Dr. Caballero, the bars his prescribed medicine and bed rest.

But they do not know. You have a little strength and, probably, a little time left. You must husband the first, use the second. There are a few changes that have to be made, and only you can make them.

He wondered if the conspirators, almost forty years ago, would have sent Captain Bebb in the Dragon Rapide if they knew what he was thinking now.

That the cloying, suffocating scent of Africa no longer belonged in Spain. That Spain was European. That Spain's destiny waited in the north, across the Pyrenees. That decisions would be made in Paris and London and Amsterdam on the basis of what happened in Madrid, and that those decisions would affect Spain in a way that the Admiral did not, and never would, understand.

He began caring again. He even began to be amused. If they could deceive him, he could deceive them. Unwittingly, they had unlocked the prison door.

The government would not pack bag and baggage and move en masse to Puerto Real, the way it moved to San Sebastián for the summer. The many-tentacled bureaucracy would remain behind.

But important elements of the aristocracy, of the business community, of the intellectual community, of Opus Dei, of the younger military, of the younger priesthood—all would be in Puerto Real for the fiesta. He could reach them there as he could not in his sickroom here in the Pardo Palace.

He could sound them out. He could . . .

He did not know exactly what, any more than he knew why Rojas Millan and the others really wanted him to visit Puerto Real. The abrupt hammer blow of the stroke, the closeness of death, the weeks of being unable to talk or even think in a straight line, the memory of incense and the hand of the Archbishop of Toledo touching him with the cautionary oil of extreme unction—all that had changed him in ways he did not fully understand.

He heard a roaring, beating sound. He looked out the window. Like an ungainly bird, the helicopter settled to the ground.

The former Civil Guard Pedro Ramírez lived with his son's family in the village of San Julián. It wasn't much of a village, the few streets unpaved, the whitewashed houses small, chickens scratching at the bare earth between them, brown and black goats foraging in refuse piles in the ditches. San Julián's working population spent long hours in the laundry that took in work from the big hotels in Torremolinos a few miles away, or cut sugarcane, or earned their pesetas at the Coca-Cola bottling plant or across the road at the San Miguel brewery. A few of them, including the former Civil Guard Pedro Ramírez's son, were employed in the subdevelopment that lay at the edge of the sea beyond the fields of sugarcane. Ramírez's son was a plumber at the subdevelopment, working for the rich Madrileños, Americans and Filipinos who lived behind their brick walls in the big villas there.

Every afternoon after his siesta Pedro Ramírez would walk along the dirt track past the high cane rustling in the breeze to the subdevelopment gate. The gateman was from San Julián and of Pedro Ramírez's generation. Sometimes Ramírez thought he should have found such employment himself, but he had decided he could help the family of his son in other ways. Occasionally he was paid to run errands, like that past Sunday when he had visited the great bullfighter Ricardo Diaz in Puerto Real. Occasionally he watched the children while his son and daughter-in-law visited her family up in Granada. At such times he felt useful.

Better yet was the boat. He left it on the beach between the subdevelopment and the first distant high-rise buildings of Torremolinos. He had a kerosene lantern for the boat, and at dusk a few hundred yards off shore the fish would rise to its light. There was no telling what his net might catch. Sardines, boquerones, salmonete, sometimes a large, sweet-fleshed merluza. Going out with the boat, pulling at the oars and feeling the good looseness in the muscles of his back, watching the dusk drop on the sea, lighting the lantern and casting the net, became the big part of Pedro Ramírez's day. He went whenever the weather permitted, unless his son had gone to Granada. Whenever the weather permitted, in May, meant every day.

On Tuesday, carrying his lantern, he greeted the gateman with a cheerful "Hola, Paco," and they chatted a while before Pedro Ramírez went along the paved road past the rarity of apartment houses built on stilts. The gateman Paco had told him the apartment houses on stilts had been designed by a Filipino, and ever since Pedro Ramírez thought of the Philippine Islands as a rare place, like a planet he would never see. But he had some knowledge of it, and that pleased him: He knew they built their houses on stilts.

Ramírez went past the Filipino buildings and skirted the large parking lot of the Holiday Inn. A stiff onshore breeze blew the flags of many nations out stiffly above cars that were all gleaming chromium and steel. Ramírez wondered for a moment about the people unseen in the lighted windows of the Holiday Inn. He was both amused and pleased that they had come to his tierra for their vacations, although he did not know quite why they had come.

Then Ramírez smelled the sea, and his steps quickened. Soon he was striding along the sand in the dusk. It was the only stretch of empty beach left between the bay of Málaga and the buildings that had spread out northeast from Torremolinos, and Ramírez liked to walk there. He could almost imagine it like the old days, when gypsies lived in the caves carved out of the soft rock that rose behind the beach. The gypsies were gone now. Perhaps they forgot they were gypsies and worked in the big hotels in Torremolinos.

Ramírez passed a few other fishing skiffs that belonged to friends of his in San Julián, and then he saw his own boat, beached above the high water mark. It would take Ramírez fifteen minutes to drag the boat across the sand and into the sighing tide. It was hard work, and sometimes his friends who owned the other boats helped him, but they didn't come every day.

Ramírez saw the figure of a man silhouetted near the high prow of the boat against the last glow of the twilight. Good, he thought. He wouldn't have to drag the skiff down to the water alone after all.

"Are you Sr. Ramírez?" the man asked. He spoke with the lisping accent of Madrid.

"I am Pedro Ramírez, yes."

"The former Civil Guard?"

"Yes, señor." The Madrileño was no man Ramírez knew.

"My name is López. I'm a friend of your friend the Civil Guard sergeant Juan Alvarez."

"I did not know Juan had friends in Madrid." Juan Alvarez

had given Ramírez the envelope for the bullfighter Ricardo Diaz.

"I'm vacationing at the Holiday Inn," López said. "Juan told me about you, Sr. Ramírez."

Ramírez had a patient mind and a slow way of speaking. "Told you what about me?"

"That you went fishing most evenings. That this boat is yours."

"That's true," said Ramírez.

"Juan thought you wouldn't mind if I went with you. What do you use?"

"Net," said Ramírez. "It's in the boat. This lantern attracts the fish. Is it true that you wish to join me?" It was a rare thing for a Madrileño, almost as rare as the Filipino buildings on stilts.

"I'll pay you for the pleasure, señor."

Pedro Ramírez shook his head. "Señor, how could I accept the money of a friend of Juan Alvarez? Come, help me drag this monster of a boat into the sea. That's payment enough."

Ramírez had beached the skiff on logs at right angles to its keel. It was easy getting the boat as far as the wet sand of the high water mark by removing the logs in back and then placing them in front, and difficult after that. The two men struggled, the skiff's keel gouging a furrow in the wet sand.

"You're strong," said Ramírez.

"I don't have your years, viejo," López told him.

Ramírez liked the man. He did not talk much while they struggled with the boat, and he bent his back as much as any of Ramírez's friends would have done.

They rolled up their pants and tossed their shoes into the skiff. Soon it had buoyancy. It bobbed in the gentle surf.

"Come aboard, señor," Ramírez said formally, and the Madrileño awkwardly climbed into the boat.

Ramírez rowed for fifteen minutes straight out to sea. López sat in the stern, silhouetted against the lights of the Holiday Inn.

When he decided they had gone far enough, Ramírez removed the oars from the tholes.

"What do we do now?" López asked.

"The lantern. The net. And then we row back. It is very simple, señor."

Ramírez lit the kerosene lantern. He set it on the thwart in the prow of the skiff and stood to cast the net. It hissed into the water, sinking quickly through the glow cast by the lantern.

"Can I help?" López asked.

"We could both row. It isn't necessary."

"I'd like to."

They sat side by side and began to row. They rowed for three minutes back toward the beach.

"What will we catch?" López asked.

"Ah, who knows, señor?" Pedro Ramírez said. "A monster of a whale, perhaps," he laughed, and those were the last words he ever spoke.

He felt a quick movement to his left, and was aware that López had half risen from the thwart. Something, he realized it was López's elbow, hit his face, and then something else, he did not realize it was López's hip, thrust hard against him, and suddenly he was up and over the gunwale and in the water.

He coughed and looked up at López. He treaded water and grasped the gunwale. López, standing, the skiff swaying, kicked at his hands, and he let go. López kneeled and pushed down hard against his shoulders. Ramírez went under and came up. López pushed again. He went under and struggled and came up again. He tried to turn his head and bite López's hand. He could not. He went under again and thought of his son and his daughter-in-law and the grandchildren waiting in San Julián.

He came up once more, but he was weak then. The hands pushed. He went down and saw the lantern light and tried to fight his way back up to it. He saw Ricardo Diaz signing the tattered copy of *El Ruedo,* the proudest moment of his life, and he saw his son coming home past the tall sugarcane, and he saw the rare buildings on stilts, and then convulsively he breathed, he could not help it, but what he breathed was salt water, and he had time enough to wonder, knowing he would never learn the answer, why the man from Madrid had wanted to kill him.

Jesús Quintana sat alone in the skiff. Even if no one used the oars, the onshore breeze and the rising tide would carry it back to the beach. That meant Quintana would not have to swim. He could row toward the lights of the Holiday Inn and let the skiff beach itself. Later that night the tide would wash away his footprints in the wet sand.

He felt mild satisfaction in the killing of Pedro Ramírez, like the satisfaction he might feel waking in the night to the whine of a mosquito and with one swat of his palm killing it and going back to sleep knowing he wouldn't be bothered.

Ramírez had been a loose end. The danger of letting him live would have been minimal, but Quintana believed in caution.

It was almost like the meeting six months ago to decide how to eliminate the Caudillo. They had all agreed on the necessity, but none of them was willing to do the job himself and it was finally determined that was a good thing. It was also determined that whoever did the job should be caught doing it, killed doing it, and certainly none of them saw himself in that role.

Quintana had volunteered to study the problem. He knew he would have to hurry. The others were less certain about the need to kill Franco than he was. Six months ago the changes in the Caudillo had been more apparent to Quintana than to the others: The total downgrading of the Falange, the increasing favor in which the old man held the Opus Dei faction, his growing interest in the plans of the moderate technocrats.

Someone, Quintana had thought, with no political ax to grind. Someone with a grudge. Someone capable of performing the act and then forced to perform it. He had been surprisingly easy to find, which was another way of saying that things came easily to Jesús Quintana.

But, by almost dying, Franco perversely took it away from them. It was only a matter of days, and then of weeks. Dr. Caballero made tests and administered therapy, and the old man shocked them all with his recovery. It was only a partial recovery, but the brush with death had accelerated the changes in Franco. A political liberal, Quintana knew, often became a cynical conservative in his old age. The reverse was no common thing, but Franco had always been unpredictable.

It satisfied the others that Franco should live a few more months, duped into believing he still ruled Spain. They would merely bide their time. It did not satisfy Jesús Quintana. Finally his will had prevailed. Someone suggested Dr. Caballero. It would be simple for Caballero to hold a pillow over the old man's face while he slept. Franco was weak. His struggles would be minimal and an autopsy would show only that he had died in his sleep of natural causes. But still, they had all vetoed the idea of Caballero. The important thing was that nobody associated with the cabal perform the act. Caballero had seemed relieved.

The others believed the succession would come about as Franco had ordained, with the vacuous Juan Carlos as Chief of State and the unpopular Admiral as head of government. It would, for a time.

But Jesús Quintana was a student of history, and he saw himself playing Colonel Nasser to the Admiral's General Naguib. The Admiral was a cautious man, in some ways even more cautious than Quintana. His caution could have been a problem, had he been aware of the plot to assassinate the Caudillo. Quintana and the others had not made him aware of it. But they knew that the Admiral, presented with the gift of Franco's death and his own rise to power, would check the increasing influence of Opus Dei and the technocrats. Quintana himself knew more than that. In a year, or two, or five—he was only a little older than Nasser had been when the Egyptian army deposed King Farouk—he would emerge from the shadows. Spain needed a strongman, and there was none stronger than Jesús Quintana. His patient infiltration of the bureaucracy on behalf of the Admiral would guarantee his ultimate rise to power. The dossiers he had compiled on the others would make them pull their forelocks in obedient peasant servility.

Quintana went forward on his knees to the kerosene lantern and extinguished the light. He began to row slowly, a thoughtful look on his face. The skiff would be found, or it would go out on the next tide. Ramírez's body would wash up on shore or sink or be swept out to sea. An old man goes fishing alone. There is an unfortunate accident. His heart, or even an attack of vertigo. There would be no investigation, and no way to link the death to Jesús Quintana.

Even the others, settling in now at Castillo del Moro in Puerto Real, knew that Quintana had two meetings, the first at the Málaga army garrison, the second at Radio Peninsular. He had already seen the general. He had left a change of clothes in his rented car in the Holiday Inn parking lot. He would change; he would see the radio director and drive back with

109

him to Puerto Real, half an hour late perhaps. In Spain that was not late at all.

Quintana pulled on the oars. The dragging of the net made the work more difficult than he had expected. He wondered if the final catch of Pedro Ramírez's life had been a good one.

9

◇◇◇

On Wednesday afternoon Ricardo Diaz stood in the callejón, the narrow passageway between the two red wooden fences of the Puerto Real bullring, and watched the corrida. Angel Teruel was fighting as senior matador, Teruel who could use the big percale cape with a heart-stopping slowness if he approved of the bull, and who could kill beautifully, thanks to his height and long arms, but who lately had not trusted any animal emerging from the toril gate and was inclined to get the cape work over with quickly, to chop with the red serge muleta and then kill any way at all as long as the method presented no danger to Angel Teruel. He had shown promise in the old days. They said another Ordóñez, or another Ricardo Diaz. They were always saying that.

Teruel could fool the tourists, who probably thought it unsporting that the bull always had to die, and he could fool the Spaniards who had to save their pesetas for the bullfight and saw perhaps one or two a year. The knowledgeable aficionados knew better.

What they knew, and what they waited for, and what they saw less and less these days, was the approach to death. A matador must smell death in the hide and excrement and breath of the rushing bull, he must see death in the mean dark eyes, he must feel it in the whack of the horns against his belly as the bull follows the lure of the cape, and finally he must take it and transmute it, making the closeness of death an approach to immortality, feeling the immortality in himself as he stands with the smaller cape, the killing cape, facing the bull, urging the bull to pass, turning a quarter circle pivot as the bull comes by and whirls and comes again, until the feeling of a temporary immortality stretches out, stopping time, and he is both himself and all men, and the bull is that dark nothingness we all move toward with every tick of every clock in the world, but he can, and he does, fend it off in the passing but held, graceful but deadly, tragic instant of a felt and conveyed immortality.

"It's not Angel's day," Ricardo Diaz said.

Antonio Buenavista was glaring over the wooden fence. "It's a pretty damn good bull."

The crowd came to its feet then, shouting olé! to a deceptive pass in which Angel Teruel leaned in close after the horns of the big Pablo Romero bull swept by. The picing had already been done and the banderillas placed, and Teruel got a smear of blood on his suit of lights. That always brought the crowd to its feet. But it was a pass of value chiefly to Angel Teruel's dry cleaner.

And aren't you a cynical bastard, Ricardo Diaz thought. You did that sort of thing yourself, four years ago, when the fear grew. Except for those two fights in Madrid and a few others. A very few others.

He had an excuse. He was already older then than Teruel was now, and his wife was dying. The marriage had already gone sour but there had been no thought of divorce because Virginia had converted to the faith Ricardo Diaz had been born to, and she had taken the conversion seriously. She had taken other things seriously too. The danger, for one: a year after they were married she refused to see him fight. His long, on-again off-again affair with Maria Teresa for another.

Virginia had come to Spain from Texas, eighteen years old, on her junior year abroad, to study at the University of Madrid. She met Ricardo Diaz at the Salvatierra caseta during Holy Week in Sevilla. He had just taken his alternativa as a matador, very young, very sure of himself. His father, who had worked as a banderillero for Antonio Buenavista, died of tuberculosis when the boy was five. He had never known his mother. She had died in childbirth. Buenavista had raised him as his own son until the boy was fourteen. Then—he hardly knew why even now—he had run away. He cut sugarcane in Almería, he picked oranges on the flat green huerta of Valencia, he wandered north and worked as a bootblack in Barcelona, then crossed the border into France and found work as a busboy in the Carlton Hotel in Cannes.

He learned two things there: how nice it would be to be rich and seated at the tables he cleared, eating food and drinking wine that cost more than he earned in a month; and that, quite improbably, he had a voracious appetite to learn. He read what he could in Spanish, and soon he learned to read French and English. He wanted to *know.* He had no idea how the knowledge would serve him, the bits and pieces tucked away in his brain, but he had to discover them and own them. And then he learned a third thing. He was very attractive to women, to the beautiful, jaded women from Paris and London and New York who stayed at the Carlton Hotel. He visited their rooms at first fearfully, then with confidence. He was seventeen. He worked at this new and reasonably pleasant profession for a year. The women gave him gifts. For the first time in his life he had money.

On the beach of the Croisette one day, his day off, a flabby Frenchman he had never seen before walked up to him and without a word hit him, rather ineffectually, and called him names, and the names were quite accurate but even so at seventeen you have to hit back. He was tall and rangy and he punished the man with a swift efficiency. A crowd had gathered and the police came. Ricardo Diaz ran. They found him that night in a barn near a village above the middle corniche. They took him to the local gendarmerie and administered what the French call a severe correction. Then they drove him to the border. He had entered France with no papers and no money and left the same way. He crossed at night a few miles from La Junquera and worked his way south. He had the knowledge of the delights of being rich, and the knowledge he had got from the books in Spanish, French, and English, and he returned to Antonio Buenavista's home in Marbella.

Buenavista greeted him as if he had hardly been away.

"I want to be a bullfighter, Don Antonio."

"Naturally. It took a little longer than I thought, that's all."

Virginia King was not King Ranch, Texas, but she had money, or her family did. They were married three months after meeting during Holy Week in Sevilla. Virginia was tall, blond, intelligent, a warm laughing beauty. She loved Spain and she loved Ricardo Diaz. It was very easy to fall in love with her.

Her father flew over from Texas, furious. "I can have it annulled," he said.

Ricardo Diaz said nothing.

"How much money will buy you off, you son of a bitch?"

"Virginia's going to have a baby, sir."

The big Texan looked suddenly five years older. "I ought to cut her off. I probably will. Jesus God, a baby."

Ricardo Diaz did not need the King money. In his final year as a novillero, an apprentice fighter of bulls, he had earned fifty thousand dollars, more than most matadors.

By then he really did love Virginia. "We don't need your money," he told her father. "We don't want it."

"This is no life for her."

Virginia disagreed. She was stubborn. Her father flew back to Texas. Ricardo Diaz never saw the man again. Virginia's share of the King wealth was to be held in trust until she was thirty-five, but she did not live to be thirty-five.

The life, after all, had been no life for her, certainly not after the Duchess of Salvatierra, whom they had first seen with braces on her teeth at the caseta in Sevilla, grew up. She wasn't beautiful, not beautiful the way Virginia was or Kate Cameron, but she had that quirky sense of humor and that mind with its own darting logic and a sensuality Ricardo Diaz could not resist. The problem, he could tell himself later, was that Virginia stayed home in Puerto Real while Maria Teresa followed his corridas when she wasn't going to illegal political meetings. He could tell himself that to avoid blaming himself. Virginia's face became flaccid with alcohol. She took to that American foolishness of communicating with him through their older son Alberto. "Alberto, ask your father to give me a little more wine, please."

She became something he left behind at the ranch, like the first of his Ferraris or the failure of the avocado trees. He hardly saw her, and then he went for months, especially during the temporada, without seeing her at all.

Her liver failed. She died of internal hemorrhages in the Segovia clinic in Torremolinos—having chosen it, probably, because Dr. Segovia had been trained in the States—while Ricardo Diaz was winning two ears twice at San Isidro in Madrid.

He cut the pigtail after San Isidro. Four years ago. He had never stopped blaming himself after the first year of conveniently blaming Maria Teresa.

He had killed Virginia as surely and as crudely as Angel Teruel was now slaughtering the bull by going in around the side and stabbing for the lung in the Puerto Real bullring.

10

◇◇◇

From the Strait of Gibraltar
northeast past Málaga, Spaniards will tell you, the weather is
as unpredictable as a beautiful woman who does not believe in
God. It never rains on that stretch of coast in May. Well, señor,
almost never. But if it should rain in May, señor? And the
Spaniard draws in his breath. Ah, señor, then you will see a
storm.

The clouds piled high, roiling upward, less than an hour after
the first bullfight of the fiesta. The air was sultry and hot and
at first there was no wind, and then the wind came hard and
suddenly, and the temperature dropped fifteen degrees in fifteen
minutes.

Not until ten o'clock did the first tentative raindrops fall, big as silver duros. Soon thunder ripped the darkness and bolts of lightning plunged into the luminous sea. Then the rain came heavily, in sheets, like a waterfall. It was no night for fishing in a small boat, and no night for a party in the garden of a villa in Benalmádena. The unexpected thunderstorm that might have saved Pedro Ramírez's life the night before, or at least postponed his death, sent Kate Cameron's guests scurrying for the shelter of the villa.

Kate was no compulsive party-giver. Once a year would do quite nicely, she always said, and that once a year was the first night of fiesta. It was a big party, and looked forward to since the previous autumn in London, when one of the Beautiful People, after the theater curtain fell, might have said, "Well, my dear, I'll see you at Kate's in May." It was an exciting party, and the previous winter on the Piz Nair slopes above St. Moritz another of the Beautiful People, poised at the top of the run in Bogner finery, kicking air-cushioned boots into Spademan bindings on Rossignol skis, might look over her shoulder at the man she had met and slept with the night before and say, "Darling, you really must come to Kate's in May." "May, where's that?" "Benalmádena, silly. It's in Spain," and the Beautiful Person would tilt forward and the unvirginal body would glide down over virgin snow. It was a party that struck sparks, because Kate with a perverse amusement would invite all the right and all the wrong guests, and the Beautiful People, weary of New York, jaded with Paris, unimpressed by Sardinia, would say, "Last year she had this fellow Max, God knows where she got him. I think he's a Spaniard. He weighs three hundred pounds and talks with an accent like Sid Caesar German and is the world's biggest collector of miniatures, miniature anythings, and he never stops talking."

Kate Cameron's guests, this year, came in costume. They were Moors or they were Spaniards. They wore turbans and

118

sashes and pantaloons and soft Moroccan slippers with toes upcurved like the prows of tiny boats. Or they wore black cloaks and doublets and silk stockings and Velázquez ruffs around their necks.

The party's theme suited the fiesta of Puerto Real. Kate Cameron had simply moved it fifteen miles along the coast and a thousand feet up into the hills. The fiesta commemorated that day in 1492 when Caliph Boabdil had looked back on Granada and wept before leading his men down through the mountains to the sea. The rear guard, with Ferdinand and Isabella's cavalry breathing down their necks, had left from Puerto Real. It had not been called Puerto Real then, but Ferdinand and Isabella had quickly changed the ridiculous Moorish name of the small port the way Spaniards, since 1939, have changed the names of five hundred streets in the peninsula to Avenida Generalissimo Franco.

Franco himself, asleep in Castillo del Moro, did not attend the party.

Richard and Elizabeth were there, Elizabeth wearing a harem costume that would have given a eunuch some ideas he thought had been nipped along with an essential part of his anatomy.

Jean Paul flew down from London in his Lear jet. His friends called him Paul and he was eighty years old. Thanks to his oil interests, the depletion allowance, and a brigade of tax attorneys busily performing financial and legal legerdemain in a dozen countries, he was the world's wealthiest man.

Dale Wassermann was there, and a man who lived in Paris and was no longer the boy wonder of American novelists.

A long-haired, mustached tennis player, who had the potential to and one of these years would beat Stan Smith consistently, was there.

Two British M.P.'s were there, without their wives. An

Academy Award-winning actress who liked her girls any way at all as long as they were willing was there. The Emir of a Trucial State, the deposed head of a military junta in South America, a poetry-writing former candidate for President of the United States were there. A Jewish violinist who lived in the Bernese Oberland with his sister was there, as was Andrés Segovia.

Miss Kitchen, who had contrived to miss her plane in Málaga, was there. The Spanish aristocracy, in the persons of some of the Medinacelis and Albas and Don Alfonso de Salvatierra, was there.

The man who had said Fuck you, Mr. Ernest Hemingway, was there.

A fat, garrulous man with a deep rolling laugh, who had terrified the eastern seaboard of the United States with a radio program at about the time Franco came to power in Spain, was there.

Half a dozen bullfighters and Don Eduardo Miura, whose bulls no one wanted to fight, were there.

Another man named Eduardo had come with Don Alfonso. He had a shaven skull and he looked Prussian except for the incongruously liquid eyes and soft mouth. He was Eduardo Santo Domingo, Director General of Security.

"Understand, I'm not defending you," the man who had said Fuck you, Mr. Ernest Hemingway, was telling the Don Eduardo who bred bulls, "but you Spaniards are no worse than anyone else. Historically, I mean. You have to suffer the legacy of Henry VIII, that's all. The so-called Black Legend. Oh, I'm not saying Torquemada and the Inquisition didn't do a hell of a lot to keep Spain in the Dark Ages, but what the hell was going on in the rest of Europe at the time, that's what I want to know? For every Spanish heretic burned at the stake they burned a hundred witches in Westphalia and Scotland and

Salem, Massachusetts. The same goes for Franco, that's all I'm trying to say. He's no better and no worse than the rest of them. He's just a politician. Fuck all politicians," said the man who had said Fuck you, Mr. Ernest Hemingway.

"I never discuss politics," said the Don Eduardo who bred bulls, and followed his champagne goblet to the wall where the Picasso portrait of Kate Cameron hung and where Ricardo Diaz was talking with his son.

"One of these days, Ricardo, you must fight my bulls again," Don Eduardo said.

Ricardo Diaz smiled. "I'd be a hundred forty years old by the time you bred the nervousness out of them."

"Ah, the nervousness," said Don Eduardo. "Always the nervousness. What about you, young man?"

"Better ask me after Sunday, Don Eduardo," José Carlos said. He still had that Texas Longhorn quarterback look, despite the nights in Torremolinos.

Miura laughed, and the last note of his laughter merged with the first abrupt chord of Andrés Segovia's guitar, and for the next half hour Kate Cameron's guests listened to Bach as only Segovia could play him.

Miss Kitchen was tone deaf and waited impatiently for the recital to end. Then she sought out Don Alfonso. His face had a pinched look over the Velázquez ruff when he saw her.

"I thought you were back in London."

"I couldn't miss the party, could I, sweetie? Aren't you a little bit glad? I thought maybe another set of tennis or a visit to that cute little tower of yours, so I drove back. The police shooed me away. Sweetie, why do you have the police there? They can frighten a delicate girl like me."

It was no secret. Far from it. The idea was to publicize Franco's visit. The Caudillo, in more than decent health, had come to Puerto Real for the fiesta. He had looked in less than decent health the one glimpse Don Alfonso had caught of him when they whisked him in a wheelchair from the tennis courts to the villa.

"I have Franco as a houseguest," Don Alfonso said.

"Franco!" cried Miss Kitchen in a strident voice, and she caught Don Alfonso's arm above the elbow and expertly gave him an instant of exquisite pleasure. She could see his eyes change in the pinched, worried face as Eduardo Santo Domingo joined them, bowing over her hand and kissing air during the introductions.

His velvet-soft eyes looked at Don Alfonso, though his words were for Miss Kitchen. "Yes, dear lady, the Chief of State himself," he said in excellent English. "I regret the necessity of the police but I'm sure, as an American, you understand."

"I'm British," Miss Kitchen said. "Saint Sunday, what a lovely, what a terribly Spanish name. Are you really chief of police of the entire country?"

"Director of Security, dear lady. It isn't quite the same."

"With dungeons and ways of ferreting out all the little radicals and clever devices for making them talk?"

Don Alfonso's face became more pinched. She was saying those things to needle him, he knew.

"Dear lady," said Santo Domingo, "I'm afraid you read too many thrillers." He inclined his chin in a small bow and left them.

"I'll kill you if you talk like that in front of him again," Don Alfonso said in a furious whisper.

"Sweetie, don't make me laugh. I'm black belt. I could mop up the floor with you, and you'd love it."

Ricardo Diaz was talking with his son and with Antonio Buenavista when Santo Domingo joined them under the Picasso portrait.

"This is the boy, eh, Don Ricardo."

122

"José Carlos," Diaz introduced them, "I'd like you to meet Colonel Santo Domingo."

"He has afición—for a cop," Antonio Buenavista chuckled.

"Sure, the Security Chief," José Carlos said very quickly in English. He smiled. "I'll bet he goes on the freebie list. You can't be too careful with a big wheel in Security."

"Precisely," said Santo Domingo in his precise English. "Especially since the Security Chief really does enjoy the bull-fights, José Carlos."

"Whoops," José Carlos said.

Of all Kate's guests, Santo Domingo alone was not in costume. He wore one of his dark Savile Row suits and, now, a look of amusement on his face.

"I look forward to your alternativa on Sunday. Don't speak English to the bull, though. He wouldn't understand it."

Santo Domingo turned to Ricardo Diaz. "Don Ricardo, if you have a minute?"

The two men went to the broad sweep of window wall. The drapes had not been drawn. Lightning speared into the sea far below.

"Quite a spectacle," Santo Domingo said.

"They'll be fighting knee-deep in mud tomorrow."

"I'd like your opinion on something. If you were Maria Teresa de Salvatierra and if you had returned to Spain secretly and wanted to hide, where would you go?"

"Is she back?"

"We think so. Where, Don Ricardo?"

Ricardo Diaz looked at him. "My place," he said.

Santo Domingo's soft mouth pursed in the faintest of smiles. "Thank you, Don Ricardo. That was wise of you. It would have been unpleasant to arrest the duchess while Franco accepted her hospitality. Or her cousin's hospitality, anyway. We don't want to make a fuss, and I see you don't either."

"What about her cousin?"

"The cousin doesn't have to know. When the fiesta ends, the Caudillo will grant the usual political amnesty. He invariably does, you know, during these charity affairs. She'll be included."

Ricardo Diaz did not doubt that. Any list of political criminals to be amnestied would be drawn up by the Director General of Security.

"Provided," said Santo Domingo, "she keeps out of trouble between now and Sunday. Could you help us there?"

"I don't know."

"She's family—the old grandees. During the inevitable period of transition we'll need their cooperation."

"You'd get their cooperation no matter what happens to the duchess. They gave up on her a long time ago, Don Eduardo. That isn't what's bothering you."

Santo Domingo sighed. "She has a following. Among the worker-priests, the peasants, the students. That's where trouble will come during the transition."

"Grant her amnesty now and what's to stop her from picking up where she left off, organizing their riots?"

"Nothing," Santo Domingo admitted, and then Ricardo Diaz understood.

"You want her to stay out of trouble now so you can use her later. The best agent provocateur is the one you don't have to pay, isn't it?"

"Did you know," said Santo Domingo, "that the man responsible for the death of your son was murdered?"

Ricardo Diaz waited, perhaps a second too long. "No, I didn't know that."

"He was murdered in Málaga last November. The crime has never been solved." The velvet eyes studied Ricardo Diaz guilelessly. "We would appreciate any help you can give us with the duchess."

Ricardo Diaz wondered if he could convince Maria Teresa to leave Spain for good. "I'll see what I can do," he said.

"I'm glad you see things my way," Santo Domingo told him.

"There's one thing you can do for me," Diaz said. He described the man he had met outside the Gran Corillo in Madrid. "You wouldn't happen to know him?"

"It could be a lot of people." Santo Domingo considered for a moment. "You said he has a way of looking at you as if you weren't there? That sounds like Jesús Quintana."

"Who is he?"

"He works for the Admiral. He's down in Puerto handling security during the Caudillo's stay. Where'd you happen to run across him?"

Ricardo Diaz looked out at the darkness. "In Puerto," he said.

Santo Domingo waited for elaboration, but none was forthcoming.

Kate Cameron's guests eddied about the remains of the lavish buffet. Dale Wassermann and the former boy wonder novelist argued about the death of the novel as an art form. The richest man in the world allowed himself a third glass of champagne, against his doctor's orders. The fat man who had terrified the eastern seaboard of the United States with a radio program recounted how he had introduced Marlene Dietrich to Greta Garbo in Hollywood. The Jewish violinist from Switz-

125

erland learned, to his surprise, that the Emir of the Trucial State was not anti-Semitic. The man who had said Fuck you, Mr. Ernest Hemingway, cornered Richard and Elizabeth and related the incident in loving detail. Ask Ava Gardner, he said, she was there. But Ava Gardner, at that time, had been following Luis Miguel Dominguín all over Spain and Dominguín, who had done the bullfighting sequences in *Around the World in Eighty Days,* had not fought in Pamplona that year, Richard pointed out. "Fuck all actors, they're all the same," said the man who had said Fuck you, Mr. Ernest Hemingway, and Richard, somewhat drunk, wanted to throw him through the window wall, but Elizabeth talked him out of it. The poetry-writing would-be President of the United States decided he might write a book about Spain. He would change his mind in the morning: Brennan and Pritchett and Michener had already said it all. The tennis player who would beat Stan Smith consistently one of these days flirted with Miss Kitchen, to no avail. She eyed the man who had said Fuck you, Mr. Ernest Hemingway, speculatively. The deposed head of the South American junta told anyone who would listen that he intended to go back when his people needed him.

"Your father's worried about you, Joey," Kate Cameron told José Carlos.

"I knew a guy once in school in the States," José Carlos said. "His old man was a surgeon, his uncle was an internist, his older brother a cardiologist. It was all laid out for him. He'd go to med school. The only trouble was, he couldn't stand the sight of blood."

"Did he go to med school?"

"He died of serum hepatitis from a dirty needle. Mainlining. You just can't figure it all out for a guy. He has to figure it out for himself."

"Yes, I can understand that."

"My father can't. He got it from his old man, and Buenavista I guess. That makes me the third generation. What if I don't want to be a goddamn bullfighter?"

"Don't you?"

"I don't know what I want. He won't give me the chance to find out. I don't even know if I'm Spanish or American."

"I could talk to him, Joey."

"No! That's even worse. I have to work this out for myself. He's so damn Spanish. You know what I mean?"

"I know what you mean, Joey."

José Carlos said nothing for a while. Then he said: "You're in love with him, aren't you?"

Kate said: "I never discuss my love life after two o'clock in the morning." She looked at her watch. "It won't be easy following Segovia, but it's about time for the dancers."

"Flamenco?" José Carlos made a face.

"The jota. I brought a troupe down from Aragón. They're very good. Flamenco's been corrupted. The jota goes all the way back to the Moors. It's the most typically Spanish dance of all."

"Yeah," José Carlos said.

"Don't you like it?"

"Sure I do. That's the trouble."

11

◇◇◇

On Thursday afternoon José Carlos parked the Dodge wagon on the broad paseo of the Alameda in Málaga. Sunlight filtered through the leaves of the plane trees and fronds of the date palms, picking out color on the mosaic-tile sidewalk. José Carlos gave the uniformed parking attendant a duro, and the man put a slip of paper under the windshield wiper.

"Spain," Maria Teresa was saying as she got out of the station wagon, "is incapable of having political parties as they're known in France or England or the United States. Do you know why?"

Maria Teresa was wearing a sober black dress and low-heeled shoes. She looked tiny standing next to José Carlos.

"I know my father will hit the roof when I don't show up to cape Diego Puerta's bulls."

"Because," said Maria Teresa, "once a Spaniard becomes involved with a political party, the party means more to him than the country. A Spaniard doesn't send a congratulatory telegram to the man who beats him on election day. He's more inclined to shoot him. That's what went on before the Civil War, more or less."

"Then what was all that stuff you were feeding me in Paris about parliamentary democracy?"

"Oh, maybe in the year two thousand," Maria Teresa said as they walked along the Alameda. "Meanwhile, we need a strong paternal leadership."

"I thought you hated Franco's guts."

"I never said I hated Franco. In fact, I admire him. I just happen to detest his government."

"They always say," José Carlos said in English, "that dames don't have the most logical minds going."

"Politicians are basically hypocritical," Maria Teresa told him. "Right-wing, left-wing, middle-of-the-road, it doesn't matter. They all claim they're serving the best interests of the people when what they're really doing is helping themselves to the biggest slice of pie. If you make enough waves, they have to give a little of it away. The more waves you make, the more they have to give."

Maria Teresa took his arm. "They're mostly mediocre time-servers, often stupid, who—"

"You think Franco's stupid?"

"Not at all. In some ways he's brilliant. The most brilliant touch of all is that he's always been basically nonpolitical. The ideology buffs are definitely not for him. But he uses them. Discards them too, when he no longer needs them. That's what happened to the Falange. Franco used them, then buried them

130

in the Movimiento. They have about as much power in Spain today as Trotskyites have in Russia. Franco's no fascist. He never was. He's just an old-fashioned right-wing dictator. His cronies are something else again—political hacks who tend to see enemies everywhere. They're almost paranoid, which means you have to be careful."

"Since when have you been careful?"

"Well, if you're too careful you can't get anything done, can you? I have to take calculated risks. Besides, it's fun. Being a duchess can be pretty dull. But you only take a risk when it stands to gain something. Politicians can't function without stability, you see, and they'll grant concessions to keep it. Some professor makes a speech against the Army, and the students riot. What happens then?"

"They close the university."

"They'll open it eventually, and the Army will be a little less sacrosanct." Maria Teresa glanced quickly up at his face. "I used the wrong example, didn't I? That's how Alberto got killed."

"He was a funny guy. Much more Spanish than me. You could never tell what he was thinking. He was going to get into trouble whether you came along or not."

"And you're not Spanish?"

"Look," José Carlos said, suddenly angry. "People keep telling me what I ought to be. My father. Kate Cameron. Now you. If you all left me alone maybe I could figure it out for myself."

"Well," Maria Teresa said lightly, "I'll begin by leaving you alone for half an hour anyway. I have to see a worker-priest whose father was killed in the—"

"I don't want to know who you're going to see."

They had walked from the bullring end of the Alameda past the city hall and the post office to where the plane trees and date palms gave way to orange trees and sidewalk cafés and the gleaming façade of the Málaga Palacio Hotel.

"If only you knew how Spanish you really are." Maria Teresa smiled at the stubborn expression on his face. "Find a table in the shade and have a drink, José Carlos. I won't be long."

She patted his arm and turned the corner past the big hotel, looking demurely anonymous in her sober black dress.

Miss Kitchen walked past the hotel doorman and blinked in the bright sunlight. The young woman in black just going around the corner looked familiar. Kate Cameron's party? Miss Kitchen wondered. No, that wasn't it. Miss Kitchen frowned and remembered. She had seen portraits of the woman hanging in Castillo del Moro. Not in the tower, of course. The woman, she was sure of it now, was Alfonso's cousin, the exiled duchess. Pretty little thing, Miss Kitchen thought. She decided it would be amusing to tell Alfonso she had seen her in Málaga.

There was no wind that afternoon, and no need to work the bull near the cliff that loomed over one side of the miniature bullring at Rancho Andaluz. It was just as well. That part of the arena was still a quagmire from last night's rain.

The bull was a novillo, a three-year-old animal a hundred kilos or so off its full weight, but the horns were good and the bull, not force-fed on grain, had strong legs and considerable staying power. Ricardo Diaz swung the large, stiff percale cape slowly before the charging novillo in the classic pass, the veronica, which is both the foundation of the bullfighter's art and the measure of his skill.

It was a good veronica, and Ricardo Diaz turned to execute it again as the bull came by in the other direction. This time he cut the sweep of the cape short and snapped it in so that the cloth wrapped itself around his body. The bull, instead of rushing by and wheeling to come back again, attracted by the lure, galloped past and pulled up short. Diaz strutted away, his back to the animal, with a stylized arrogance he did not feel.

He waved Antonio Buenavista into the ring. "You take him a while," he said, and leaned against the fence to watch the older man, moving slowly but with grace, approach the bull with his own cape. Then he turned and looked down the unpaved road toward the highway. No sign of the Dodge wagon, no sign of José Carlos. The boy had left the ranch before Diaz had returned for lunch, and a quick check had revealed that Maria Teresa was gone too.

Turning back to the ring, holding the collar of the rose and gold cape in both hands, ready to run across the sand and divert the bull if Buenavista had any difficulty, Ricardo Diaz felt his anger grow. José Carlos apparently thought he could walk into the Puerto Real bullring on Sunday without any preparation at all. Maria Teresa apparently was encouraging him.

Diaz lit a cigarette. The anger gave way to an empty feeling, like the first words out of a peasant's mouth when he wanted to show his contempt for the futility of life: "Nada, hombre. Nada."

Nada: nothing. But more than that. It was a word that encompassed the bleak, dessicated Spanish landscape, the hard weary days of the peasant's life, the naïve folly of thinking that anything was of consequence in a world guided not by a benign

133

deity but by an indifferent fate. Nothing and nothing. And again nothing. Not even despair, not now, because the end of it all, the nada, hombre, nada of the peasant's metaphysical contempt, was waiting for him on Sunday.

Not according to Jesús Quintana. According to Quintana, whom he had seen that morning, a fortune awaited him after Sunday, and a new identity if anything went wrong. It all had been arranged carefully—the escape route, the phony passport, properly visa-stamped, the money in a bank in New York.

He had met Quintana at the foot of the street that went down from the Puerto Real town hall to the beach. It was early and the cafés that lined the beachfront promenade still empty except for the waiters unstacking chairs and setting them around the small tables. A few beach boys moved slowly across the sand, opening umbrellas, placing cushions on the slats of the beach chairs, preparing the day for tourists who thought their hangovers would be baked out by the brutal sun and rinsed away by the polluted sea.

Quintana got there five minutes after he did, behind the wheel of a nondescript Renault.

"Get in, matador."

Quintana made a quick U-turn and drove back up the hill past the town hall. They drove in silence for fifteen minutes, Quintana handling the little car with the careless disdain— nada, hombre, nada—that is so natural to Spanish drivers. The coast highway was already crowded with trucks. The Renault threaded its way among them as if they weren't there, cutting in and out of lane, crossing the double yellow line to pass a semitrailer and then darting back in, buffeted by the slipstream of a truck coming the other way, missing a head-on collision by a split second.

Not that Quintana was in any hurry. He just drove that way. A professional racing driver, an Englishman, had once told

Ricardo Diaz that most Spaniards ought to be outlawed from the roads. "It's not a game to them, as it is to your Italians," he had said, "and they don't consider it a challenge, as the Krauts do. They simply refuse to believe that any other driver would dare get in their way. It's your damnable Spanish mentality. There's the individual, and the universe, and very little else between. It's almost impossible to convince a Spaniard that anyone else really exists. Sometimes on the road he learns it the hard way. Head-on collisions tend to be fatal."

They drove through Torremolinos and then climbed a potholed blacktop road, leaving the garish strip of the Costa del Sol, international and tastelessly modern, and going back two hundred years among the olive groves and almond trees and peasants with their plodding burros beyond the first range of hills. Spiky aloes grew along the roadside, and whitewashed red-tile-roofed villages fled by, and the small churches waited, starkly white in the morning sunlight, for fewer communicants every year because the priests could only offer the hope of salvation, but the owners of the hotels and restaurants on the coast below offered the hard reality of good wages.

Quintana turned off the potholed road and drove a few hundred yards along a dirt track into an olive grove. Last night's rain had eroded the red clay here and there, exposing gnarled ancient roots. Ricardo Diaz could just make out the glint of sun on sea through a cut in the treeless hills.

Quintana got out of the car and breathed deeply. "I like this place," he said. "It's a nice spot," he elaborated, looking around, "unless you happen to be a peasant."

His admiring glance took in the bare hills and the blue sky. "Did you know that murderers are rarely caught in the act when witnesses are present? Half the time, in a crowd, they're not even identified. There are a few moments of stunned inaction, while everyone waits to see what everyone else will do.

It's like fixing the bull in place with—what do you call that pass?"

"A media veronica," Ricardo Diaz said.

"Right. A media veronica. It ought to give you five seconds anyway, and if anything goes wrong five seconds are all you'll need. Here," Quintana said, removing what looked like a map from his breast pocket and unfolding it on the hood of the Renault. "Take a look at this."

This was a one to two-hundred scale drawing of Castillo del Moro, the main house and the grounds.

Quintana touched the drawing with his index finger. "The ballroom. Two hundred guests, give or take a few. It can hold more. The windows face south. French doors, actually. Figure dinner starts at ten-thirty—that's the dining room, over here."

The well-manicured finger moved. "Whether Franco attends the dinner or not depends on how he's feeling, but he'll be in the ballroom by twelve-thirty. The usual speech. Then two hundred people crowding around, congratulating themselves on being there, paying homage to the Caudillo. They'll be smug, and they'll be curious. In a way he's coming back from the dead, you know. They'll be studying the old man the way an entomologist studies a bug."

That, Ricardo Diaz thought, was the way Quintana was studying him.

"They'll have eyes for nothing else." Quintana paused. He looked away from Ricardo Diaz. "That's when you put the knife in him. That's when you leave it in and just fade into the crowd." Quintana's mouth smiled. "A fifty-fifty chance. Maybe better. You ever bet on the frontón? Any time I ever pulled a slip from the tennis ball and knew the odds were fifty-fifty, I felt pretty good. You handle it right, nobody will ever know you did it."

The finger returned to the scale drawing of the Castillo del

Moro ballroom. "If you have bad luck, there's a contingency plan. You kill him and you go through the French doors. That puts you"—the finger jabbed—"here. From this point it's three hundred meters uphill, it's not a very steep hill, to the tower. Now, see how the contour lines almost come together just behind the tower? That's a cliff."

"I can read a map, Sr. Quintana," Ricardo Diaz said.

If Quintana was surprised that Diaz knew his name, he didn't show it. He went on: "A hundred twenty-five steps are cut in the rock down to the sea. They're floodlit at night. Security's very tight, of course, and that helps you. You won't break your neck going down those stairs."

"What do I do then, assuming I get that far? Swim to Africa?"

"A boat, twin Chrysler engines. She can do almost forty knots. You go to Tangier, central police station. You see a cop named Mahmoud Zeid. He'll hide you. A month, two months. That's up to Zeid. You spend a lot of time in the sun tanning yourself. You grow a mustache, gray your hair. They'll take a picture for your new passport. In late June, maybe July, you fly to New York. The money will be waiting for you in an account under your new name at the Manufacturers Hanover Trust, Fifth Avenue and Forty-third Street. Ricardo Diaz disappears if he has to. After that, you're on your own."

Ricardo Diaz wondered about the good frontón odds, wondered at what point along the meticulously detailed imaginary escape route they would kill him. He had to die, of course. His death guaranteed Quintana's safety. Quintana, fifty-fifty odds, one to two-hundred scale drawing, French doors, floodlit steps, Chrysler engines, Tangier, the Manufacturers Hanover Trust and all, knew that. You do not let the man who kills Franco for you remain alive.

He tried to put himself in Quintana's place. The sooner the

better, he decided. The machine pistols of Civil Guards waiting just outside the French doors would do nicely.

He said: "Say I gave a letter to a friend and told him to deliver it to the Director General of Security or the publisher of *ABC* if he didn't hear from me at a specified time."

Quintana waved a hand deprecatingly. "Nada, hombre. Nada. You'll get away with it."

"But if I didn't."

"When a chief of state is assassinated there's always talk of conspiracy. This won't be any exception. The talk never amounts to anything. Nobody will want to rock the boat, believe me. And if anybody tried, he'd get nowhere. Write your letter, send it to the Pope if it'll make you feel better."

Quintana flashed his teeth in a pleasant smile. "Before you know it you'll be breeding fighting stock again, or buying yourself a ranch in Texas or somewhere. You'll live the good life, matador."

A few minutes later they drove back to the coast road and west to Puerto Real. Quintana had nothing more to say. It was as if, for him, Ricardo Diaz had ceased to exist.

Now at Rancho Andaluz, Diaz watched Antonio Buenavista finish his work with the three-year-old bull. One of the ranch hands opened the toril gate and with a series of quick, artless, retreating passes Buenavista led the animal there. The ranch hand shut and bolted the gate and Buenavista, sweating, walked slowly across the hard-packed sand. Diego Puerta tossed him a towel. He mopped his face.

"I'm not as young as I used to be."

"Is anyone?" Puerta asked.

"But you know something? I enjoyed it. We'll show them something on Sunday, eh Ricardo?"

Kate Cameron and Ricardo Diaz sat at a table in the Seven Seas Restaurant overlooking Puerto Real's small yacht basin. The decor was nautical. Fishnets hung from the ceiling, and a display of seafood was set out on beds of ice on the deck of an old fishing skiff at the entrance to the large, crowded dining room. The windows were portholes, and through the one nearest their table Ricardo Diaz could see a barge floating in the floodlit yacht basin. At midnight, just a few minutes off, fireworks would erupt from the deck of the barge.

A pair of strolling musicians had come to their table. With guitar and mandolin they played the theme song from Kate's last film. Then they broke into the paso doble "Cielo Andaluz." It was bullfight music and over the years had become Ricardo Diaz's song, played by the drums and brass of the banda taurina in the bullring when his performance merited musical accompaniment. He listened with a polite smile on his face and acknowledged the applause of the other diners in the restaurant with another smile when the last chord was struck. He wished the musicians hadn't recognized them.

He stuffed a hundred-peseta note into the guitarist's hand and watched them move to another table.

"I've made up my mind," Kate said. "After fiesta I'm going to put the place in Benalmádena up for sale. I'm restless, I guess. Some people take it out on other people. I take it out on places."

"Where will you go?"

"Well, do the movie first. Then maybe Gstaad for a while. Richard and Elizabeth know a chalet I can have near theirs. I want a real winter. I want snow ten feet deep. I want to make every ski run in the Bernese Oberland and sit exhausted in front of a fireplace and drink hot mulled wine."

Kate leaned across the table, brushing at a strand of her wheat-blond hair. "They have fondue parties at night on the mountaintops, and you ski down by torchlight," she said. "Or before that, in the autumn. The colors. The air's like dry white wine. You can walk a hundred miles on the top of the world. The cattle come down from high pasture then and all you hear is the tinkle of cowbells."

"You sound like the Swiss National Tourist Bureau." Ricardo Diaz grinned. "Have you ever heard one of those Swiss cowbells? They don't tinkle, they clank."

"Let a girl dream, will you? Did you ever see the Alps in winter, under a full moon? The snow's an eerie electric blue. It's so bright you can read outdoors in the middle of the night."

"And freeze to death."

"Cut that out, Ricardo Diaz. They have little country inns near the trout hatcheries, and in winter the taxis are sleighs, and they light their Christmas trees with real candles. They—"

On the barge in the yacht basin the first Roman candles whooshed upward and burst into geysers of color.

Kate reached across the table for his hand. "Come with me, Rick. You'll love it, I know you will."

He stared at her face, the lovely, guileless American face, the eyes wistful, the jaw stubborn, and because it was a future that could not be he suddenly wanted it. Wanting it could get him through the rest of the week. And whatever they said about him afterwards, whatever she thought of him afterwards, at least he could leave her the memory of tonight.

"The taxis are sleighs?"

"Yes."

"And tinkling cowbells?"

"Yes. I swear they tinkle." She was beginning to smile.

"Real candles on the Christmas trees?"

"Yes. Yes, Rick."

"Oiga, waiter," he called. "Let's have some Carlos Primero."

"En seguida, maestro." The waiter brought the bottle and performed the ceremony of heating the huge snifters over an

140

alcohol lamp, letting the mellow brandy burn for an instant with a fluttering blue flame.

Ricardo Diaz raised his snifter. Pinwheels of gold and red, the colors of the Spanish flag, spun hissing on the barge. The staccato cracking of fireworks filled the air.

"It's pretty damn tempting," he said. "Let's drink to it."

He could see, he could almost see on Kate's smiling face, the future.

12

◇◇◇

Anarchists are rarely found outside Spain. But, Spain being Spain and anarchy being anarchy, the proponents of a government of no one, by no one, and for no one are not only numerous but divided among themselves.

In Catalonia, which is Spain only geographically and where the tempo of life is more French than Spanish, the anarchists believe with a quick nervous French passion in what they call anarcho-syndicalism. It is an anarchy in which the workers own the factories and reserve for themselves the decisions usually made by a parasitic political apparatus.

That anarchy, which is not anarchy at all, except of course in Catalonia, which is not Spanish at all, is looked upon with contempt in the south of Spain. In Andalucía the anarchy is of a purer and hence less practical sort. It is a naïvely mystical peasant anarchy, not unlike the communal movement of the nineteenth-century Russian mystic communist Bakunin, which was swept aside by the Marxist–Leninist totalitarian broom in Petrograd and Moscow. It is an anarchy which says if every peasant has his own small holding to farm, each will help the others and, faced with the purity and goodness of their lives, the corrupt government—all government being corrupt—will wither and die.

The former Civil Guard Pedro Ramírez had been an anarchist all his adult life, a fact unknown to Jesús Quintana and irrelevant anyway when he killed him. Scratch an Andalucian of a certain age and you are likely to find an anarchist. The fact that Pedro Ramírez had worked thirty years as a Civil Guard had not been inconsistent with his political beliefs. A man has to earn his pesetas somehow.

His friend Paco Oliva, the gateman at the subdevelopment who had informed Ramírez that the strange buildings on stilts were of Filipino design, was also an anarchist.

On Friday night he awaited the visit of a duchess. For Paco Oliva no gap existed between an elderly widower who lived alone in a hovel on the southern edge of the village of San Julián and the bearer of one of the oldest and noblest titles in Spain. Or, if a gap did exist, he stood above it and she below. He was a man, she a woman. He had twice her years. He remembered the at first glorious and then brutal days of the Civil War. She hadn't even been born then.

Promptly at nine o'clock he heard the car. Her promptness brought a smile to his gaunt face. She had spent too much time in all that France to the north. Who ever heard of a woman being prompt?

Oliva, who wore a shirt with collar and the one jacket he owned but no tie, moved quickly about the single small earth-floored room of his home. Two chipped glasses for the table and a bottle of red Valdepeñas wine. A plate, also chipped, laden with chunks of country-cured ham. An unopened package of cigarettes for the duchess, although he did not approve of a woman smoking. He lit three candle-ends, melting the wax so the candles would stand upright on saucers. He had no electricity. What did he need electricity for?

He heard the car door slam. Quickly he straightened the picture of the Virgin on the wall. He did not believe in God or the Virgin and he assumed the duchess didn't either. But it was a pretty picture.

He wondered what orders the duchess would bring him from the party in France. It alone of the old revolutionary parties still sent messengers across the Pyrenees. It hadn't died, like the others. It was only waiting. Gelignite bombs were the latest thing, a man who had visited him a few years ago had said. Gelignite, what a rare name. He had used TNT, almost forty years ago, to derail the ferrocarril Madrid–Córdoba. The engine, still puffing smoke, had shot off the tracks to the left. The troop-carrying cars had shot off to the right, tumbling over and over down a ravine. After the war he had been detained only a few months. Officers were shot. He had been young, only a recruit. The derailing of the train had been the big moment of his life, but he had had nightmares about it ever since. He did not like to think about the soldiers, screaming as the cars tumbled into the ravine. There ought to have been a better way, even if the soldiers had fought on the wrong side. Why didn't the government simply wither and die, as it was supposed to? He knew he would set no TNT charges again, and his interest in that explosive with the rare name was only theoretical. He liked the slow rhythm of his life. No one bothered him. He supposed he hated Franco because he had hated Franco in his youth, but even Franco wasn't so bad, really. He hoped the duchess had interesting news to bring him from the party.

He heard footsteps and a knock at the door. He already stood there, just inside, and opened it quickly. The duchess came in carrying a briefcase. Paco Oliva's smile showed the three yellowed teeth that remained in his mouth.

"Doña Maria Teresa," he said, and was going to bow. But the duchess offered her hand and he shook it. She was small and dark and quite pretty, but she shook hands like a man. He indicated a chair with a sweeping courtly gesture, and she sat. He opened the bottle of Valdepeñas and filled both glasses. He sat, pushing the plate of country-cured ham closer to her side of the table. She picked up a chunk and began to eat.

"Delicious, Sr. Oliva," she said, taking the briefcase from her lap and setting it on the table. It seemed heavy. It began to worry him. Maybe it contained gelignite.

He had met the duchess once before, through a young priest in Málaga who, with his worldly ways, had hardly seemed a priest at all. That was when she had organized the demonstration demanding a university in Málaga. It was an odd parade for Paco Oliva to march in. A university holds little importance for a man who cannot read. But he had marched. The Civil Guards dispersed the marchers only after they began to demonstrate outside the ayuntamiento, the city hall in Málaga, but the demonstration must have served its purpose. A year later stickers appeared on car bumpers demanding the university. The Civil Guards paid no attention to them. A year after that the university was founded.

They spoke for fifteen minutes. Paco Oliva realized he was doing most of the talking. The duchess was a good listener and he liked to talk. There were many funny stories he could tell about the rich foreigners who lived in the buildings on stilts, and he told them. The more he talked, the more he thought the duchess was preparing him for something he would not like.

His eyes kept going to the briefcase on the table. He hoped it did not contain gelignite. If it did, and if the duchess asked him to use it, he would. But the idea did not please him.

The duchess opened the package of cigarettes and took one. Paco Oliva leaned across the table and lit it with a candle. He hoped the duchess would not smoke too many cigarettes because they were Regalías, and Regalías cost a lot of money.

The duchess rested a hand on the briefcase. Paco Oliva's heart began to pound hard. She unfastened the buckles.

Paco Oliva cleared his throat. "Did you bring me gelignite?" he said. "I only wanted to ask." His palms were damp.

"What's gelignite?" the duchess asked.

"You don't know?"

"I'm afraid not."

"It's not important," said Paco Oliva.

The duchess took a sheaf of paper from the briefcase. "If you could paste these on walls in Málaga in the usual places," she said, "you will be serving the cause."

Now that he had learned the briefcase did not contain gelignite, Paco Oliva was somewhat disappointed. "Is it permitted to ask what is written on the notices?"

"The university in Madrid has been closed for months. These demand that it be reopened. They'll be posted in cities all over Spain."

It was, once again, something of importance about a university, entrusted to a man who could neither read nor write. Paco Oliva smiled, and then he heard a sound outside. The door burst open and a tall young man with blond hair came in. Behind him, one of them shoving him with the butt of a machine pistol, came two Civil Guards.

José Carlos supposed the Civil Guards had parked their car outside the village. He hadn't heard them coming. The first thing he knew, a flashlight had shined in his eyes.

"Get out of the car."

He could not see the uniforms in the darkness but the voice of authority was unmistakable. A cop, and not likely a tráfico. He obeyed the command.

"Face the car. Put your hands on the roof. Step back two steps."

He stood awkwardly like that while one of them frisked him. He was carrying no papers of any kind.

"Who are you?" the voice asked.

His first thought was of Maria Teresa. They knew she was inside there. He could not help that. His second thought was of his father. He did not want to implicate his father.

He spoke halting Spanish when he answered, using an American accent. "My name is Joseph Charles. I'm an American."

"Your passport?"

He turned around slowly. "In Torremolinos."

"What hotel?"

"I'm staying with friends."

He thought he could make a run for it in the darkness. But that would leave Maria Teresa to face them alone.

"We will see about your friends in Torremolinos later."

Something prodded the small of his back. He began to walk. He reached the door and it was pushed in suddenly and something hard shoved him through the doorway. He saw Maria Teresa and an old man seated at a table. The old man got up.

"Sit down, viejo. Put your hands on the table. Remain absolutely still."

The old man obeyed.

"Your papers," one of the Civil Guards said.

The old man asked: "Is it permitted to move my hand?"

"Your papers."

The old man reached into a pocket of his jacket and produced an identity card. One of the Civil Guards looked at it and tossed it on the table. The other one picked up one of the posters and squinted at it in the candlelight.

"Nothing," he said. "A thing of the university in Madrid. To open it, Roberto."

"To educate anarchists like these," grinned the Civil Guard named Roberto. He looked down at Maria Teresa, who had remained seated. "And now you, señorita."

In atrocious Spanish Maria Teresa said: "I demand that you call the French consul in Málaga."

"You're French?" Roberto asked, still grinning. "Would you say she is French, Fernando?"

"She looks Spanish to me," said the Civil Guard named Fernando.

Both Civil Guards were young, Roberto plump in a rumpled uniform and Fernando small and gypsy-looking in a uniform that might have been pressed half an hour ago.

"Is this Spanish?" Maria Teresa asked, tossing a French passport on the table. "Can you read? My name is Marie Pongerville. I am a citizen of France."

Fernando studied the passport. "There is no entry stamp."

Maria Teresa shrugged. "They didn't stamp it at the border. Sometimes they don't."

"You brought these posters?" Fernando asked.

"They are mine," Paco Oliva said.

Roberto leaned over and cuffed him backhanded across the face, not hard. "When we ask you a question, answer it, viejo. Your name is known to us."

149

"The milk of your mother," Paco Oliva said.

Roberto cuffed him again, harder, and Maria Teresa said quickly:

"I brought them from France."

Paco Oliva rubbed his nose and looked at a smear of blood on his knuckles. "The Frenchwoman is lying to protect me," he said.

Roberto hit him a third time, getting his shoulder behind the blow. Paco Oliva fell off the chair. He coughed out some blood and a tooth and scrambled to his feet, flailing at Roberto with both fists.

Roberto extended his arm stiffly, planting the palm of his hand against the old man's forehead and holding him off. Roberto was grinning.

Paco Oliva ducked suddenly and scooped one of the candle saucers off the table and hurled it at Roberto. It struck his shoulder. Hot wax splashed his face. Roberto shoved hard with both hands and sent the old man tumbling across the overturned chair.

The violence did not please the gypsy-looking Fernando. "Since we are going to take them in anyway," he said, placing a restraining hand on his partner's arm.

Roberto pulled away from him and kicked Paco Oliva in the side. The old man groaned and drew his knees up toward his belly. Fernando sighed. Maria Teresa got between Roberto and the old man.

"You're very brave," she said with no French accent. "Do you hit women and children too?"

Her teeth flashed white in the candlelight. Then she spat in Roberto's face.

His arm jerked up and José Carlos caught it and turned him and hit him a clubbing blow with his fist under the left ear. Roberto's knees buckled but he did not go down. He brought

150

his slung machine pistol up in an arc and the butt caught José Carlos' jaw, jerking his head back. José Carlos swung again, Roberto ducking under the blow and driving the butt of the machine pistol at José Carlos' belt.

Maria Teresa cried out. Fernando said Roberto's name, wearily, three times, as if he had had to put up with his partner's violence before. Roberto used the butt of the machine pistol each time his name was spoken, smashing it into José Carlos' ribs and his face.

José Carlos could hear the ribs cracking. He could feel the cartilege of his nose crushing under the buttplate of the machine pistol. His knees hit the floor and Roberto kicked him twice.

A voice said, over the roaring in José Carlos' ears: "He was trying to get away," and another voice said, "Yes, Roberto," wearily, and the first voice said, "You saw it, he was trying to get away."

Then José Carlos fainted.

With the window of the Ferrari down, Ricardo Diaz could smell the open ditches that carried sewage from the village of San Julián to the sea. His headlights picked up the sign to the Golf Parador and Radio Peninsular and the Holiday Inn. Then there was a stretch of empty road with sugarcane growing on one side and fields stretching flat to the sea on the other. He saw lights in that direction and braked to a stop, climbing out of the Ferrari and raising the red and white striped barrier at the head of a narrow road that led toward the lights. A no-trespassing sign was nailed to the barrier to discourage but not prohibit visitors. The Civil Guards, after all, served the people as well as the state.

Ricardo Diaz drove toward the lights. Soon in the moonlight he could make out the two-story brick building that housed the Civil Guard substation. He saw half a dozen cars parked outside and as many motorcycles. A Civil Guard came out and gave him a slow cop look and mounted one of the bikes and went blasting into the night. Diaz went up the steps and inside into a brightly lit room with whitewashed walls and a wooden divider and a few desks and chairs and filing cabinets and on the wall behind the divider a large portrait of Franco.

Two Civil Guards stood on the near side of the divider, heads down, one of them overweight in a rumpled uniform and the other slender and dark as a gypsy. Behind a desk on the other side of the divider sat a bald, burly Civil Guard sergeant droning softly in a monotonous voice. He looked like a bored priest until he saw Ricardo Diaz. Then he leaped to his feet and lunged through the hinged section of the divider.

"So they were trying to escape," he shouted in a booming voice. "How could they have escaped? You were armed."

"They were going to run," said the overweight Civil Guard sullenly. "It is true, I swear it. Tell him, Fernando."

The Civil Guard named Fernando mumbled something.

"An old man," shouted the sergeant, his face and bald head a mottled red, "a woman, and the son of the great matador Ricardo Diaz."

"They were going to run for it," the overweight Civil Guard said, more sullenly. "We did not know who the boy was."

The sergeant paraded back and forth in short angry strides, hands locked behind his back. He pivoted and stood before the overweight Civil Guard. "I shit in their going to run for it," he shouted, "and in your not knowing who the boy was, and in what you use for a brain." He struck Roberto three times with his open hand, hard. Roberto's head jerked from side to side. The dark Fernando winced.

"Now get out," shouted the sergeant. "Go kick the Bishop of Málaga in the balls. Go rape a nun. I wouldn't put it past you."

The two Civil Guards went slowly toward the door.

"Forfeiture of pay for two months," the sergeant called after them, looking like a bored priest again. Their backs stiffened but they kept going. Soon Ricardo Diaz heard the sound of a car starting and driving off.

"What can I say, maestro? What can I tell you?" asked the bored priest.

"How is he?"

"The doctor is with him now. The bullfight specialist from Málaga, Dr. Pérez Moreno. You know Pérez Moreno. Of course you do. The best, maestro. The very best for your son."

"Where are they?"

"Inside there."

Ricardo Diaz walked through the barrier and past the high desk and along a narrow hall to a dayroom furnished with a few cots and wooden chairs. An old man sat on the edge of one of the cots, his head hanging and his large hands dangling between his spread knees. José Carlos, stripped to the waist, lay on his back on another cot. Wide bands of tape bound his chest. His nose was swollen grotesquely under his blackened eyes. Maria Teresa watched while Dr. Pérez Moreno jabbed a hypodermic needle into his upper arm.

Pérez Moreno was a fat man with short-cropped white hair, a white mustache and rimless glasses. "Don Ricardo," he said formally.

"Don Agustín."

"Three broken ribs and of course you see the nose. They are

153

green fractures, the ribs, but he should not fight on Sunday. Even a small tossing—"

"I'll fight," José Carlos said. His voice sounded far away and hollow. "This year anyway. I promised."

Diaz realized Pérez Moreno had given him a sedative. "We'll talk about it in the morning."

"You used to fight with horn wounds still draining," José Carlos said in that faraway voice.

Pérez Moreno, who had put in the drains on more than one occasion, shrugged. "He'll stay here tonight," he said. "In the morning you can drive him back to the ranch."

"All right. Good."

Maria Teresa, her back turned, had yet to acknowledge Ricardo Diaz's presence. Now, still not looking at him, she said: "I don't know what to say, Ricardo."

"Don't say anything."

"They were only posters," the old man sitting on the cot said. "A thing about the university in Madrid. Of such gravity, posters for the walls of Málaga? That they should beat someone like that?"

José Carlos' breathing became regular. His blackened eyes were shut. Maria Teresa covered him with a coarse woolen blanket.

The burly sergeant and another man appeared in the doorway, the sergeant standing back deferentially. The other man was Jesús Quintana. He nodded at Diaz. "Tell them, sergeant," he said.

"The events of this night," the sergeant said in his bored priest's voice, "did not occur. The woman, the Frenchwoman Marie Pongerville, is free to go. The man Paco Oliva is free to go."

"You mean I can leave?" Paco Oliva asked. "What a rare thing." He got off the cot and touched Ricardo Diaz's arm.

"Matador, I am sorry about your son. It was a monstrous thing, what they did."

"Get out of here, viejo," said Quintana.

Oliva looked at him, and at Maria Teresa apologetically. "If you ever need me again, Doña Maria Teresa."

"Get out," said Quintana, and Oliva looked at Maria Teresa again and left.

"He's hurt," Maria Teresa said. "He may not be the son of the famous matador Ricardo Diaz, but they hurt him too, doctor. You *do* treat the poor?"

Pérez Moreno picked up his black bag and went outside with Maria Teresa. Quintana moved his head an inch, and the sergeant followed them.

"Is she always like that?" Quintana asked.

"How did you find her?"

"Yesterday she was seen in the company of your son in Málaga. She visited a priest named Galan who had been in trouble before. Other contacts were obvious. Early this afternoon she left some posters with an old woman who had fled Málaga with the Republican refugees during the Civil War. Then your son drove her to San Julián."

"Who was the informant?"

Quintana waved the question aside. "Leave that to me. After Sunday you may not have the time to do anything but run. I hope you appreciate what I did for you, killer. I had to go to the top, the Civil Guard commandant of the province. Me, Jesús Quintana, with my hat in my hand. Now I owe him one. I don't like owing favors. You have to pay them back sooner or later."

"What happens to José Carlos?"

"You heard the sergeant. The events of this night did not occur. You don't think that was his idea, do you? Don't worry about the boy."

155

"And the duchess?"

Quintana shrugged. His eyes studied Ricardo Diaz. "The same. She's free. That wasn't my idea."

"Santo Domingo," Diaz said.

"Sure, who else? She'll do it again. Santo Domingo knows that. She'll do it again and we'll land on her with both feet. That wouldn't exactly bother you, would it, killer? First your older son, now this. You satisfied? I wouldn't want you bearing a grudge, on Sunday."

"Nothing's changed," Ricardo Diaz said after a while.

"You're not so dumb," Quintana told him. He looked down at José Carlos and back to Ricardo Diaz, his eyes going expressionless, as if he had lost interest in both of them. He lit a Vencedor cigar, turning it slowly in the flame of the lighter, and followed Diaz through the hall to the front room where the others were waiting.

José Carlos moved his head. He tried to sit up. He was drifting in and out of a morphine stupor. He tried to fit together the bits and pieces of conversation he had heard.

13

◇◇◇

The reviewing stand, assembled from iron pipe and pine boards during the night, stood somewhat closer to the church than to the town hall of Puerto Real. By ten o'clock Saturday morning most of the dignitaries had taken their places: the mayor, the priest, the commandant of the provincial Civil Guards, the Director General of Tourism, the Director General of Security, the five biggest landowners of the region, and a few international celebrities including Kate Cameron, Richard and Elizabeth, and the garrulous fat man who had once terrified the eastern seaboard of the United States with a radio program.

By ten-thirty they were broiling under the hot sun and looking with envy at a platform raised a foot off the cobblestones where, in the shade of a velvet canopy fluttering in the hot wind that blew down off the mountains, half a dozen grandees of Spain sat on comfortable chairs sipping cool sherry and looking as if they wouldn't mind waiting another hour or two.

Those in the reviewing stand could see the cliffs above the town, the entire length of the steep Avenida Generalissimo Franco that went down to the beach, and a fair stretch of the beach itself. By craning their necks at appropriate times they would miss none of the pageantry. But the cannon that signaled the beginning of the events had yet to be fired. The cannoneer, like everyone else, was awaiting the arrival of Generalissimo Franco. The Caudillo, already an hour late, would make his first public appearance anywhere since the stroke that had almost killed him. The dignitaries were far more interested in the state of the Caudillo's health than in the pageant of Puerto Real.

In borrowing the legend of the flight of the last Caliph for their fiesta, the people of Puerto Real were no sticklers for historical detail.

For one thing, Caliph Boabdil had probably never set foot in Puerto Real. His fleet of galleys had set sail further along the coast, in what is now the province of Granada.

For another, no army of Spaniards had hurled stones from the heights above the port, whatever port it had been, in 1492. Boabdil and his court had marched in an orderly fashion to the sea, embarking with several hundred Spaniards who preferred life among the civilized Moors to life among the barbaric Christians.

The people of Puerto Real even had the time of the year wrong. The Caliph Boabdil had sailed in January, not May, but January with its uncertain weather was no time to hold a fiesta.

Nor was the traditional next-to-last day of the fiesta as ancient a celebration as the brochures commemorating the event, translated badly into four languages and distributed to the tourists, maintained. Most Puerto Realeños remembered a time when the festivities centered around a cattle fair and a few third-rate bullfights in a portable ring transported from Sevilla for the occasion. But a cattle fair does not attract tourists and no one would spend a thousand pesetas for a seat in a rickety portable bullring to watch a third-rate bullfight.

The festival was created out of whole cloth in 1958, the year the peseta was sufficiently devalued to become a stable currency, by a mayor of Puerto Real named Sanchez Prieto. Its success had led to the construction of Puerto Real's own bullring five years later.

Very few citizens of Puerto Real pointed these facts out to the tourists.

A not very prepossessing statue of Sanchez Prieto, who had been a not very prepossessing man, stood in the plaza between the church and the town hall. The bronze plaque on the pedestal made no mention of taking strenuous liberties with history. It merely gave Sanchez Prieto's dates of birth and death, followed by two words: *Con gracias.*

After Marbella and Torremolinos, Puerto Real had become the richest town on the Costa del Sol.

The longer he kept them waiting, Franco decided, the less the people would notice his infirmity. The dais was low, the car could park close to it. He would mount the two steps and cover the short distance to his seat swiftly with his aluminum canes. He wanted them to see, or think they saw, a reasonably healthy Caudillo. And he *was* feeling well. He should have come here

159

months ago. He looked at his wheelchair on the poolside terrace of Castillo del Moro. A few weeks in the healing southern sun and he could have thrown that abomination away. He smiled. Yes, he thought, isn't it nice to dream?

Beyond the pool and the manicured lawn he could see his chauffeur giving a final chamois-leather rub to the fender of the black Rolls-Royce. The car already gleamed. Half a dozen motorcycles stood on their kickstands near it, and two open Dodges that would carry additional Civil Guards. Franco's personal bodyguards would jog alongside the Rolls as the motorcade made its slow way to the plaza in Puerto Real.

In the old days Franco's bodyguard had come from the Army of Africa, grim-faced Moors wearing Moroccan khaki and the red berets of the Navarrese requetés. They had been an elite group, all well over six feet tall, intensely loyal to their commander-in-chief, who had led them out of Africa to save Spain from the Antichrist. They had not been Christians themselves and had spoken very little Spanish. Their presence reminded the people of the part they had played in the Civil War, and Franco, with his Gallego shrewdness, had got rid of them.

Now his bodyguard consisted of six brothers from Málaga who served with the Civil Guards. Their name was Gómez. They had never been put to the test as bodyguards—no attempt had been made on Franco's life in the more than thirty years he had ruled Spain. It was, he supposed, an indication of the people's acceptance of the regime. Well, perhaps not the regime. Most Spaniards opposed the idea of government on principle, any government. They tolerated it because it was a thing men must tolerate. But the people, finally, had accepted him. He had given Spain more than thirty years of peace.

One of the Gómez brothers brought his canes, and he began the slow walk to the car. He wondered whether Prince Juan Carlos de Borbón y Borbón, the tall handsome young man now walking across the lawn beside him, would do as well. Juan Carlos, grandson of the last Spanish monarch, would be proclaimed king after Franco's death. Well-educated and possessing an undeniable charm, he lacked his father's assertiveness. That was why the father had been passed over in favor of the son. Franco wondered whether that had been a mistake.

"It's going to be a scorcher today," Prince Juan Carlos said. He had white, even teeth and a matinee-idol's smile. He looked cool and composed in the uniform of an admiral of the Spanish Navy.

"It already is," said Don Alfonso de Salvatierra. "Summer comes suddenly down here." Don Alfonso wore a morning suit that already looked somewhat wilted. An attenuated young man, like so many of the old aristocrats, but harmless enough, Franco thought as a Gómez brother helped him into the Rolls-Royce. Not at all like his cousin. She'd be up to her old tricks as soon as she set foot on Spanish soil again. Oddly, the prospect did not displease him. There was something appealing about a pretty young woman flouting ten generations of family tradition with so much to lose and so little to gain.

The duchess' father had been a hard drinker and a womanizer, like Franco's own father. Probably she hadn't liked the sybaritic duke any more than he had liked the naval paymaster Nicolás Franco who had deserted his family in Galicia more than fifty years ago. When the naval paymaster had died in 1942, the Civil War over and Franco already Chief of State, the funeral had been a small, private affair. Adolf Hitler, not knowing Franco had hated his father, had sent a large, tastelessly Teutonic wreath. It had brought German troops no closer to Gibraltar.

"Will you see the fights this afternoon, Excellency?" Don Alfonso asked as the motorcade drove toward the gates of Castillo del Moro.

161

Franco frowned at the car's fourth passenger. "Dr. Caballero tells me I can see only one corrida. I'm waiting for Sunday."

"Ricardo Diaz and his son, isn't it?"

Franco nodded. He hoped Diaz would have a triumph, hoped the son would show some promise. The meeting aboard *Maria de la O* after the death of the older son still troubled him. He liked Ricardo Diaz.

"The older boy turned out rather unfortunately," Don Alfonso said. "My cousin's influence."

So this one wants to be Duke of Salvatierra, Franco thought without surprise. "Do you like the bullfights?" he asked.

"They're very Spanish," Don Alfonso said. He glanced anxiously at Franco to see if he had said the right thing. Franco's face remained impassive. "Rather too Spanish, I sometimes think."

"I like them," Franco told him, and looked quickly at the prince. Did he see a faint gleam of amusement in the dark eyes? He wondered whether Juan Carlos would eventually confer the title on this tanned, decadent aristocrat. He hoped not. The look of amusement was encouraging.

"I didn't mean to imply I disliked them," Don Alfonso said quickly. "But my cousin always adored them, and I suppose that prompted me to have reservations. We are—so very different."

"You don't like your cousin, Don Alfonso?" Franco asked.

Again that look of amusement in the prince's eyes.

"I don't like her politics. She's a disgrace to the Salvatierra name."

"Because she's an anarchist? That bothers you?"

"Naturally, Excellency." A half-formed smile waited on Don Alfonso's face. He looked confused.

"But anarchy is so Spanish," Franco said, "and it makes Spain so easy to govern. Anarchists disagree with one another

162

even more than they disagree with me. In a way I'm grateful to them."

Don Alfonso laughed uneasily. "I do see what you mean. The not-so-loyal opposition *is* rather splintered."

"Without leadership, that's true," Franco said thoughtfully. "But don't forget Opus Dei and the new technocrats. They could mount a real challenge to the Movimiento one of these days, and the anarchists might surprise us all by forgetting their differences and joining them in a new political alignment."

"Unthinkable," said Don Alfonso.

"I'm not so sure," the prince said as the Rolls-Royce turned onto the road toward town. "When a country is ready for political parties it gets them."

That was a conclusion Franco himself had reached in the long solitary months at the Pardo Palace. He hadn't expected the prince to share it.

"Forgive me if I disagree," said Don Alfonso coolly. "The Church and the landowners"—he glanced quickly at Franco —"and of course the Army, are the natural rulers of Spain. They always will be."

"That's one viewpoint," the prince said mildly. "I can see why a bishop or a general would hold it. Or a member of the landed aristocracy, Don Alfonso. But aren't you leaving someone out?"

"Surely not the people?" A droplet of sweat rolled down Don Alfonso's long aristocratic nose.

The prince smiled at him, a most open and engaging smile. "I was thinking of the Caudillo now," he said, "and myself later."

Don Alfonso's face went sallow under the deep tan. "Naturally, Your Highness, I only meant. . . ."

Francisco Franco settled back comfortably against the

163

leather cushions. He studied the deceptive matinee-idol good looks of Juan Carlos de Borbón y Borbón.

For the first time he could hope that Spain would be in good hands after he died.

It would be estimated later that more than fifty thousand spectators jammed the plaza and lined the streets and overflowed onto the beach of Puerto Real to watch the spectacle. What with the reviewing stand, the bunting-draped platform, the statue of Sanchez Prieto, and the space cordoned off for the official motorcade and the pageant, only a few thousand could squeeze into the plaza itself. Some of them had arrived before dawn to watch the construction of the reviewing stand and the placing of stanchions and ropes.

Among them was Paco Oliva. Until last night he had not planned on making what was for him the considerable journey —it was almost forty miles—from San Julián to Puerto Real. He was still surprised to find himself there in the crowded plaza as the motorcade rolled in and the Chief of State emerged from the enormous black car and, supporting himself with two canes, took his place on the platform.

It had been no impulse on Paco Oliva's part. He had lived too long in the slow Mediterranean rhythm of his life to be an impulsive man. He had thought about it for hours and finally decided: Well, if they put me in prison for it, they put me in prison, and if they don't, they don't. He had taken a few duros from the water jug under his bed and walked into Torremolinos, where he paid the few duros for a ride on one of the buses shuttling back and forth between the Noche y Dia

Terminal and Puerto Real. It was one of the first buses, and his early arrival gained him a place as close to the reviewing stand as the stanchions and ropes would allow.

The spectacle would be of much interest, and so would the viewing of the rare people—dukes and generals and film stars and the Chief of State himself—who came to see it. But Paco Oliva had not come for that, although if his heart weren't pounding so rapidly in his throat he would have enjoyed it.

He did not enjoy watching the Civil Guards holding the crowd back. They reminded him of last night. That they could take pleasure in beating an old man and a boy, and drive them to the Casa Cuartel in the middle of the night and then, astonishingly, release them. And why had they done all that? Because of some notices printed on flimsy paper, a thing about the university in Madrid. And then what had they done? Why, they had forgotten all about the notices, they had left them on the table in Paco Oliva's house.

He still did not understand the importance of the notices, but if the duchess said they had a value, then they had one.

Posting them on walls in Málaga was one thing, but how many people, Paco Oliva asked himself, would actually read them? The Malagueños scurried this way and that so quickly that they would hardly see the notices at all.

Paco Oliva had wrapped them in an old newspaper and brought them on the bus to Puerto Real. A gusty wind blew down off the mountains and when the moment was right he would unwrap the notices and hurl them up into that wind. They would spread and flutter and drift down on the crowd. A million people? Paco Oliva wondered. Well, maybe not a million, but more than he had ever seen in one place before.

The duchess would be very pleased with him.

He heard the boom of the cannon and for a while forgot the package tucked under his arm. It was like a motion picture theater, except that the screen was all around you and not a screen at all. It was really happening.

High on the cliffs above the town, so small they looked like insects, people began to hurl stones. They threw them toward an empty area of the beach, and of course no one was in any danger. It was, Paco Oliva knew, a hurling of stones at the Infidels, the Moors being driven out of Spain by King Fernando of Aragón so long ago that Paco Oliva's great-great-grandfather had not even been born.

Soon, to the beating of small drums, he saw the Moors coming. The men wore turbans and pantaloons and broad bright sashes, the women robes and veils. They marched along the cobbled street that entered the plaza alongside the town hall. Leading them, riding a white Arabian stallion, came the last Caliph—his name, Paco Oliva remembered, was a rare thing, hard to pronounce. Boabdil, that was it.

The Moors following him, even though they were citizens of Puerto Real dressed for the occasion, seemed so real that Paco Oliva still forgot the package under his arm. He watched the Moors pass along an aisle roped off in the plaza and enter the steep street that went down to the beach. He watched King Fernando's soldiers leave the heights above the town and hurry in pursuit. They were very convincing too in their doublets and plumed hats and silk hose, and Paco Oliva could almost imagine himself back in that ancient time when King Fernando chased the Moors from their last foothold in Spain.

Standing on tiptoe he could just see above the heads of the crowd the narrow street that ended on the beach, where a few score Moors waded into the surf and boarded three galleys with dark red sails and eyes painted on their prows. Oars dipped and splashed as the galleys moved a few hundred symbolic yards out to sea in the general direction of Africa.

166

What a rare sight! thought Paco Oliva, still forgetting the package under his arm as twenty fine horsemen representing King Fernando's army galloped far below along the beach, pennons fluttering from their long lances.

The cannon boomed again, signaling the foot soldiers who had hurled rocks from the cliff to strew roses and carnations among the spectators in the plaza of Puerto Real.

The throwing of the flowers brought Paco Oliva back to the present. He thought of the duchess, who had treated him as an equal, and he thought of the Civil Guards, who had beaten him. He took a deep breath and unwrapped his parcel and with both hands he hurled the notices as hard as he could up into the wind.

They floated and fluttered, soaring on updrafts and dropping and soaring again. They filled the air like confetti, like white doves, like snowflakes in the mountains above Málaga. Paco Oliva grinned like a little boy as a thousand hands reached for the notices, and a thousand more. Everybody thought them part of the spectacle, he realized. First the roses and carnations, then the white papers with the words printed on them that Paco Oliva could not read. Ai! the duchess would be proud of him.

Something jolted his back and he stumbled but did not fall because a big hand grabbed his arm. He looked up at the face of a Civil Guard. He slowly stopped smiling.

Eladio, the eldest Gómez brother, caught one of the notices as it floated down. His eyes scanned the printing quickly. He saw two Civil Guards rushing an old man away through the crowd, half-carrying him. Well, thought Eladio Gómez, if that is the only disturbance we have to contend with, we are hardly earning our pay.

He felt something touch his shoulder and craned his neck to see what it was.

The Chief of State was leaning down over the red and gold bunting-draped railing.

"Bring the man here, Eladio," he said.

Francisco Franco watched Eladio pushing his way through the crowd after the retreating backs of the two Civil Guards and the old man. Old? Yes, certainly old—he's only a few years younger than I, Franco thought as Eladio and the Civil Guards came back through the crowd with their prisoner. If a man could look proud and bewildered at the same time, that was how the old man looked.

The notice, which Franco had read quickly, contained a dozen short questions and a single answer. The questions were addressed to the Chief of State. They were rhetorical questions, concerned with the need to educate Spaniards to think for themselves and the fact that the University of Madrid was closed. The answer, for anyone dense enough not to supply it himself, was printed at the bottom. University City must be reopened, and the Chief of State alone could unlock its gates.

Franco could hardly disagree with that. He had wanted to open University City and, until Carmen brought the rector to the Pardo Palace, thought that he had. The rector's visit had opened his eyes and replaced a comfortable illusion with a difficult reality, and all he had done about it thus far was journey south to the fiesta of Puerto Real at Admiral Rojas Millan's suggestion. Since the Admiral was one of the designers of the illusion, if not its chief designer, that was hardly doing anything about it at all.

Still, Franco had all his life weighed options carefully before acting. Weighing options and applying subtle pressure instead of acting impulsively and applying unforgivable pressure had kept him in power more than thirty years. In the beginning he had been ruthlessly efficient in punishing enemies of the regime, but after a Civil War such ruthless efficiency was necessary. The other side, had they won, would have shot him as surely as they had shot General Goded in Barcelona. Franco had never, in the years since, victimized the country or imperiled the regime with a Stalin- or Hitler-style purge. It would have been unthinkable.

The careful weighing of options and the almost Oriental subtlety of pressure had become a habit. Probably a good habit in his fifties, in his sixties, even in his seventies. But now? Now he had no time for that.

He wondered what had prompted the old man to carry his handbills to the fiesta of Puerto Real and distribute them on the wind. What had the old man to gain? He did not, being dragged now to the bunting-draped railing, look stupid. He did not look fanatical. It would have been difficult for an old peasant who had probably never attended school in his life to be fanatical in the matter of opening a university. Then why?

The old man blinked up at him. He could move his head and very little else the way the Civil Guards were holding him. It was suddenly very quiet.

"What is your name?"

"Oliva," said the old man in a whisper. He cleared his throat. "Oliva, Excellency," he shouted. Don Alfonso de Salvatierra laughed.

169

"You read these things, Sr. Oliva?" Franco asked.

The old man's eyes dropped. "I cannot read."

"But you know what they say?"

"The university in Madrid. To open it, Excellency." The eyes looked up again.

Franco had a momentary feeling of unreality. What was he doing here, questioning this old man about a few hundred inconsequential handbills the old man hadn't even been able to read? Didn't he have more important things to do? The answer, and it came immediately, was that he did not. He was old, like the handbill man. The oil of extreme unction had touched his brow, but he still lived. Sending Eladio Gómez after the old man had been an impulse, unexpected, out of character, and strangely satisfying.

"You want the university opened?"

"Yes, Excellency. It would be a good thing, to open it."

"Who printed the handbills?"

Paco Oliva tried to wave an arm. The arm was held fast. He managed to wave a hand. "In all that France to the north."

"Let go of him," Franco said. The Civil Guards exchanged glances and released Paco Oliva.

"You have friends in France?"

"No, Excellency. I have never been out of the province of Málaga."

"You have done this sort of thing before?"

"Yes."

"Why?"

"I have often asked myself that question." Paco Oliva thought for a moment. "Must there be an answer?"

"No," said Francisco Franco, smiling.

"Is it permitted to ask what you will do about the university, Excellency?"

"You fought in the Civil War?"

"Yes."

"Which side?"

"The other."

Franco sighed.

"But you'll open the university?"

"As soon as possible, Sr. Oliva."

Oliva grinned. He had only two teeth in his mouth. He glanced at the pair of Civil Guards, as if surprised they were still there. He said: "Enjoy the fiesta, Sr. Caudillo."

"Go with God, Sr. Oliva."

Paco Oliva walked off, at first slowly. He turned around and half raised a hand as if to salute, then let the hand drop as he walked jauntily away until he was lost in the crowd.

Franco sent to the reviewing stand for Eduardo Santo Domingo.

"Find out who gave the old man the handbills."

"We already know," Santo Domingo said, his soft dark eyes expressionless. "The Duchess of Salvatierra."

"Dios mío, is she back in Spain?"

"She returned illegally this week."

"See that she receives an invitation to the banquet tomorrow night."

The soft dark eyes widened.

"After all," Francisco Franco said, "in a sense she's my hostess."

He regarded the look of amazement on Santo Domingo's face. Twice in the space of a few minutes he had yielded to impulse, and it pleased him. He wondered where his next impulse might lead.

14

◇◇

The mayoral of the Concha y Sierra ranch scrawled the numbers 7 and 48 on a slip of cigarette paper. He scrawled the numbers 27 and 15 on another, and 38 and 11 on a third. He removed his broad-brimmed Córdoba hat, folded the papers and dropped them in.

It was Sunday morning, the hour after dawn, and three men stood with the mayoral above the bullpen in the plaza de toros of Puerto Real. They could smell the six bulls that would be fought in the afternoon and see the sheen of their coats and their horns, thick as a man's upper arm at the base and dark there, and tapering to a white sharpness. The bulls, secure in one another's presence, nuzzled grain or rested calmly on their haunches. On the narrow walkway above the other side of the

173

bullpen a group of twenty men looked down at the bulls. They had come to see the sorteo, the sorting. Among them was the man who had said Fuck you, Mr. Ernest Hemingway.

"It's a pity about the Diaz kid," he said, and then amended that: "Or maybe he's just as well off. They look pretty rugged—for Concha y Sierra stock."

Another spectator slammed his hand on the high wall of the bullpen and called, "huh-huh, toro!" but the bulls ignored him.

"You're not much of a bull caller, friend," the man who had said Fuck you, Mr. Ernest Hemingway, told him. The unsuccessful caller of bulls, who had paid good money for his place on the walkway, uncorked a bottle of brandy and took a long pull.

On the other side of the bullpen the mayoral waited with the papers in his hat. The three men with him were the confidential banderilleros of Ricardo Diaz, Miguel Márquez and Palomo Linares, who would substitute for the injured José Carlos in the last corrida of the fiesta.

"You're all satisfied with the pairing?" the mayoral asked. The question, hardly necessary, was part of the tradition. The three confidential banderilleros had studied the bulls for half an hour and agreed among themselves on the pairing.

The small, well-formed 7, with medium-size horns, a good coat, a damp muzzle, and no defects any of them could see, was first choice of all of them. It had been paired with the bigger, huge-horned, nervous 48, the bull that had escaped the steers at the corral. You might get a magnificent fight from the 48, they all agreed—or the 48 might send you to the bullring infirmary.

The 27 was much like the 7 and had been paired with the 15, which pawed the sand restlessly from time to time and might turn out the most cowardly of the bulls. A manso, a coward, is a dangerous bull that charges unpredictably.

174

The 11 had short, slightly inward-curving horns which would minimize the danger of a goring. They had all decided to pair him with the 38. They did not trust the 38's left eye. Not that he was totally blind in the left eye. If he had been, the municipal veterinarian would have sent him to the slaughterhouse. But still, he seemed to have some difficulty with it. If the left eye failed to follow the muleta, the killing cape, when the matador went in with the sword, the matador might find himself up on the horns.

The three confidential banderilleros, all past their prime as bullfighters, nodded to the formal question. They were paid not for their ability to run a bull with a cape or plant the barbed banderillas, two activities they would perform perfunctorily later that day, but for their knowledge of bulls. The pairing was important. Their matadors' lives might depend on it.

A failed matador called Azaña Long Nose was serving as Ricardo Diaz's confidential banderillero. Working for the senior matador he got to choose first. Reaching into the mayoral's Córdoba hat, he withdrew a slip of paper. He opened it.

"The 7 and the 48," he said, rubbing his long nose. Ricardo Diaz would fight the 7 and the 48 that afternoon.

Palomo Linares' confidential man drew next. He got the 27 and the 15. Provided the 15 was not too cowardly, it was probably the best draw of the lot.

The confidential man of Miguel Márquez said: "I think I'll take the 11 and the 38," and the other confidential men laughed at his expected joke. "Maybe we'll give the 38 a pair of spectacles," he added, and they laughed at his unexpected joke.

"Huh-huh, toro," called the unsuccessful caller of bulls, fortified with brandy. The bulls continued to ignore him.

"You're all satisfied with the drawing?" asked the mayoral.

The confidential men of Palomo Linares and Miguel Márquez were most certainly satisfied. The practice of the pairing and drawing had been corrupted over the years, and a senior matador would often select the two bulls he wanted to fight. A senior matador as famous as Ricardo Diaz could get away with that, but it was not Diaz's style. He settled for the luck of the draw, and Azaña Long Nose had drawn him his luck, good or bad.

"A drink," said the mayoral, "to settle the dust."

He produced a bottle of Anís del Mono, the traditional before-the-bullfight drink. Each of the confidential men took a swallow of the sweet aromatic anís, and each wiped his mouth. The mayoral took a drink. "Much luck to you all," he said. Later, using long prods, the mayoral and his Concha y Sierra ranch hands would drive the animals from the bullpen into separate cages where they would wait out the final hours of their lives until one by one they entered the arena through the toril gate, the Gate of Fear.

"You may have a real bull of bulls with the 48," one of the other confidential men told Azaña Long Nose.

"That's possible," Long Nose admitted, but he did not look happy. There was something about the 48 that bothered him. It was an instinctive judgment. Had Ricardo Diaz been the other sort of senior matador, Long Nose would have avoided the 48.

The three confidential men and the mayoral turned to go, but before they could reach the wooden stairs they heard someone coming up.

"It's Antonio Buenavista," said the man who had said Fuck you, Mr. Ernest Hemingway, from the other side of the walkway.

Buenavista greeted the mayoral and the three confidential men and followed his paunch across the narrow walkway to get a look at the bulls. He stood perfectly still and studied them for five minutes.

"Give me a drink of that anís," he said, and the mayoral passed the bottle. Buenavista took a long swallow, a real swallow, and turned slowly.

"Tell Palomo he can buy a seat in the shade," he said.

Bound by wide bands of adhesive tape, José Carlos' chest felt stiff as plywood. Under the stiffness he could feel a dull ache that became a sharp pain when he moved. He had gone to bed early Saturday night and slept fitfully three or four hours, dreaming that Maria Teresa was in bed with him.

He woke from the dream disturbed and drank two glasses of water and went back to sleep, immediately dreaming again of Maria Teresa. She lay in his arms and said, "If only you knew how Spanish you are," and in the illogic of the dream he said, "An athlete and a bullfighter aren't the same thing," knowing those words had been spoken before, not by him but about him, and knowing suddenly when he awoke from the second dream that, broken ribs or not, broken nose or not, he wanted his time on the hard sand under the hot sun in the Puerto Real bullring.

He got out of bed and switched the light on. He sat on the floor smoking a cigarette, not letting himself think about the dreams. He took the top sheet off the bed and folded it until it was the size of a fighting cape, and he stood in front of the mirror and watched himself drawing the folded sheet back slowly along his right side in a veronica. The movement hurt his ribs, but not much. He drew the sheet past his left side, and that hurt more. He folded the sheet again, smaller, until it was the size of a killing cape, and he tried the pass of the dead one and the natural pass to the left, linking four or five natural passes before pulling the imaginary bull from behind him with a recorte that finished the sequence. That one really hurt his ribs.

He studied his face in the mirror, the strip of tape across his nose, the discoloration around his eyes. He thought Dr. Pérez Moreno could give him something, a shot of cortisone perhaps, to bring the swelling down.

Unable to sleep, he sat on the floor again smoking. He thought finally about the Maria Teresa dreams. He wanted her. He had wanted her in Paris, and he wanted her now.

He watched the faint blue dawn coming in through the windows. His father would not let him fight, or would at least try to talk him out of it. He wondered if his father still loved Maria Teresa. No, probably not. There was Kate. There had been Kate for a long time. But he couldn't help thinking his father would still be in love with Maria Teresa if Alberto had not been shot dead in Madrid. Was that Maria Teresa's fault? Well, he thought, yes and no. About as much as what had happened to him in San Julián.

A half hour after dawn he went to the guest room where Antonio Buenavista was sleeping. Buenavista was snoring gently. José Carlos shook his shoulder.

"Don Antonio."

Buenavista came instantly awake, looking up at José Carlos and nodding. He did not have to be told. "It's late," he said. "There goes breakfast. Thanks a lot, kid." He smiled.

Yawning and scratching the sides of his hard barrel-like paunch he got out of bed.

"They'll draw before I can get there."

"I'll take whatever Palomo's man gets."

"Want me to tell your father?"

"No," said José Carlos. "I'll tell him."

Antonio Buenavista began to dress. "I hope to hell you know what you're doing."

"I've got to do it, Don Antonio."

Buenavista went outside to his car and drove to the bullring.

15

$$\diamond$$

"Actually, these are damn fine seats," said the man who had said Fuck you, Mr. Ernest Hemingway. He grinned engagingly at his companion, who was wearing a big floppy-brimmed sunhat although they sat on the shady side of the arena. "Above the exit like this, nobody will block our view. And, as it's your first bullfight," he lectured, "a barrera seat wouldn't do. You'd see the action closer up, of course, but you'd miss the spectacle as a whole."

Handsome rather than pretty, he thought, looking at his companion. Very English in that long-toothed horsey way. Minor aristocracy perhaps. She had drifted into Harry's Bar late last night and had a couple of drinks. They had talked. He said he had an extra ticket to the bullfight, and she accepted the

181

invitation. She might turn out somewhat kinky—these blooded British types often were.

"That gate over there," he said. "It'll open promptly at five. The bullfight's the one thing on time in Spain."

Miss Kitchen looked at the big clock across the arena. "Two minutes," she said. "This is terribly exciting for me, you know. I mean, they say you're a real aficionado."

"Oh, I've seen my share of bullfights, Kitty. You get cynical after a while. They breed the valor out of the bulls and the matadors fake the action when they can. With the kind of crowd they have these days they can get away with it. They avoid danger like the plague. Here they come."

The band sitting on the sunny side of the arena struck up a paso doble. The crowd cheered as the big gates of the patio de caballos swung open. Behind a mounted bailiff in Renaissance costume the bullfighters began their march across the sand, embroidered dress capes on their left shoulders and arms, right arms swinging stiffly free as they strutted out.

"The one on the right in the blue suit, that's Ricardo Diaz. Márquez is the one in green. Diaz's son is wearing white, and no hat. For the next few minutes he's still an apprentice, you see. Keep your eye on Márquez. He should be the best of the lot. Diaz is all washed up and the boy's an unknown quantity."

"He's a beautiful young man. He hardly looks Spanish."

"Mother was American. Behind them are their peones. They'll nail the sticks."

Miss Kitchen looked her question at him.

"Sorry. Banderillas. They have barbed points. Matadors don't put them in themselves these days—another example of the decadence of the fiesta brava. Behind them's the cavalry, the picadors. Horses about ready for the glue factory, but that's normal. See how they're blindfolded? They'd bolt if they could see the bull. Those lances the picadors are carrying have shields behind the point so they can't penetrate too far. Which doesn't stop the picadors from trying. I've seen bulls piced so hard they almost bled to death. Another way of eliminating the danger."

"What are the mules for?" Miss Kitchen asked.

Three mules harnessed to a wooden bar followed the bullfighters across the sand. Behind them came three men in red shirts.

"To drag out the dead bulls. The types in red are the monosabios, the wise monkeys. Call them lackeys and you'll get the picture."

The man who had said Fuck you, Mr. Ernest Hemingway, held a wineskin at arm's length and squirted a jet of red wine into his mouth. He offered the skin to Miss Kitchen and she proved adept at it. "Several things you ought to notice," he said. "See the shields in front of those four openings in the fence? They're called burladeros. The bullfighters can squeeze in behind them but of course the bulls can't. You couldn't have a bullfight without them. And the alleyway between the two fences, that's the callejón. See down there? Those wicker baskets contain capes and the leather cases, swords. They'll be using the water in those clay jugs to wet down the capes. It's windy, and the weight will help."

The bullfighters had approached the shady side of the arena. Miss Kitchen watched Ricardo Diaz and Miguel Márquez sweep off their black woolly hats and salute with them.

"Saluting the president," she was told. "See? Behind the bunting, that's the president's box. The little fellow on the left I suspect you recognize."

The little fellow on the left was Francisco Franco.

Miss Kitchen awarded her companion a smile.

"President's in the middle. He's usually a landowner or the mayor or someone like that."

"It's Don Alfonso de Salvatierra," Miss Kitchen said, surprised. "I didn't think he liked the bullfights."

"He doesn't have to. The one on the right with the big smile

183

and the dangling forelock, that's El Cordobés. He'll tell the president what to do, when to change the acts of the fight, when to give a trophy. They do it with a handkerchief," Miss Kitchen was told.

"A what? You did say handkerchief?"

"The president hangs it over the railing. You'll see. Now, what else? That gate over there. It's the toril. The bulls come out there. They call it the Gate of Fear, and you can bet Diaz is feeling some of that fear now. He hasn't fought in close to four years, and he's doing it this time only to give the sword to his son."

"Those uniforms must cost a fortune."

"Trajes de luces. Suit of lights. They do. More than a thousand dollars each. Silk and satin and a tremendous amount of gold thread. Those jackets weigh twelve pounds."

"You really think Diaz is afraid?"

"He hides it, but you can tell. If he was a religious man he would have been in church this morning, praying. But they say he's an atheist. There was a time he believed in himself. He doesn't believe in anything now. No reason to feel sorry for him. He made a fortune with the bulls."

The parade went back across the arena, the mules and picadors leaving. Miguel Márquez unfurled his embroidered dress cape and handed it to a plump woman in the first row of seats.

"His mother," Miss Kitchen was told. Señora Márquez spread the cape on the railing in front of her.

Miss Kitchen smiled. "Doesn't he have a girl?"

"A bullfighter? He probably has to fight them off."

Ricardo Diaz gave his cape to a beautiful blond woman, and she spread it in front of her. There was a smattering of applause.

"Kate Cameron," Miss Kitchen was told unnecessarily. "Who's the little brunette?"

José Carlos had presented his dress cape to a small dark girl.

"It's the Duchess of Salvatierra," Miss Kitchen said in a startled voice. "That's funny."

"You're right, it is the duchess."

Miss Kitchen wondered what she was doing in the bullring when she should have been in jail.

"Look at the Diaz boy's face, Kitty. Am I mistaken?"

"I don't—oh, his eyes, I see. It looks like he's been beaten."

"I can take a guess," said the man who had said Fuck you, Mr. Ernest Hemingway, in a spiteful voice. "His father."

"You mean his father beat him up? Oh, come now."

"No, it's a decided possibility. The boy just gave his cape to the duchess, didn't he?"

"What's wrong with that?"

"Before he took up with Kate Cameron, Ricardo Diaz was her lover. You know these hot-blooded Spaniards. This could turn out to be an interesting afternoon at that."

The ring had been cleared. The two matadors and the apprentice matador went into the callejón for their fighting capes and emerged to station themselves behind the planking of the burladeros. A fat bullfighter in a tobacco-brown suit of lights stood alone on the sand.

"Buenavista," Miss Kitchen was informed. "He'll run the bull one-handed with his cape so Diaz can get a look at the way it moves."

"Diaz fights the first bull?"

"Well, ordinarily as senior matador he would. In this case he'll take it through the first part of the bullfight and then give his sword to José Carlos. He looks nervous, doesn't he? Watch the red door now, Kitty. The bull's about to come out."

185

In the still hot late afternoon sun, in the gusty wind, in the march across the bullring, in the formality of the ritual of death still to come, in the knowledge that everything one way or another would soon be over for him, Ricardo Diaz felt at peace with himself. It was not indifference; it was an acceptance of the implacability of fate which, in the western world, only a Spaniard truly understands.

Waiting behind the burladero he hoped he could maintain the mood. It would keep at a distance the fear that had driven him from the bullring at the height of his career. Now he had no time for fear. He had no time for anything, which really was saying the same thing. He had no time for anything but to be Ricardo Diaz, whoever Ricardo Diaz had become in this forty-first year of his life, with all the other years behind him which had made him who he was. He had known that instantly in the morning, and already the morning seemed a long time ago.

It had begun in church. Father Joaquín was serving the wafer to three old women dressed in black as Ricardo Diaz entered and sat in a back pew. Three old women in black to take the body of Jesus Christ in their mouths as they knelt before the railing in a small whitewashed church in Andalucía while Ricardo Diaz, lapsed Catholic, lapsed bullfighter, lapsed human being, watched.

Father Joaquín drank the wine and wiped the chalice with a linen napkin. He made the sign of the cross and droned words Ricardo Diaz could not hear and, hearing, would not have heeded. Diaz found himself walking toward the altar and the wooden Christ while the three communicants went past him and outside.

"Father," he said softly, but his voice had a fullness in the church and Father Joaquín gave the chalice to the acolyte and peered into the dimness, his round face ruddy over the white surplice.

"Ricardo Diaz," he said in a surprised voice as Diaz reached the railing. "You're fighting today, aren't you?"

"I don't want to talk in here, Father Joaquín."

The priest smiled faintly and looked at the wooden Christ. "He doesn't always listen, you know. Or He can listen anywhere. Will the vestry be all right?"

They went through a door into the small vestry, where Father Joaquín removed his surplice.

"There's something I have to know, Father." Ricardo Diaz looked up at the small crucifix on the wall. "Were you with my wife when she died?"

Father Joaquín neatly folded the surplice and put it in a black chest. "Why did you wait four years to ask me, Ricardo?"

"I'm not much of a Catholic. I have to know now, that's all."

"She sent for me, yes," the priest said. "She died in a state of grace."

"I don't care about that," Ricardo Diaz said. "Listen, Father—did she say anything about me?"

"I confessed her, Ricardo. I can't talk about that."

"Did she forgive me?"

"Virginia Diaz was a good woman, a good wife."

"I wasn't a good husband."

"I'd be pleased to hear your confession, Ricardo."

Ricardo Diaz laughed harshly. "It would keep you pretty busy, Father. I'm a lousy Catholic. I killed her."

"Haven't you enough sins on your conscience without inventing any?"

"I drove her to her death."

"There is a weakness of the flesh anyone can fall victim to. People die before their time."

"Those are platitudes."

"To those who don't believe, I deal in platitudes. I'm sorry."

"I guess you don't get many atheists, in here."

187

"I don't know what an atheist is, Ricardo. There are many paths to God."

"That's a platitude too."

"What do you want to hear, that an atheist could lead a life Christ would approve?"

"I'm not smart enough to be an atheist," Ricardo Diaz admitted. "And not smart enough not to be. Where does that leave me?"

"The Lord likes a challenge, I like to think," said Father Joaquín. "He's pretty human that way, you know. He understands uncertainty."

"I don't know how to put this," Ricardo Diaz said uneasily. "Say a man is caught up in something—circumstances, fate, I don't know. Say he's driven to do something you'd call the ultimate sin."

"What is the ultimate sin, Ricardo? Sometimes I think it's despair, the total despair that drives men to suicide."

"Damn it," Ricardo Diaz said, and Father Joaquín looked at him sharply and then pursed his lips in a faint smile. "There's something I have to do. There are people who'll suffer if I do it, and they'll suffer if I don't do it. They have faith in me and either way I'm going to destroy that faith. What kind of advice does God have for that, Father? Look it up in the book. Show me a way out."

"There's always a way out, here. Let me confess you."

"I can't. I'm sorry, Father."

"Then I'll say a prayer for your soul, Ricardo."

"Sure, you do that, Father."

Ricardo Diaz opened the door, and Father Joaquín preceded him out of the vestry and past the altar.

"And I'll pray for the souls of those who love you, Ricardo. I wish I could do more. I wish you'd let me do more."

188

Diaz took all the money from his wallet and thrust it into the priest's hand. "For the poor box."

"Well, the poor can use it."

They looked at each other. Ricardo Diaz had a sudden impulse to drop on his knees and ask for a blessing he could not receive. Instead he went past the railing and lit a candle and set it with the others glowing before the altar.

"That's for someone who'll die outside a state of grace," he said. "Would you pray for him too?"

"Can you give me a name, Ricardo?"

"Does it matter? Say a prayer for him, Father. Can you do that?"

"I'll pray for him. Go with God, Ricardo."

Ricardo Diaz left the church not knowing if the candle was for Francisco Franco or for himself.

Miss Kitchen looked across the sand to the opening of the toril. The bull had not emerged. An old man stood there flapping his hat in the entrance of the tunnel.

"It's dark in there," the man who had said Fuck you, Mr. Ernest Hemingway, told her. "The light attracts him, or movement."

The man jumped and flapped his hat against his leg. Still the bull did not appear.

"Look at Diaz," Miss Kitchen was instructed. She saw the matador standing behind a burladero, head and shoulders above the planking. He was gazing across the sand, not at the toril but at another burladero, where his son stood. "Here, take

189

the field glasses." Miss Kitchen took them. She brought Diaz's face into sharp focus.

"His own son," said her companion. "See the way he's looking at him? That's hatred if I ever saw it. I believe I was right about the duchess, Kitty. And the beating. Diaz does have a reputation as a hard-nosed son of a bitch, you know."

On the sand Antonio Buenavista waited with his cape. Ricardo Diaz watched the slate go up over the toril gate. He saw the number 27 written on it in chalk. A good, routine bull, nothing spectacular, Buenavista had told him earlier. The 27 was the first of the two bulls José Carlos would kill. On the slate it said the 27 weighed four hundred eighty kilos. Not very large, not like the monster 48, but certainly big enough for José Carlos' debut.

The old man was still waving his hat, trying to attract the bull. Ricardo Diaz stared at his son, head and shoulders above the burladero, collar of his cape between his teeth. He looks like a matador, standing like that, Ricardo Diaz thought.

He had looked very young and more American than Spanish when they ate a light lunch at Rancho Andaluz, his blond hair uncombed and his striped shirt open at the collar. Buenavista had joined them for lunch. They talked very little over the meal. They did not mention the bulls until Buenavista put his coffee cup down and said, "Well, me for a siesta. That's what the bulls are doing now, and I'm older than they are."

Ricardo Diaz got the bottle of Carlos Primero from the sideboard. "One drink?" he asked his son.

"No, but you go ahead," José Carlos told him.

190

Neither man spoke while Conchita cleared the table. She would not look at Ricardo Diaz. She did not like it that he was angry with Maria Teresa.

"To your first fight as a matador," Ricardo Diaz said stiffly, raising his glass.

"Broken ribs, broken nose, and all. Some debut."

"You can still pull out."

"I kind of pulled out of being an American," José Carlos said, "and I pulled out of being a Spaniard. I don't know what the hell I am. You know something? I'm going to find out today, with a pair of Concha y Sierra bulls."

"Still planning on school in the fall?"

José Carlos didn't answer the question. He poured himself some cognac after all. "We used to talk about her a lot, Al and me," he said.

Ricardo Diaz thought he meant Maria Teresa.

"After she died. Al was closer to her than I was, I guess. But it's funny, it hit me harder. At least I think it did. Al was a hard guy to know what he was thinking. But he said one thing. He couldn't figure out what you were doing in Madrid when she was dying down here. He never forgave you for that."

Ricardo Diaz had never forgiven himself. When Pérez Moreno sent Virginia to the clinic in Torremolinos he had thought there was a lot of time left. But Virginia sank very fast. She hadn't wanted to live.

"If she'd lived, would you have got a divorce?"

"Your mother didn't believe in divorce. She would have left me, though."

"Because of Maria Teresa? That's funny too, you know? Because I like her. So did Al. He knew you were having an affair with her and he knew what it was doing to mother. But that didn't matter. Figure that one out."

"I stopped trying to figure things out a long time ago."

191

"I ought to take my alternativa more often. You don't usually listen like this." José Carlos flashed a sudden grin. "Come to think of it, I don't usually open up like this."

"Spanish reserve," Ricardo Diaz said. "It's a lot of crap, of course. Dignity and decorum, and courage if it kills you. Sometimes something hurts too much to talk about, that's all. So you retreat inside a shell and call it dignity. Or you get roaring drunk without letting anybody know you are. That's decorum. Or you watch the bull and feel the fear gnawing at your belly, but you go in after him anyway. That's courage. Sometimes I think what makes a Spaniard tick—or a man—is how he goes through life deluding himself."

"We don't like who we are, you mean?"

"Your age, it's different. Or younger. A child dies, and what do they say? He died full of illusions. The world didn't have the chance to take them away from him. Or he didn't have the time to take them away himself."

"Old lighthearted, optimistic Dad," José Carlos said without mockery. "Bulls getting to you?"

"Going back after four years, that's a long time."

"You'll knock them dead," José Carlos said.

"I'd better. They'll expect it. Old Juan Belmonte came out of retirement and had three seasons like he never had before, and they said it was all tricks. Once you're on top they want you to fall. They wait for it. That's one thing you can't escape. Not in Spain and maybe not anywhere. Nothing makes more enemies than success does. *You* figure that one out."

José Carlos whistled. "You better have another drink, Dad."

"No, listen. They'll expect the impossible from you too, because your name happens to be Diaz. You'd better go in there knowing that."

"I know it. I always knew I had to live up to you."

Not after tonight, Ricardo Diaz thought. After tonight you'll

192

have to live me down. He put back the second glass of Carlos Primero in one gulp. "The ribs bothering you much?"

"Well, as long as we don't let the bulls know they're broken."

"Palomo will still go in there for you, if you want."

José Carlos tapped a finger against his temple. "He can't go in here."

"Goddamn Spic," said Ricardo Diaz, and they smiled at each other in a way they hadn't in a long time.

"Look," José Carlos said, "I wasn't going to bring this up. I thought I'd mind my own business, but we're rapping, you know? Go easy on Maria Teresa. It wasn't her fault I got beat up on." He looked at his father levelly. "Or that Al got killed. We're just not living in a time you can go tilting at windmills. She never did learn that."

Ricardo Diaz didn't say anything.

"She's one of the good ones. What the hell," José Carlos said, and poured himself another cognac. "I wasn't going to say this either. Maybe I better not."

"No, go ahead."

"Well, if she wasn't your girl in a way, I think I'd go after some of that myself."

Ricardo Diaz waited five seconds, then he threw back his head and laughed. The color drained from José Carlos' face.

"She's not my girl," Diaz said. "She never really was, mine or anybody's. You don't really know her, you just think you do. You don't go after some of that. Some of that goes after you."

"Maybe that's what I need." José Carlos managed to laugh too. "Teach me humility, you know? I never had much trouble in the girl department."

"Goddamn Spic," Ricardo Diaz said. He suddenly wanted very much, more than anything else, to see how his son would turn out.

193

"Hey, Dad. There's a name," José Carlos said. "Quintana. Jesús Quintana? Who is he anyway?"

"I don't know any Quintana."

"Sure you do. When Pérez Moreno put me under Friday night you were talking to a guy named Quintana. It was like a dream when you wake up you can't quite remember it, you know? He said some funny things."

"Oh, that Quintana. He's just a guy who works for the Admiral."

"No kidding? What was it all about, anyway?"

"Nothing much. He owed me a favor. That's how you all got out of there."

"What do you know," José Carlos said. "My old man moves in pretty exalted circles."

Ricardo Diaz lit a cigarette. "We'd better get into our fighting gear," he said.

Ricardo Diaz's sword handler Rafaelito laid out the clothing while his matador showered. At the foot of the bed were the black slippers, on the bed pink silk stockings, gold-embroidered blue satin breeches and vest, a ruffled white shirt, a narrow silk tie and sash. The heavy brocaded jacket with its broad epaulettes hung inside the closet door. The dress cape was draped on a chair with the black hat, the montera, on top of it. Rafaelito knew it would take half an hour to dress his matador.

His hair wet, Diaz came out of the bathroom in a white terrycloth robe. There was a knock at the door and Rafaelito said, "Yes?"

"It's me. Maria Teresa."

The sword handler looked at his matador.

"All right," Diaz said after a while, and Rafaelito opened the door.

In the old days it had annoyed the afición that Ricardo Diaz had not made a public spectacle of dressing to meet the bulls. He was the only one who didn't, and the hangers-on missed the chance to wish their matador good fortune or observe his face carefully to see if there was any fear in him.

It very quickly became part of the Diaz legend. He was a private man and finally, reluctantly, the afición came to respect him for it.

Maria Teresa had come in from the pool. She was wearing a black bikini and her dark hair was plastered to her head like a helmet. Droplets of water beaded her skin.

"All right, Lito," Diaz said again, and the sword handler left the room.

"This is one of the parts I used to like," Maria Teresa said with a tentative smile. "Giving your sword handler apoplexy because he didn't think there'd be time to get you dressed."

She walked across the room barefoot and climbed on tiptoe, bringing her arms up around his neck and pulling his head down to kiss him on the lips. "I used to like this part too," she said.

Well, he thought, looking down at her, there was time. In a way she was entitled to it even more than José Carlos. José Carlos hadn't been offered a choice of fathers.

Suddenly she drew away from him. "I'm doing this all wrong. I don't know how to say this. I'm not very good at apologizing. I'm sorry, Rick. I'm so damned sorry."

"José Carlos doesn't blame you."

"He should. So should you. Forgive me, Rick?"

He put his hands on her shoulders and felt how she was trembling. "Cold?"

"No, I've got stage fright. That's a laugh, isn't it? One of these days I'll grow up. One of these days maybe I'll even stop playing at politics. Tilting at windmills."

"That's the way José Carlos put it."

"That I'd better stop?"

"No. Tilting at windmills."

"Well, I'm going to stop. I mean it. I was going to catch a plane for Paris tonight, after the corrida. But there's a small complication."

"What kind of complication?"

"Didn't you see the official car? No, that's right, the Ferrari was out. An invitation to the banquet tonight, signed by the Generalissimo himself."

"What the hell!" Ricardo Diaz said.

"That was pretty much my reaction."

Diaz's arms dropped to his sides. He felt the skin of his face going taut.

"What's the matter?"

He could picture the banquet at Castillo del Moro, the chandeliers glittering over starched linen and old crystal and china, the waiters wearing white gloves, the politicians and generals and a bishop or two, the sharp-eyed, dedicated techno-crats with their computer minds, a few of the new crop of dollar millionaires, and at the head table Maria Teresa seated near Franco, and afterwards in the ballroom she would see him do what Quintana had made it impossible for him not to do. He blinked that vision away and saw Maria Teresa on the lawn at University City, Alberto's head on her lap, his face destroyed by three slugs from a machine pistol. Maybe, while the others stood in stunned silence, she'd have the chance to cry over his dead body too. That would give her something to remember. That would make it easy for her to catch a plane for Paris.

"What is it, Rick? You look so strange."

196

"Don't go there. Get on that plane."

"Of course I'm going. Nothing could keep me away. I just don't understand—what will they do, give me a medal for my activities against the state?"

"I'd better get dressed," he said.

"Remember that year in Bilbao?" she asked quickly. "Dominguín was there, and I suppose I did flirt with him a little. If you want to know the truth, I liked making you jealous. I wasn't sure I could."

She stood with one hand on her bare hip above the narrow band of the bikini bottom and stared up into his eyes. "In Bilbao, you said, they like bulls more than bullfighters. They buy the biggest bulls they can find and hope you'll do everything wrong. I guess you didn't particularly like Bilbao. I did what I could to change that. Didn't I, Ricardo? Didn't I, Rick?"

She shook her head suddenly. "I talk too much. I always say the wrong thing. I . . ." Her eyes blurred with tears. She's going to cry, he thought, and saw her shake her head again. Her damp hair fell across her eyes.

He cupped her face with his hands and kissed her lips gently. She brushed the hair away from her eyes and reached behind herself to unfasten the bikini top.

"There's time," she said. "Isn't there?"

"Sure, baby. Plenty of time."

They made love on the bed, on the blue and gold embroidered suit of lights. Under her head lay the crimson sash, almost the color of blood.

16

◇◇

K-Hito, the dean of Madrid's bull-
fight critics, once wrote that Ricardo Diaz had the slowest cape
in the history of bullfighting. Timing the movement of the cape
to the rush of the bull and then controlling the bull's charge
by slowing the motion of the cape so that man and bull seemed
suspended together for an impossibly long time was one way
of producing that heart-stopping emotion which is the essence
of bullfighting. Another way was to fight close to the bull, too
close to the bull really, in the bull's terrain it is called, so that
while the matador makes a plastic unity of himself and the
animal, the bull is in a position to disrupt that unity by destroy-
ing the matador with his horns. Ricardo Diaz fought in the
bull's terrain better than anyone else too, K-Hito had written,

and the combination made him the finest bullfighter of his generation.

Some small percentage of the ten thousand spectators who filled the bullring of Puerto Real understood that. They came to see the slow cape and the plastic unity and the fighting in the bull's terrain, as only Ricardo Diaz could show them those things. They watched while Antonio Buenavista zigzagged backwards across the sand, running the number 27 one-handed with his cape so that Diaz, behind the burladero, could study the bull's style. A considerably larger percentage of the spectators thought Buenavista was the matador they had come to see, and his age and girth and gracelessness disappointed them.

Buenavista took three running strides and heaved his bulk behind the burladero where Ricardo Diaz stood. The bull kept coming, hooves thudding on hard-packed sand, horns banging against the wood while Buenavista and Diaz looked over the top at him. They could feel the strength of those horns each time they struck the burladero. Around the curving barrier Azaña Long Nose flapped his cape and shouted to attract the bull's attention.

Ricardo Diaz stepped out onto the sand.

"You see, I told you," said the man who had said Fuck you, Mr. Ernest Hemingway. He looked down toward the sand scornfully. "That's about what you can expect from Diaz. He's let Buenavista do a lot of one-handed running, if you see what I mean. Now he'll make a halfhearted pass or two and call for the cavalry. He's just going through the motions."

Miss Kitchen nodded. A malicious type, her new friend, she

decided. They were often better than the athletic ones like Alfonso. The malice covered an uncertainty about themselves, a weakness that could be probed and used. You could do a lot with that kind of man, a lot he never dreamed of, and never mind Alfonso and his silly props. You could really turn a malicious man into a plaything. You could have him crawling, begging for it.

Ricardo Diaz walked across the sand, feeling his cape flutter and sculpture itself for a moment against his right leg as a gust of wind whipped down from the northern side of the amphitheater.

Twenty yards away the bull turned, and the small eyes saw the man in his blue and gold suit of lights. Diaz had waited for that moment, knowing what he could expect from the bull but less certain of his own reaction. He raised the cape and snapped it down hard so that it flapped like a sail in a sudden crosswind. Attracted by the motion, the bull started toward him.

He waited for the fear that had driven him from the bullring almost four years ago, and the fear did not come although the bull very definitely was coming now at a hard, sand-spurting gallop. He passed it easily on his right side, drawing the cape back slowly, diverting the bull's charge from his own body to the cloth. Still there was no fear, no need to will his legs to remain in place, and he spun and jerked his right wrist to attract the bull with the flutter of the cape, and drew the bull past again with another veronica, closer, but still in his own terrain, not the terrain of the bull. This time the bull kept going

201

and Ricardo Diaz, swept up by the ease with which he had executed the first two passes, almost called him back. But the applause and the few olés he heard would have to do for now. This bull belonged to José Carlos.

He removed his montera and lifted it in the direction of the president's box. A faint smile touched his face when the applause gave way to booing and whistling.

In the president's box Alfonso de Salvatierra leaned toward El Cordobés. "Does he want me to change the act already?"

"Bring in the horses, yes."

"But he hasn't done anything yet."

A matador's request for a change of tercio could be obeyed or ignored by the president.

"It's his son's bull, Don Alfonso," El Cordobés explained.

"I suppose I see what you mean. The more he does, the more they'll expect from the boy."

"Something like that."

"Is the boy any good?"

"We'll find out soon enough," said El Cordobés with his usual beaming smile.

Don Alfonso draped a handkerchief over the railing, and a trumpet sounded to summon the picadors.

The middle-aged hippie who owned Sally's Alley in Torremolinos watched the two picadors riding into the arena from the patio de caballos. She did not like the part with the horses, even though they wore protective padding and were only rarely disemboweled by the bull. The reserve picador stationed himself just outside the patio de caballos. The other rode his blindfolded nag around the ring and reined up a few yards from the shut toril gate. From her seat on the shady side of the arena Sally watched Ricardo Diaz cape the bull without grace toward the horseman. The crowd responded with more booing. Diaz did not seem to mind. He retreated behind the horse as the horns thudded into the padding and the picador leaned far out of his saddle, driving the point of his long lance into the bull's back just behind the crested tossing muscle, using his weight to force the steel deeper until it was stopped by the crosspiece separating point from wooden haft of the lance. After a while Diaz caught the bull's attention and caped him away, artlessly again, merely flapping the cloth and pulling the bull off with the motion. The booing was less strenuous this time. It wasn't a bad performance, it was merely indifferent, and the crowd responded with an indifference of its own.

Sally drank cognac from a leather-covered flask. She had been impressed with Diaz that night he had come for his son. Now she felt sorry for him. Well, she thought, the cognac warming her, he's not exactly a spring chicken. He doesn't look scared, though—just as if he doesn't care. Cynical, maybe, because he's ten years past his prime and knows the one thing you can't do is get the years back. You could cry over them, and how you wasted them, and sometimes you could even deceive yourself.

The kids like me, Sally thought. I'm one of them. But then she had another swallow of cognac and smiled bitterly. Like hell I am. I sell them pretty good Moroccan kif, that's all, and I give them a place to smoke it. I've been here too goddamn long. I'm not fifty, I'm forty-four. Big fucking difference. This coast belongs to the very young and the very rich. Fool yourself long enough and it gets to be a habit. What I ought to do is get the hell out of here. She gulped more cognac, some of it dribbling down her chin. There are no old-folks homes for foreigners in Spain.

The only trouble was she had nowhere to go. No goddamn where at all. With Diaz it was different. That ranch of his, a few hundred thou in a Swiss account probably, and whatever he did today, all the long years ahead of him to reap the rewards of his fame.

Sally no longer felt sorry for Ricardo Diaz. The bull had been piced three times and Diaz had signaled with his hat that three would be enough. She found herself hating the bastard, lifting his hat to the box where Franco sat and instructing them what to do and they did it.

One of these days they'd catch her with the good Moroccan kif on her, and then what? Slam the prison door behind her and drop the key into the goddamn Med.

"I am not fifty," she said out loud, and the fat Spaniard sitting next to her glanced in her direction. She realized she was a little bit drunk.

She watched the horses leaving the arena. She hoped Ricardo Diaz would get a little bit careless.

Antonio Buenavista ran across the sand, raising the harpoon-pointed sticks and, as he crossed the line of the bull's charge, planting them in the animal's back. Buenavista loped off in one direction and the bull in another, the banderillas clattering against each other. Buenavista had driven them in too low on the right side.

Behind a burladero Ricardo Diaz asked: "You ready?"

José Carlos nodded, licking dry lips. "It's a better bull than Antonio thought, isn't it?"

"It was better. Or maybe it just looked better. Watch this."

This was the second, younger banderillero, a man named Maldonado. He jumped, light-footed, raising the sticks high as his feet left the sand. The bull came toward him at a quick trot. On his toes Maldonado brought the sticks up higher, over his head, and drove them close together into the bull's back. The animal trotted past, bellowing, head swinging, and then its forelegs gave out, buckling, and it went skidding across the sand.

"Jesus," José Carlos said.

"Too many bullfights, not enough real fighting stock to go around," Ricardo Diaz told him. "This one's less than four years old, grain-fed to get it big enough. It's run out of gas. You won't get much of a faena out of it. Don't try. Chop it down some. Kill it in a hurry."

"I guess," José Carlos said. "Some debut."

Ricardo Diaz said the only thing he could say. "There's another bull waiting for you."

"What if it runs out of gas too?"

Diaz looked at his son. "There's always the sobrero."

The sobero was the substitute bull, used if one of the six animals fought that day turned out to be defective or if—equally rare—one of the matadors decided he'd had bad luck he wanted to change or good luck he wanted to maintain, and bought the sobrero to fight after the six bulls of the corrida had been killed.

"The sobrero's a Miura," Ricardo Diaz said, "and Miuras don't run out of gas. Just take it easy, kid. If your second bull's a dud we'll shock the hell out of Don Eduardo. We'll buy the Miura for you."

José Carlos grinned, and then the trumpet sounded.

"Why doesn't the bull charge?" Miss Kitchen asked.

The bull was on the sunny side of the ring, facing a burladero behind which Antonio Buenavista stood. Every now and then the bull would hook his right horn at the planking. Every now and then he would turn away, and Buenavista would call him and wave his cape over the boards.

"He hopes he can get a shot at Buenavista," the man who had said Fuck you, Mr. Ernest Hemingway, explained. "Which gives the boy time to get his doctorate."

"His doctorate?"

"That's what they call it. A doctorate of tauromachia. He gets it from his padrino, his godfather. In this case, his own father. And Márquez is there as testigo. Pretty little ceremony, isn't it? It ought to be, anyway. But here—take the glasses and look at Diaz. Wouldn't you say he looks angry? There's bad blood between them, I tell you."

"The duchess?"

"It's not just the duchess. Something that happened in Torremolinos earlier this week. The boy got himself involved with—I'll tell you later. There goes Diaz for his sword."

The red leather scabbard went suddenly limp as Ricardo Diaz drew the sword, feeling the familiar felt-wrapped hilt, seeing the gleam of Toledo steel and the downward-curving tip. Beyond where José Carlos and Miguel Márquez were waiting stood the bull. A red ribbon of blood striped the black heaving flank, result of the picing. A pair of banderillas was still in place, too low on the right side, clattering when the bull hooked at the fence. The sticks would make right-hand passes difficult, whacking against José Carlos' chest every time he tried them. The bull's gray tongue protruded and he looked over the planking at Buenavista and bellowed. He'd run out of gas, all right.

Ricardo Diaz approached his son. He held the sword in his right hand and gave José Carlos an abrazo, pulling him close. "He's finished," he said in English. "Just get it over with. Never mind the crowd."

As José Carlos took the sword from his father the crowd applauded politely.

"Better not pass him on the right. Antonio nailed the sticks too low."

José Carlos' lips were dry. "Yeah, okay," he said.

Miguel Márquez came over, offering José Carlos an abrazo of his own. "Hey, speak a language a guy can understand." He smiled a quick shy smile and stood back. "Sometimes the patient's too far gone, doctor. You'll have others."

José Carlos looked at both of them. "That's all?"

"Well, I was supposed to make a speech. That's what they think I'm doing now," Diaz told him. "Let's save it for another bull."

"Many ears," Miguel Márquez said, and Ricardo Diaz gave his red serge killing cape to his son. The muleta was furled over a notched stick. Márquez and Diaz walked across the sand and slipped behind a burladero. They went through and kept walking along the curving callejón between the fences. They would come out on the other side of the ring behind a burladero close to where José Carlos would confront the bull.

José Carlos stood alone. Sword in hand, muleta under his arm, he marched to the barrier below the president's box. He raised his head and saluted with the sword. He saw Franco looking down at him then, smiling. Setting the montera squarely on his head for the first time, he walked across what was suddenly an immensity of sand, a desert, to the center of the arena. He took off the montera and slowly pivoted, holding it aloft. Then he tossed the hat over his shoulder, dedicating the first bull of his career as a matador to the ten thousand spectators.

He went to where the bull waited, and unfurled the muleta. The notched stick felt slippery in his sweating hand.

"Toro," he said softly, and then louder: "Toro!"

The bull swung away from the red planking.

High on the sunny side of the amphitheater the blond girl wearing granny glasses had to shout to make herself heard. "I feel so sorry for him, you know?"

A fresh wave of booing and whistling swept over the packed stone benches.

José Carlos in his white suit of lights stood in front of the bull. The bull was down but not dead. José Carlos spread the muleta on the sand below the black muzzle and raised not the killing sword but the descabello, the execution sword with the crossbar behind the point. He had tried to cape the bull, but it had stood like lead. He had tried short chopping passes, but the bull had only swung its head, tongue protruding. He had squared the bull, forelegs parallel, and gone in with the killing sword. He had hit bone. He had tried again and hit bone again, sword buckling and spinning away. He had tried three more times. The bull was made of cement. Cushions had been hurled into the ring. Finally the bull had collapsed near the barrera. José Carlos had exchanged sword for descabello.

Buenavista and Azaña Long Nose stood on either side of the fallen bull, their big capes spread. José Carlos brought the descabello up and then down, missing the spinal cord at the base of the bull's skull. The bull stood and settled on its haunches again. More cushions hit the sand. José Carlos forced the bull's head down with the point of the descabello and tried the execution thrust again. The bull twitched and stood and swayed and settled on its haunches again. José Carlos tried once more. The bull did not die.

"I thought he was supposed to be pretty good," said the boy whose father sold Pontiacs in Worcester, Mass.

"Look at him," said the other blond girl. "The poor guy. He's crying."

The crowd hooted. A cushion struck José Carlos' leg. He spread the muleta again.

"Christ," said the boy. "After this selling Pontiacs won't be so bad." He had run out of money. His father had sent him a plane ticket home. "Or college."

"Or anything," said the girl with granny glasses.

They watched José Carlos spreading the red serge cape. A short man wearing a white jacket and white cap came out through a burladero. He had a dagger in his hand. José Carlos shook his head. Ignoring him, the short, white-jacketed man leaned over the bull behind the horns and drove the dagger in. The bull jerked and rolled over on its side and was dead.

José Carlos walked away with his muleta and descabello, not looking back.

"Poor J.C.," said the girl with granny glasses. She felt like crying too.

17

◇◇

The sun sank lower behind the western rim of the plaza de toros. The minute hand of the big clock jerked a two-minute segment of the past into the present, and another, and another.

Ricardo Diaz had his twenty minutes in the sun with the number 7 bull. The number 7, sleek, well-formed, with a good spread of horns, proved a disaster. The number 7 broke his charges, hooking to the left and upward, catching the cloth with his horns, letting Diaz complete no passes. The number 7 charged the picador once, tasted steel, and would not charge again. The number 7 bellowed and stood his ground and got a pair of badly planted banderillas from Azaña Long Nose and another pair from Maldonado. Diaz, eyes bleak, tried no faena with the killing cape. He chopped five times, six, lowering the number 7's muzzle.

The crowd screamed "No!" and Diaz ignored them. He was out around the horn before going in with the sword. He stabbed for the lung, in no danger himself, and the bull shuddered and hemorrhaged from the mouth and died. Diaz walked into the callejón.

The minute hand of the clock jerked again.

"Didn't I tell you he was all washed up?" said the man who had said Fuck you, Mr. Ernest Hemingway. Miss Kitchen didn't hear him. His voice was swept away by the boos and whistles and catcalls.

Sally, quite drunk now, was smiling. It serves the bastard right, she thought. A real debacle. Let him see how the other half lives.

The girl with granny glasses was pale. The sight of blood gushing from the bull's mouth sickened her. She left her seat quickly and ran for the exit.

In the president's box El Cordobés was not grinning. Lousy bicho, he thought. You couldn't get a fight out of a bull like that if your life depended on it.

Francisco Franco shook his head as he watched the mono-sabios clear the litter of torn paper and cushions and bottles that had been hurled into the arena. They forget so fast, he told himself. Once Ricardo Diaz had been their hero. Then, twenty minutes of bad luck in the sun, and this. Soon, perhaps, they would say Diaz had been a fraud even in his good days. And what, Franco wondered suddenly, will they say about me? After I die, after enough time has passed so they can say what they think? Not twenty minutes in the sun with bad luck Almost forty years. Will they remember the mistakes only Dios mío, yes, I have made mistakes.

Miguel Márquez, wearing a big smile over his bottle-green suit of lights, went trotting around the arena. He stopped here and there, lifting that smile up to the packed benches, holding aloft the ears of the bull he had just killed.

Trailing behind him, his banderilleros picked up bouquets of roses and carnations. They retrieved Córdoba hats and berets, tossing them back into the stands. One of them caught a hurled wineskin, and their matador paused in his circuit to squeeze a stream of tinto into his mouth. The crowd was on its feet roaring. Márquez trotted out to the center of the ring and held the two ears high. He shook his head, as if he felt unworthy of the crowd's acclaim, and began another circuit of the arena.

The number 38's vision had not been defective. The 38 had been a bull that charged on railroad tracks, back and forth, back and forth every time Márquez swung the big percale cape, every time he executed ayudados and naturales with the smaller killing cape. Márquez had profiled with the sword and gone in once, right over the horns, and the bull took the sword in to the hilt and went over, all four feet in the air.

After his second circuit of the ring Miguel Márquez went into the callejón. He mopped his face with a towel and drank water from a clay jug.

"I had a little luck," he told the Diazes.

***

The minute hand of the big clock jerked, the sun dropped, the shadows lengthened across the arena.

"Ricardo's second bull could be the best of the lot, Excellency," El Cordobés told Francisco Franco. "Buenavista liked the look of him."

213

A second bull, a second chance, Franco thought, hoping El Cordobés was right.

There would, of course, be no second chance for the Caudillo of Spain. With his actions, good and bad, he had made his place in history. When the judgment was rendered he would be in his crypt in the Valley of the Fallen.

The dark opaque eyes narrowed. How much time had he left? Did he have twenty minutes in the sun with another bull?

The crowd came to its feet. The toril, the Gate of Fear, opened. A magnificent coal-black bull came exploding out.

"It's the old adage," Miss Kitchen's companion said contemptuously. " 'When there are bulls there are no bullfighters, and when there are bullfighters, no bulls.' This one is what they call a toro-toro, a bull of bulls. Look at him."

Miss Kitchen looked at him.

"And see what Diaz is doing with him. It's criminal."

Diaz was passing the bull with a veronica and skittering back out of danger.

A few minutes later: "And look at that."

Leaning far out of his saddle, the picador was punishing the bull, insisting with the steel, getting the weight of his shoulder behind it while the bull wanted to break contact.

And later: "Does he call that a faena? It's a damn disgrace."

And finally: "That's no kill, it's a slaughter. See how Diaz is avoiding the horns? In the old days the Civil Guards would have had to get down there and protect him from the crowd. You see what I mean?"

Miss Kitchen saw what he meant. So did the crowd.

So did two Civil Guards in the detachment, forty strong, seated high on the sunny side of the amphitheater. Plump Roberto glanced at the gypsy-looking Fernando.

"For that he became rich," Roberto said.

"And the son. The son was no better," Fernando said.

"A toro-toro like that. The bastard. I wish we'd had him that night along with the boy."

Fernando thought of the forfeiture of pay. He nodded slowly.

"Never mind the towel," Ricardo Diaz said in the callejón. "I want a drink."

Rafaelito handed him the clay water jug.

"I said a drink."

Rafaelito went away and came back with a bottle of Fundador. Diaz tilted it, letting the harsh brandy scald his throat.

"What was it, Ricardo?" Antonio Buenavista asked gently.

Ricardo Diaz took another drink. "I don't know. He was a pretty good bull." He could have been a great bull, Diaz thought. He had known that as soon as the 48 came hurtling from the toril.

Márquez came over. "Nothing, Ricardo," he said. He was embarrassed. "I have days like that. We all do."

Ricardo Diaz hardly heard him. He felt nothing but the gut-wrenching awareness of tonight that had overwhelmed him when the 48 came out. He had fought the bull in a daze.

He took another drink. Brushing the back of his hand across

his mouth, he looked at José Carlos. The boy was licking his lips nervously. He turned away, and they both saw the slate going up over the toril.

The crowd applauded as Miguel Márquez stepped onto the sand to fight his second bull. There was one real matador out there anyway.

"Key tay?" Miss Kitchen repeated the unfamiliar sound.

"Yes, that's almost right—*qui*-te. From the verb quitar, to take out. I gather your Spanish is a bit rudimentary?"

"It's bloody awful," admitted Miss Kitchen.

"Well, this could be worth watching. The quite used to be an important part of a bullfight. The matadors were in direct competition, you see, all three of them out there while the picador went to work with his lance. A good five-year-old bull could take as many as eight or nine pics, if you see what I mean, and if the bull insisted under the lance they had to take him out.

"They took turns executing some pretty fancy passes getting the bull away from the horse. Gaoneras. Faroles. Chicuelinas. But what really gets the crowd is the classic stuff, a series of veronicas finished by a media veronica. The only trouble is you don't see it much these days. The bull's trying to spill the horse, so the men have to get dangerously close to begin a series of quites. They avoid it when they can. Another sign of the decadence that—"

"Look," said Miss Kitchen.

The bull was hooking for the quilted padding on the horse's right side, one horn clanking against the picador's iron box-

216

stirrup as Márquez came around the horse's flank flapping his cape. The snapping sound and the movement attracted the bull, and Márquez swung his cape, pulling horns and muzzle into it.

"Olé!" cried the crowd.

Márquez swung the cape again. It swirled around his body, fixing the bull in place. Applause swept the arena. The picador waited, lance back under his right arm, horse pawing the sand nervously as Márquez led the bull back with a final long sweeping motion of his cape.

"You don't often see that," Miss Kitchen's companion admitted. "It's the crowd, really, more than Márquez. They're inspiring him, you see."

What a totally jaded man, thought Miss Kitchen. The jaded ones could be most diverting if you trained them. The way Márquez down there had trained the bull.

"Ricardo Diaz is supposed to do the next quite," she was told. "He won't. They'll blow the trumpet. Why should Diaz work up a sweat? It's a charity performance, if you see what I mean. Nobody's paying him to risk his life."

"The boy in white," said Miss Kitchen as José Carlos came around the horse's flank. With the first sweep of his cape the crowd was on its feet roaring.

José Carlos planted his feet. Left foot, then right. He could feel the hard-packed sand shift a little under the thin soles of his slippers. He could hear the crowd chanting its olés. The bull's ear twitched and the tufted tail lifted as the bull charged.

José Carlos accepted the charge, and the great black bulk

217

came at him. He pulled the cape back slowly, low on his left side. The bull went by, left flank brushing his hip. He felt a sharp knife of pain in his ribs. He no longer heard the crowd. The bull was everything. He brought it past him again, slowing the charge. The left horn whacked against his ribs. He did not feel the pain now. The bull trotted off a few paces, and José Carlos ran after him calling. He repeated the pass, the veronica, on the punishing left side. He had the bull. He had the darkness of it, and the mystery. It went past, the horns and then the long sweeping blackness jolting him. He could smell the hot carnal stink of the beast. He called it again.

Maria Teresa leaned on José Carlos' dress cape spread on the railing. God, she thought, you're your father all over again, you even look like him now, oh Christ, again again again, the way you're doing it now, sweet Mother of God look at you, Spanish even with your blond hair and those blue eyes, and I'm Spanish too, I'm not going back to Paris or anywhere, I belong here—
She stood up and she screamed.

The crowd was screaming.
It had happened too fast for Miss Kitchen to follow, but the blood, the blood on the white suit of lights, the capes flapping, the horns digging for the fallen boy, all of it lurched in her, deep inside like sexual excitement, her kind of sexual excitement, and

she grabbed her companion's hand with a man's strength and could feel the small bones grating in the trapped hand.

He looked at her, his eyes angry and then bewildered and finally submissive. She would begin her training of him tonight. He would be a very apt and willing pupil.

She looked down at the arena.

One more pass now, a final veronica to the left, José Carlos knew, would bring the bull back to the waiting lance. He watched the bloodshot eyes and saw again the anticipatory twitch of an ear. Jerking his left wrist he began the slow serene sweep of the rose and gold cape.

A gust of wind took the cloth, snapping it, and he raised his foot, nudging the cape with his toe. The bull came fast and the trailing edge of the cloth fluttered around José Carlos' slipper. As he pulled the stiff collar of the cape toward himself he tripped and fell over backwards.

The bull was on him, trampling. All he could do was fold his arms over his face. That, and feel what was happening to his ribs.

Ricardo Diaz got there first, slapping the hot heaving flank, pulling and twisting the thick tail while the horns gouged sand, seeking José Carlos. Diaz saw blood on the jacket of the white suit of lights, saw Márquez and Buenavista running across the sand, waving their capes.

Shouting, he got both hands on the tail and pulled. Head and horns lifted, turned, and the eyes saw Buenavista's cape. The bull swung toward it, was lured away.

Ricardo Diaz crouched over the white suit of lights. José Carlos was unconscious. Azaña Long Nose helped lift his shoulders. Two monosabios came and grabbed his legs. All four ran with him through the slot of a burladero and along the alleyway to a tunnel that went below the stands to the infirmary.

Francisco Franco was on his feet in the president's box. He raised his cane and touched the shoulder of a man seated to his left at the edge of the box.

"What are you waiting for, man?" Franco said. "The boy's badly hurt."

Franco watched Dr. Caballero hurry from the box. The injured boy was already out of sight in the callejón. Franco grasped both canes. He had to go there too. Ricardo Diaz was his friend. If the boy had to be moved to a hospital he could offer his helicopter.

He summoned Eladio Gómez. "The chair, Eladio."

The canvas and aluminum folding wheelchair was propped against a rail at the back of the box. Franco had not wanted the chair brought to the plaza, but Dr. Caballero had insisted.

Eladio Gómez snapped the frame open and Franco seated himself. "Hurry—the infirmary."

The other Gómez brothers formed around them. Civil

Guards materialized out of nowhere. They went quickly, the chair rolling toward the exit. Everybody was silent, everybody standing as he passed. He saw faces turning, watching him. He did not care. Let them see he was old and infirm, half a cripple. Perhaps it would help him realize it himself.

Seated a few rows from the president's box, Jesús Quintana saw the Civil Guards clearing the way, Eladio Gómez pushing the wheelchair. The sudden call of a trumpet startled him. The bullfight. Of course. The bullfight would go on. The picadors entered the patio de caballos. The banderilleros got their sticks at the fence. Márquez was caping the bull in the center of the arena. The crowd was noisy, talking too much, fending off the nearness of death with their voices.

Jesús Quintana got to his feet. He had not counted on a meeting between the assassin and the victim. Not under these circumstances. Not until later, when all would go as he had ordained.

He walked along the aisle behind the barrera seats, pushing a white-coated ice-cream vendor out of his way. He walked faster. He was almost running.

221

18

◇◇

The harsh glare of lights on the whitewashed walls. The smell of ether. The two doctors, fat Pérez Moreno and the tall thin one from Madrid, Franco's doctor, leaning over the operating table. The gold-embroidered white jacket, stained with blood. The white shirt, cut from José Carlos' body, dripping blood. The wide bands of tape, blood seeping through them. Surgical scissors to cut the tape, black in the brightness with José Carlos' blood. Franco there, out of his chair, behind the doctors. The sounds of the arena, muffled, the muted thunder as Miguel Márquez fought his bull. Voices outside the infirmary door. Antonio Buenavista out there, and the Civil Guards, and the mob with its morbid curiosity. Eladio Gómez's hand heavy on his shoulder, and the sympathy in the man's face. "Hombre, it will go well. You'll see."

The doctors' surgical masks, their hands moving deftly in tight rubber gloves, the small sharp instruments glinting, the bottle of plasma catching the light.

"More ether?" asked the doctor from Madrid.

"No, basta. It is enough."

The mask covering José Carlos' face, the hiss of oxygen. A needle in José Carlos' side, puncturing the flesh, penetrating between the ribs, and from the needle a rubber tube running to a jar under the operating table. Water in the jar, bubbling every time José Carlos breathed.

The quick cut of a scalpel, like tracing a red line on the pale skin. The flesh parted and clamped.

"Here, the bone."

"And here."

A pair of clippers, like wire cutters, a snipping sound, bone coming loose and tossed into a pail.

I wanted him to be a bullfighter, and for three minutes with a cape he held the terror and the joy in his hands. Eighteen years of living for three minutes, because they were the three minutes I wished of him. Did I ever ask him what he wanted?

Standing there helpless in the heavy brocaded jacket, the cold sweat on his body, watching Pérez Moreno and the doctor from Madrid.

He turned away and stared at the wall. He heard the drums and trumpets faintly. Márquez was having himself a day.

He saw the aluminum canes, the uniform of a Captain General, the medals, the small, almost lipless mouth, the large opaque eyes—Franco.

"You remember the hunting lodge in the Gredos, Ricardo?"

The head trembling, as close to death as the body on the table.

"Yes."

Franco was speaking again. He did not hear the words. "What?"

"The boy will like it there. When he is strong enough you must bring him. You can hunt, you and the boy. You'll come? It would give me great pleasure, Don Ricardo."

He said something. He turned back to the table. The voices from the passageway were suddenly louder. "Eladio," someone called. He saw a black patent leather hat in the doorway. Eladio Gómez went there, and outside. The door shut behind him.

"I don't care who you are," Eladio Gómez said. The passageway was jammed. Civil Guards, a few reporters, a priest who had not been summoned and who, God willing, would not be needed. And the populacho, the mob. Always them.

"Is he dead?"

"Will he live?"

"Is the Caudillo really with him?"

A woman's face. That face Eladio Gómez knew. The Duchess of Salvatierra. She was crying.

"You know me, Gómez. Don't be a fool."

He knew the man: Quintana. He worked for the Admiral. Eladio Gómez was not particularly fond of the Admiral. He was not fond of the way the Admiral was waiting for Francisco Franco to die. He did not like Quintana at all. There was something about the man's eyes, the way he looked at you. Even now, when he wanted something, looking at you as if you were a thing, not a human being.

"Yes, I know you."

"I'm going in there."

Eladio Gómez leaned his broad back against the door and stared into those eyes. The man spoke and the eyes tried to reduce Eladio Gómez to an inanimate object, and Gómez listened and watched, patiently shaking his head.

The thought came like a giant hand that grabbed Ricardo Diaz's soul and shook it. He shut his eyes and clenched his fists and felt the cold sweat, and the thought would not go away.

José Carlos on the table. Pérez Moreno and the doctor from Madrid, their backs turned, their shoulders hunched, their heads down. They would see nothing.

He was as good as alone with Franco.

Castillo del Moro was an impossibility. Not that he could not do it. He could do it, and he could die. The dying was of no importance. He had prepared himself for that. But the others. José Carlos, if he lived. To live with the knowledge of what his father had done. And Kate. And Maria Teresa. No, he thought, it is impossible, and the hand shook him again.

He could reach out and touch the scrawny neck. He could touch the medals and the sunken chest. He could—

Jesús Quintana talked, and saw the stubborn peasant face of the bodyguard Eladio Gómez, and knew that nothing he said would change the peasant mind. It really does not matter, he told himself. Franco's unexpected visit to the infirmary had unnerved him. Nothing had changed. Nothing would change. He had only to wait a few hours longer.

—strike with the edge of his hand, behind the blow the strength of the shoulder and the arm that had brought death to three thousand bulls. It would not take much to kill a man as frail as Franco. Even the shock could do it. He would fall. Ricardo Diaz could almost see him falling. He would hit the stone floor hard, and that would certainly kill him. The doctors would turn, hearing it. Only then. Not before. Turn to see Ricardo Diaz kneeling dismayed at the side of the Generalissimo.

"My apologies, Sr. Quintana," said Eladio Gómez. He was warming to the argument, hoping to prolong it. He had never liked the man and liked him less now. Quintana did not answer.

"I'm sure you can understand, señor," Eladio Gómez said. Quintana glared at him.

And if I don't kill him? Will he live another week, a month? For what? He's finished. I owe him nothing. When I needed help he turned his back. No, if I don't kill him, now or later,

227

there is the small matter of the patent leather soul in Málaga, the puntillo in his neck. There is the small matter of Jesús Quintana. How can I not kill him?

⁂

"If all the world wanted to go in there," said Eladio Gómez, "could I permit it? No, señor, you see that I have my responsibility."

⁂

Ricardo Diaz heard the music faintly, the drums and trumpets, the marching rhythm and lilting melody of the paso doble *Gallito.* It was Miguel Márquez's song, played by the banda taurina when Márquez dominated the bull and the mob, as he had done today. He would be fighting what should have been José Carlos' second bull now, the last bull of the afternoon. He would be with ten thousand people, but alone, in communion with a red serge cloth and a blade of Toledo steel, and with his own body he would fend off the death all men face. They would hear *Gallito* today, Little Rooster, but they would not hear the other—no brass band would play *Cielo Andaluz,* the song of Ricardo Diaz, in the lengthening shadows of the plaza this afternoon. Nor ever again. It was foolish, he told himself, to think of that now. But the melody went through his head, and he felt the weight of the sword, and he drew back the red cape, and the hot deadly blackness came rushing at him over golden sand under the blue sky of Andalucía.

Eladio Gómez came into the infirmary. The doctors were still hovering over the table under the bright lights. The bullfighter whose son lay on the table stood close to Franco. Eladio Gómez did not like the way he was looking at him. He was sweating. His eyes were slits. He seemed a man who had awakened from the violence of a nightmare, bringing the violence with him. Eladio Gómez reached for the holster on his hip.

Francisco Franco hoped the boy would live, hoped it so hard he realized he was praying. Well, he thought, if you had to put your faith in a doctor or in God, there really wasn't much choice. He had never liked doctors. He felt something touch his shoulder, hard. He looked up into the face of Ricardo Diaz.

It was lucky, Dr. Caballero thought, that the boy was strong. They had given him dextrose, saline, and a blood-pressure elevator intravenously, and his body had come out of shock quickly so that they had been able to operate. The closed thoractomy system had relieved the pressure on the pleural cavity. The lung had not collapsed. Pérez Moreno had snipped away the splintered rib with a rongeur and was now oversewing the lung. They would leave the tube in place, to remove air and serum from the pleural cavity.

Caballero prepared a pair of needles. He jabbed them into the boy's arm—tetanus toxoid and a broad-spectrum antibiotic.

The boy was young, the ribs would mend. His pulse was slower, heavier, steadier. He was out of danger. In a few weeks, Dr. Caballero knew as he stripped off his surgical gloves, he would be as good as new. He half turned, smiling, to tell the father, but then he heard what the father was saying to Franco.

Eladio Gómez let out his breath. Nerves, he told himself. You're getting too old for this job. He heard the doctor, the fat local one he did not know, telling Ricardo Diaz that his son would live. He saw Diaz go to the table slowly and look down at the boy, then walk across the hard stone floor, tall in his blue suit of lights. Diaz opened the door but before he could go out Jesús Quintana came in. This time Eladio Gómez did not object.

Dr. Caballero reached Quintana just as the bullfighter left. The doctor heard voices in the passageway. He heard Diaz say the boy would be all right. He felt his heart pounding. Quintana looked at him and through him. He grabbed Quintana's arm and said:

"Franco knows."

Quintana's eyes focused on him.

"Tonight. He knows. Diaz told him."

Dr. Caballero went into the passageway. He wondered what would happen to himself, to the others. In his mind he tried to make excuses. They had committed themselves to nothing, after all. It had all been Quintana. They had committed no acts against the Chief of State. They had allowed Quintana to dominate them, and if necessary they would turn on Quintana. To be calm, thought Dr. Caballero, to be calm was everything. Inform the others, await developments. . . .

He hurried along the passageway. It was deserted. Above, muffled by the thick walls, he heard a roaring sound.

Miss Kitchen was on her feet, waiting while the crowd headed for the exits. She saw a figure in blue running across the sand. Soon he stood below the president's box.

A voice squawked over the public-address system, and her companion said: "The boy's going to live."

"What's his father doing down there?"

"I'm not sure."

The roaring began near the president's box.

"He wants to buy the substitute bull?" Don Alfonso asked El Cordobés.

"He wants to fight it," El Cordobés said, grinning.

231

"And I'm to grant permission?"

"You don't have any choice. The crowd will take the arena apart if you don't."

At first the crowd pushed and shoved, trying to regain their seats. And then they sat anywhere. With one voice now they roared.

Ricardo Diaz got his fighting cape. Across the barrier Antonio Buenavista looked at him. "You sure you know what the hell you're doing?"

"Now I do."

Ricardo Diaz ran across the sand toward the Gate of Fear. The trumpet sounded, the gate swung back. Diaz dropped to his knees, spreading the cape, waiting for the bull of Miura.

19

◇◇

Ai! Paco Oliva could shout no
more with the wonder of it, the hoarse olés all ripped from his
throat. And now, now as the glinting blue and the red and the
black, the man, the cape and the bull, prepared for the final
death dance on golden sand, an enormous surge of joy
wrenched him, lifted him outside himself. He was Paco Oliva
no longer but at once the demigod in the plaza, Ricardo Diaz,
and everyone, ten thousand throats screamed raw, ten thousand
men and women standing on the stone benches under the high
blue sky of Andalucía, ten thousand souls shriven of meanness
and torment and terror, ten thousand witnesses to a miracle.

That he should see it, now, just two days after he had been
close enough to Ricardo Diaz to touch him. Ai! that he should

be privileged to see it all. Ricardo Diaz on his knees with the cape spread, waiting, and the Miura rushing like a locomotive from the Gate of Fear. The cape rising and swirling, and three-quarters of a ton of bull steaming by, jerking the crowd to its feet, where it stayed. No one else on the broad expanse of sand. Even canny old Antonio Buenavista watching from behind the planks, the proud wonder on his face. Then Diaz bringing the hot galloping blackness past him, three times, four, five, slowly with the veronica in a dream where pain and wretchedness are gone and ai! the world is beautiful. And the trumpet, lost in the gigantic smile of the arena, to bring the horses. One horse and rider caught and raised and hurled by the Miura like a sack over the barrier. The second horse down, the rider down, scrabbling on the sand in his heavy leg armor, Ricardo Diaz drawing the bull away with the floating rose and gold, away and out to the center of the ring and back, still floating back to where the horseman had remounted, pale. The Miura accepting the lance once, and well, and the horseman finding honor too, Ricardo Diaz's honor, withdrawing the lance when Diaz lifted his hat to the president. Diaz going to the fence for banderillas, to place them himself, then waiting, citing the bull, going up on his toes with the barbed sticks high. That was when the music began, the music of Ricardo Diaz, but you could hardly hear it in the thunder of the plaza. Diaz on his toes, body thrust arrogantly forward, the Miura coming fast and deadly, the man unmoving, and then his right leg going out, the bull following the lure of it as the man's body swung to the left and the sticks rose. A horn ripping gold from the right leg and the sticks plunging like twins into the black withers, together, high and perfect. Diaz doing it a second time, the same way, the dangerous way, citing and awaiting the bull with the sticks and ai! it was not perfect the first time, it had only seemed perfect.

Then the bull galloping around the plaza, the sticks clattering bright in the sunlight, dim in shadow, while Ricardo Diaz presented himself below the president's box asking permission of the authorities to kill. And Diaz with sword and red killing cape, passing the Miura once two-handed, feet unmoving, with the pass of death, the Miura going by high and hard, great horns and forelegs lifting, huge back swept by the red serge. And man and bull whirling at once with their equal pride to confront each other again.

Ai! that he should have seen the rest of it, living through it like living a life in fifteen minutes. The pase natural of Ricardo Diaz, sword in right hand, killing cape barely unfurled in left hand, legs planted, body turning ninety degrees to receive and slow the charge of the noble bull of Don Eduardo Miura. Ten times, twelve? Who could count? The man making his fluid quarter turns and the bull coming and stopping, and finally the blue and gold figure wrapping the blackness around itself like a cloak, sword high in the right hand in the cleansed air, and a recorte to finish the swirling sequence of it, the bull fixed in place so that Ricardo Diaz can go to him and stroke the muzzle between the monster horns, one single adornment to show the fated closeness between the blackness of death and the mystery of living. And ai! while the standing clamorous plaza awaits the killing, he does it all again, linking the naturales in a slow tight dangerous circle around his body, stretching time and then halting it in an instant that is forever.

Ai! Paco Oliva, what an uncle, what a lucky uncle you have been to see it.

The muleta dangled from its notched stick beside Ricardo Diaz's leg. He prodded the cloth with the point of his sword and watched the bull watching him. He knew he could go again between the horns to stroke the black muzzle, knew he could line up the Miura for the killing. Instead he turned his back and gazed up from the center of the ring at the crowd. They stood, silent now, the valor of beast and man their valor, the darkness conquered for them. Now they loved him. Now. He brushed the cynical thought away. Whether they loved him or hated him, finally, did not matter. He had given them the dangerous left-handed passes as a gift, but the giving did not mean a taking away. It had been for himself too.

Nor could he stop now. He held eternity in his hand like wine in a silver chalice. He wanted the sky and the sand and the bull of Miura a little while longer.

He turned, the sun down behind the rim of the plaza now, the sand in shadow, and faced the bull in the waiting silence. He felt a faint smile on his lips as he brought the red serge cape behind him, sword and a corner of the cloth in his right hand at the small of his back, notched stick in his extended left hand, spreading the serge behind and to the left of his body. He looked at the bloodshot eyes of the bull. He looked at the wide-spaced, upward-curving horns, pointed needle-sharp, and back to the eyes. He heard the plaza stirring.

He stood, ready with the manoletina, the pass of Manolete, who died in the bullring of the dirty industrial town of Linares, destroyed by the horns of a bull of Miura when Ricardo Diaz was a boy. The requirement of the pass, the part they faked if they did it at all these days, was that you did not look at the bull. Not once, after you started. You stared straight ahead as the bull came rushing by and you felt the closeness and of course you could see something of the black bulk, but you did not look at it. And as the bull went by under the muleta you did a half-circle pivot to face, still without looking, where he had gone. Then you made a flicking motion with your left hand,

236

and he came past again, and you turned again ready with the cape to lure him.

Ricardo Diaz moved his left wrist up and then down, half an inch, to flick the corner of the cape. He saw the crowd far away and was aware of the blackness erupting at him, and the black came and went as he raised the serge, spinning, ready for the bull to come past in the other direction, and the bull did, the darkness flowing under the lifted cape, the man turning, the darkness coming at him again in a sudden bursting explosion of sound from the plaza while he spun and was ready for the bull once more.

Antonio Buenavista stood behind the planks of a burladero with his fighting cape folded over one arm, watching the black and the gold-shot blue drawn together by the swinging red. He spread his fighting cape and held it ready.

"Crazy bastard," he said, but he felt a wild elation.

Miguel Márquez stood next to him, cape ready too. His face was drawn and pale. "He's not faking it."

"My God, no. He doesn't see that bicho. He doesn't see anything now."

They did not take their eyes off the man and the bull. They stood on the balls of their feet, prepared to rush across the sand. Both knew it would do no good. Ricardo Diaz was too far away. He had led the Miura out to the medios, the center of the arena.

"How long can he keep it up?" Márquez asked anxiously.

"Maybe they'll blow the trumpet on him."

The trumpet would warn Ricardo Diaz that he had taken

too much time with the bull. A fighting bull learns swiftly. In twenty minutes he will, inevitably, shift his charges from the elusive cape to the man.

Márquez gestured. "Not today they won't. Look at Manolo."

Buenavista raised his eyes quickly to the president's box. El Cordobés was on his feet shouting.

Buenavista felt the killing fear that Ricardo Diaz did not feel. He saw the man pivoting away from the bull's charge, saw the bull turn like a cat and come back to the cape. Suddenly the fear went away. He felt the immortality of Ricardo Diaz and himself.

"Almost thirty years," he said. "I fought them almost thirty years. I'd give all of it to do what he's doing now. Goddamn crazy bastard." Buenavista's eyes were stinging.

He had lost count of the linked passes. He heard the abrupt pounding drum of hooves on sand, and he lifted the cape over horns and crested neck and withers and long back of the blackness he no longer saw, and he turned and heard the hooves again. He moved not in the safety of his own terrain and not in the danger of the bull's. They were joined. They came together and apart in the hypnotic rhythm of it, both unable to stop. Sometimes he felt the shafts of the banderillas whacking his chest as the bull went by. Sometimes he felt the flat of a horn hit him like a club. He thought his mouth was open. He thought his eyes were shut. He did not hear the thunder of the plaza. He was the bull. The bull was Ricardo Diaz. A long time had passed. No time had passed. Time stopped. The bull would live forever, and so would he. There was no wife he had driven to her death, and no son killed at University City in Madrid, and no Civil Guard murdered in the rain in Málaga, and no illness for Francisco Franco who would remain young always, and no Jesús Quintana who led him through one death, like caping the bull, to prepare him for another. The rhythmic lift and swing of the cape took those things away. The bull took them, and they never had been and never would be. The bull gave him the future. The bull gave him José Carlos, who would live a better life than his father had. The bull gave him Maria Teresa, her quick intelligence turned to wisdom. The bull gave him Kate, and Alpine bells he would never hear.

He took the bull one final time with the cape like that behind his back, seeing nothing, seeing everything, and then he dropped on one knee, arms at his side, cape on the sand, sword on the sand, the pride on his face. He could see the Miura now. He could see the horns, three feet away. The bull stared back at him. Man and bull remained motionless.

Then Ricardo Diaz stood, and turned his back. With the cape trailing from its stick and the sword under his arm he walked across the sand.

Kate could breathe again. She had always felt the terror, and never let him know. But she had never felt it like this, the terror mingled with an odd and more terrible joy that left her mouth dry and her body limp and her fingernails clawing at the embroidery of his dress cape on the railing. Richard said something, and Elizabeth. She did not hear the words. Richard was smiling. Elizabeth leaned out over the railing, watching Ricardo Diaz exchange his sword at the barrier. He passed

239

below them. Kate thought he would look up. He did not. With his sword he went back to where the bull waited.

※

Ten paces, and then five. He stopped. He looked at the Miura. Unfurling the cape, he held it across his chest and lowered it slowly. The eyes went down, following the cloth. He raised it. The eyes lifted. A slight wind ruffled the red serge. Toro, he said gently. An ear quivered. Toro, he called softly. No sound came from the plaza.

Well, he thought, it is Sunday. It is the Sunday planned for you by Jesús Quintana. It is the Sunday of a perfect bull of Miura. What can Quintana do, against a perfect bull of Miura?

※

Jesús Quintana sat in a speeding black Renault taxi. There was almost no traffic on the coast road. Puerto Real lay behind them, Torremolinos ahead and the Málaga airport. He had money, and a false passport. He always carried it and he would use it now. He could not doubt Dr. Caballero. If Caballero, with his face like that, had said Franco knew, then Franco knew. So, it was finished. Either they would let him board the plane or they would arrest him. Either he would escape to France or he would not. He had a life waiting for him in France, should they let him leave. He had always been a careful man.

And how had Franco learned? The unforeseen accident of a boy trampled by a bull, the operating table under the harsh lights in the infirmary, the boy's father there, Franco there, and that peasant of an Eladio Gómez barring the door. And Diaz, for reasons Quintana would never know, talking.

He could do nothing about the peasant Gómez. He felt the envelope in his breast pocket. He removed the envelope and a ballpoint pen and addressed the envelope to Eduardo Santo Domingo at his office in Madrid. If the police were waiting for him, he would give them the envelope. Otherwise he would mail it at the airport.

He felt the aching in his chest now, where the sticks and the horns had hit him. He felt the hardness of steel under the felt-wrapped sword hilt. Through the thin soles of his slippers he felt the coarse uneven texture of the sand, where the bull had galloped. He saw the Miura, not five paces away, hating, saw the bright ribbon of blood, congealed now, on the black flank. He saw the four sticks, still in place, shafts decorated with puffed sleeves of green and red paper. He saw the horns, thick and black and tapering to dirty yellow and white. Dangling from the bull's right side the sticks would be a problem. When he put the sword in he would have to go around the right horn.

Again he tested the Miura by letting the furled cape drop from the stick. The eyes followed it. The forelegs were planted six inches apart and parallel. He had only to profile himself to the bull, to sight over his left shoulder and along his left arm with the sword, to rise on his toes, sword in right hand over right shoulder, and drive forward, seeking the small opening between the bull's shoulder blades, the killing place where the sword would enter to sever the aorta. For an instant, driving

241

the sword in, he would hang over and between the horns, swinging the red serge low from left to right to guide massive head and horns down and past him.

That was one way, he thought. To control the action, to bring death to the bull. But you could do it another way, with a perfect bull of Miura. You could let the bull come for the death himself. Like the pass of the manoletina, no one did it these days. Receiving the bull you surrendered domination to him and let him control the final act of his life. Once the great muscles tensed and the hooves pounded, there was no changing any of it.

Ricardo Diaz smiled. He had been wrong all along. This would not be the final bull of his life. He was still young. He could almost see the posters, in all the towns of Spain, his name on them and José Carlos'—four bulls of Miura or Pablo Romero or Conde de la Corte, to be fought mano a mano by the matadors Ricardo Diaz and José Carlos Diaz. He felt it with an absolute certainty and in the moment of feeling it, of believing it, he was himself shriven, as he had shriven the crowd in the plaza, and he was immortal.

He let a fold of the red serge drop. He profiled his body to the bull. He raised the sword. What remained was to move his left wrist to make the cape move and summon the bull to his death.

Antonio Buenavista saw what had gone wrong a split second before Miguel Márquez did. He was out from behind the burladero and running toward the center of the ring. He heard

Márquez pounding across the sand behind him. The younger bullfighter overtook him and passed him. Then Buenavista, his vision blocked by the green suit of lights, heard a single hoarse scream from ten thousand throats.

The moment of certainty extended for Ricardo Diaz. Time became not an inevitable passage of events no man could alter, but something physical. Time was the sword in his right hand, and the bull tensing to charge, and the packed benches of the plaza, and the blue sky of Andalucía, and the sea beyond, and the mountains and plains and olive groves and red earth and whitewashed towns of Spain, and the soul of the land, his land and his soul, now and always in the immortality of that moment as he jerked his wrist and heard the flutter of the serge as the blackness came at him.

He swung the cloth from left to right and let the bull take the sword. It went in with a grating, ripping sound but smoothly. He leaned over it, and over the horns. The sword blade became smaller and smaller, and then the hilt and his knuckles punched the coarse hide as he hung there, prolonging the moment, before turning on his left leg to get out past the right horn. He felt the wind. He felt the cloth flapping back against his thigh and saw that, knew that, the great head was swinging back and up, following the lure even while the Miura was dying.

Father Joaquín, standing on a bench in the third row over the Gate of Fear, felt the wind. It sprang up suddenly just as the bull charged. Father Joaquín began to pray. He saw how Ricardo Diaz hung suspended over the horns even after the sword had disappeared to the hilt. Later, Father Joaquín would tell himself, it was the wind. It had nothing to do with hanging over the horns or with what Ricardo Diaz had requested of him that morning. It had to be the wind, only that.

His feet left the sand. He was up and swinging on a horn and he did not feel it. But he felt time moving again, moving and going. He clutched with both hands for the base of the horn, but there was no horn there. The horn was in him. Then he was off the horn and floating up and then slowly down and he saw Márquez and Buenavista running and as he came down he saw the blackness and the horns waiting, the right horn red with his blood, and he saw very quickly Kate and Maria Teresa and José Carlos, and for an instant Jesús Quintana, and finally only the blackness of the perfect bull of Miura which became the whole world before it too was gone.

20

◇◇

At seven-thirty on a Wednesday evening in late July Eduardo Santo Domingo sat at his desk in the big corner office of the Ministry of Internal Affairs.

It had been a long day and a hot one. His shoulders were stiff, his eyes gritty. He rubbed a hand over his face and shaven skull. He heard the smaller offices of the General Directorate of Security emptying—a door slamming, footsteps in the corridor, conversation and laughter fading toward the exit of the suite of offices.

His staff would scatter along the Gran Via and the narrow side streets, joining the throngs of Madrileños for a cold beer or an orange juice and sherry at the city's bars. Santo Domingo wished he could linger over a tall glass of barril himself, but he had work to do. Ever since the events in Puerto Real two months ago he'd been putting in twelve-hour days, not even allowing himself a couple of hours of siesta in what had been the hottest summer in years.

Santo Domingo had cleared his desk of all but three items. He sat staring at them, then got up and opened the wall safe. Removing an envelope, he placed it on the walnut desk along with the magazine, the dossier on a Frenchman named Honoré Dubois, and the typewritten list of names and brief curricula vitae. He picked up the sheet of paper containing the list of names and scanned it. This was the seventh list in seven weeks. He stared at the last name on it. It had to happen sooner or later, of course. He had been waiting for it to happen. He read:

> Ruiz López, Heriberto. b. Salamanca, 1937. Married. Two children. Doctor of Laws, University of Salamanca, 1964. Employment: Ministry of Foreign Affairs, French desk, 1965–9; Ministry of Internal Affairs, Directorate of Security, 1969–

The letter "Z" ended the summary of Ruiz López, Heriberto's, career. An "X" would have meant that his name had appeared on the coded list found in Jesús Quintana's office on the Castillana. The "Z" indicated that Ruiz López had been informed on by another of Quintana's agents.

Santo Domingo remembered his conversation with Quintana in May, and Quintana's unsubtle attempt to plant a man in his office. The rosebud of a mouth smiled reluctantly. Unsubtle, my ass, thought Santo Domingo. He already had a man in here, and the attempt was meant to put me off my guard. But who the hell would have thought it was Ruiz? Ruiz was one of his bright young men, really going places in the Directorate. Better make that past tense, Santo Domingo amended sourly.

He lit a cigar and looked through the dossier on the Frenchman Honoré Dubois. Dubois was forty-two years old and had been born in Angoulême in southwestern France. Parents, deceased. No known family. Source of capital, unknown. Investments in real estate in the Charente Maritime. Part owner Hotel Splendide, La Rochelle, Hotel de la Paix, Royan. Stock market activity, Paris Bourse, 200,000 francs per month. Domicile, Avenue Georges Clemenceau, La Rochelle.

So much for Honoré Dubois, Frenchman for two months.

Santo Domingo picked up the magazine. It was the latest issue of the bullfight journal *El Ruedo*. He turned to the account of last Sunday's fight at Las Ventas in Madrid, and read that José Carlos Diaz had confirmed his alternativa in the capital, receiving the doctorate from Miguel Márquez. Young Diaz had fought two bulls of the Hermanos Núñez and had been awarded an ear for each one. His style was cool and confident, particularly in the suerte of the muleta. A third ear had been petitioned by the afición and denied by the authorities, but the day had been a triumph. The afición rose as one man to their feet, the article concluded somewhat hyperbolically, aware that they had witnessed an awesome spectacle, the reappearance in the body of his son of the deceased matador de toros Ricardo Diaz, destroyed by a bull of Miura at the festival in Puerto Real.

As if weighing them, Santo Domingo held the magazine in his right hand and the dossier on the Frenchman Honoré Dubois in his left. Then he tossed both on the desk and dialed his telephone.

The woman's voice was cool and confident, but it contained a note of surprise too, as if she still found it hard to believe where she was or what she was doing there.

"Dígame, who's calling, please?"

"Santo Domingo, Your Grace." He used the title in an intentional offhand manner, as if he couldn't believe it either. They'd spoken frequently on the phone lately and seen each other once or twice. She was damn good at her job, Santo Domingo had to admit. At first it surprised him, and then it pleased him. Franco needed an appointments secretary who could say no without insulting you, and she could do it.

"Still chasing down subversives at this hour?" she asked. "Why don't you go home?"

"I want to see him."

"Let me see—I think I could squeeze you in two weeks from next Monday."

"Very funny. I have to see him tonight."

"You know he doesn't work that kind of hours, Don Eduardo."

"Tonight he'd better."

"I have a little book. If they say it's important and it's not, they find it a little more difficult to see him the next time."

"I'll take my chances, Your Grace."

It was banter, mostly, but the threat was there. Santo Domingo accepted it, even admired her for it. He paid little attention to the talk around Madrid. The talk had it that if you wanted an audience with the Caudillo these days you had to be a Basque separatist, an anarchist from the Asturias, or at least a member of Opus Dei.

"Come right out then, Don Eduardo."

Her office had been one of the small family salons on the second floor of the palace. Its tall windows looked out over the manicured gardens toward the woods, where small game could still be hunted. Its walls were covered with Goya tapestries from the old Santa Barbara works. Everything was eighteenth-century except for the console telephone, the steel and linoleum desk, and the dark, attractive woman who sat behind it.

"Doña Maria Teresa," Santo Domingo said, crossing the room and bowing over her hand.

"That's not necessary any more," Maria Teresa said. "We're all really anarchists here."

Santo Domingo smiled.

"Some people do get that impression, you know. You won't believe this, but it's not my idea."

"What isn't?"

"The types who come in here these days. Cigarette? He'll be a few minutes. He wants to learn about the other side, he says. He finds their ideas—*some* of their ideas would be more accurate—refreshing. By the way, there's a refreshing appointment coming up tomorrow. A new director for the office of censorship, somewhat less of a Neanderthal than the usual occupant."

"Really? Who?"

"Vega."

"The Rector of the University? Amazing. He's a . . ." Santo Domingo groped for a word.

"Liberal? Well, almost. I gather his job will be to phase out the office."

"Your idea, no doubt?"

"Prince Juan Carlos' more than mine. Not that I resisted strenuously."

"Funny," said Santo Domingo, "you don't look like an éminence grise."

"Give me a few more months at this job and I'll be gray anyway." A light blinked on the telephone console. "He's ready for you."

"I'm not sure about your politics," Santo Domingo said, rising, "but I can tell you this much—you're better looking than the last guy who held down that desk."

Maria Teresa's smile was an automatic response to the compliment. It did not dispel the sadness in her eyes.

Franco wheeled back and forth across the large sitting room while they talked. He couldn't keep still. He tilted his jaw this way and that, gestured expansively with his arms, rolled to the window and looked out at the fading light, turned abruptly to catch and hold Santo Domingo's gaze.

How long could it go on? Santo Domingo didn't know. Franco was sick, certainly. More than sick. If he lived out this year and next it would be a miracle. He must have known that himself, the way he tried to crowd everything in to prepare for the changes he would bequeath to Juan Carlos, heir to the vacant throne of Spain. Santo Domingo hoped the miracle would come to pass. There was a feeling of expectancy in Madrid, as if Franco's political experimentation was contagious.

"Quintana has a man in my shop," Santo Domingo said. "At least one that I know of. There could be others."

"Bring me up to date, please." That was another thing about Franco these days. He didn't go in for Spanish circumlocution. He had no time for it. He got right to the point.

Santo Domingo reviewed the situation briefly. Quintana's "X" list had resulted in interrogations that ferreted out the other top-level members of the conspiracy. Of the six men involved, only Dr. Caballero had proven cooperative. He had,

250

when called in by Santo Domingo, confirmed the identity of the others.

The others had denied any knowledge of the plot. And it seemed likely that the Admiral, at least, had not been involved. Proving any of it would have been difficult in any case, even if anyone had been disposed to take such a step.

An airing of the whole business, or even a court-martial behind closed doors, was impossible. The plotters knew that and so did Santo Domingo. When the Caudillo might die at any time you do not proceed against his personal physician, the Deputy Chief of Staff of the Army, the Civil Guard Commandant, and the commanding general of the military district of Madrid. Only a fool would jeopardize the smooth transition of power by making public scandal and outrage inevitable.

Franco had understood that too at a previous meeting with the Director of Security. "Don't move against them," he had said.

"No, it wouldn't be easy. We don't have conclusive proof, Excellency."

"It's not a question of proof. The body politic is like a human being. Too much shock can kill it."

Santo Domingo had relaxed, relieved that Franco saw eye to eye with him on the impossibility of a trial.

"They could be allowed to retire," Franco said now. "Full of honors, naturally. Would that be a reasonable solution?"

Santo Domingo considered for a moment. "They'll go quietly. All but Quintana. Quintana worries me."

"Because he's disappeared?"

"Oh, we know where he is. He flew from Málaga to Paris. He spent a few weeks at the Hotel Lutetia, saw some people, manufactured a new identity. When he left Paris he was a Frenchman named Honoré Dubois. He speaks French like a

251

native, you know. As Honoré Dubois he went to the city of La Rochelle in southwestern France."

"Why does he worry you?"

"He has agents in every Ministry in Madrid, Excellency. It will take months to uncover them, and there's no guarantee we'll get them all."

The possibility of a coup d'etat during the period of succession, Santo Domingo warned, still existed. It was not likely to succeed, of that Santo Domingo was reasonably certain. But that didn't mean Quintana would not attempt it, and the attempt could divide the government into warring factions at the worst possible time.

Franco asked: "Would Paris comply with a request to extradite him?"

"I'm sure they would," Santo Domingo said, and then paused. "But that would put us exactly where we don't want to be—faced with a public trial."

Franco turned from the window and rolled toward him, the wheelchair leaving tracks in the high pile of the carpet. "Then you suggest?"

Santo Domingo did not meet his eyes. "I suggest nothing, Excellency."

"I trust your judgment, Eduardo," Franco said slowly. "Do what has to be done."

Eduardo Santo Domingo sat in the living room of his apartment on Ortega y Gasset. Night had fallen, and he heard muted traffic sounds above the hum of the air conditioner. He was hungry. He ought to go over to Serrano for something to eat.

He was sipping cognac and soda, his second. The ice had melted. He put the drink down and went to the window and looked out at Madrid. He sat again and rubbed his shaven skull. He knew what had to be done. He knew how it had to be done, and hated it.

The Public Order Police could do it. Santo Domingo had three men in La Rochelle watching the man called Honoré Dubois. But Santo Domingo did not want to use them. It would be a mistake to turn the Public Order Police into political assassins. Spain had seen enough of that during the Civil War.

The alternative that Santo Domingo had considered was a paid professional, a foreigner if possible. That could be arranged, but it would take time. Santo Domingo had waited too long. Besides, he could not make the necessary arrangements alone, and any member of his staff was suspect.

Quintana had driven him to another alternative. In a way Quintana was still pulling the strings.

Santo Domingo brought his glass into the kitchen. Then he went out to find a public telephone.

21

◇◇◇

The bullfighter sat at a table outside the Café au Vieux Port in La Rochelle, nursing his third pastis. The yellow anise-flavored drink was cloying, almost sickly sweet, but it was what most of the other patrons seated at the crowded metal tables on the sidewalk outside the café had ordered. The Ricard brand seemed most popular, and he had asked for that in a thick American accent. If anyone at the café remembered him, afterwards, they would recall a tall blond American who pronounced the two "r"s of Ricard not in his throat like a Frenchman and not trilling them with his tongue like a Spaniard but with his lips. The French were critical of how you spoke their language.

The sun had gone down over the Atlantic, but the evening

was hot and the vacationing Frenchmen here in this southwestern port city five hours' driving time from the Spanish border lingered over their drinks. Soon they would think about dinner, at Les Flots perhaps. The bullfighter could see the lights of Les Flots at one side of the Old Port. He could see the two floodlit towers that guarded the entrance to the port, the Lantern Tower and the St.-Nicolas. He could see that the tide was out. If he walked to the end of the quay past the restaurant Les Flots he would reach a staircase that descended to the beach. The beach would be wide now, its sand as hard-packed as that of a bullring. Some time between nine-thirty and ten Jesús Quintana would leave the restaurant and walk along the quay and down the stone stairway to the beach. There were lights along the beach for the first few hundred yards, and then no lights. There was no moon. Later the tide would flow and cover the beach.

Heavy in the breast pocket of the bullfighter's seersucker jacket was a fisherman's knife. It had a slit for scaling fish and the blade was broad and short, almost like the blade of a puntillo. He had bought it four days ago when he crossed the border at Hendaye.

The bullfighter watched the patrons of the café leave. They were middle-class Frenchmen on their Grandes Vacances, deserting the hot inland cities for the month of August and flocking to the seaside resorts. La Rochelle was no Deauville or Cannes, but with its arcaded streets and medieval clock gate and the two guardian towers of the Old Port, it had charm. Not too many years ago there had been an American army base nearby. The base facilities had been returned to the French, but the bullfighter would not be remembered, if he was remembered at all, as the only American in La Rochelle that night. Others came to revisit the place where they had served their country. The bullfighter had seen them in the streets and restaurants of

La Rochelle, mutilating the French language as he had mutilated it when it had been necessary to speak.

The bullfighter thought of death. The Sunday before last he had killed two bulls at Las Ventas in Madrid. He had felt it then, as his father had always hoped he would. He had felt the terror and the joy, and had conveyed that feeling to the packed benches of Las Ventas in Madrid, as if with cape and sword he could shrive fifteen thousand Madrileños. It had been a good feeling, and he knew there would be other bulls in his life. With luck there might be twenty years of bulls, three thousand bulls to receive death at his hands. His father had killed three thousand bulls in all the plazas of Spain.

There was little terror and no joy in the thought of death now. It was something he had to do. He had to execute a man with the broad-bladed fisherman's knife that was so like a puntillo.

A bull is power and thundering blackness, and you trained him to accept the death. A man is many things. A man could not be trained to accept death, unless it can be said that all the days of his life train him to accept it when it comes.

The bullfighter called for his check. He paid, watching the look of condescension on the waiter's face while he fumbled with the unfamiliar banknotes. The waiter had a narrow face and a white jacket and he was completely indifferent to the bullfighter, except for his amusement at the way the bullfighter spoke French. The bullfighter left a few small coins on the table and got up.

"Bonsoir, monsieur, merci," said the waiter.

"Bonsoir," said the bullfighter in his American accent.

He crossed the street and walked along the edge of the yacht basin. It was dark now. He could smell the sea in the still night air. He could feel the weight of the fisherman's knife.

The telephone call had surprised him. He knew the caller,

of course. He had met him at Kate Cameron's villa the night of the masquerade party. The man who killed your father, the caller said, is living in France, in the city of La Rochelle. What are you talking about? the bullfighter had asked. A bull of Miura killed my father. Perhaps, the caller had said. But perhaps the man made it necessary for your father to die on the horns of a bull. You're talking crazy, the bullfighter had said, and then he heard the question: Does the name Quintana mean anything to you? He immediately remembered the night at the Civil Guard station, and asking his father about Quintana afterwards. The one who works for the Admiral? he had asked the caller, and the answer was affirmative.

Then the bullfighter had listened. The story sounded, if not probable, at least possible. His caller said, I think I can convince you. He had driven to Madrid the next day, and Eduardo Santo Domingo showed him the photograph. There was no question of possibility or even probability about the photograph. The photograph showed his father killing a man. The bullfighter just looked at it. He said nothing and for a while he heard nothing. Then he heard Eduardo Santo Domingo telling him the man was the Civil Guard who had shot his brother at University City in Madrid, and that Quintana had delivered the Civil Guard to Ricardo Diaz so that Diaz would do another killing for him later. The bullfighter asked if his father had done it. Santo Domingo said no, he had not. Santo Domingo would not go into details, except to say that Ricardo Diaz had allowed the bull of Miura to kill him because he could not do what Quintana wanted him to do and could not not do it. Believe me, Santo Domingo said, Quintana is a murderer. Circumstances and the bull were his weapons, your father the victim.

The bullfighter had asked Antonio Buenavista about the final moments of his father's life. Buenavista hadn't wanted to talk about it. But, yes, he admitted finally, Ricardo Diaz had hung over the horns too long. And then there was the wind. You could never predict the wind.

Next the bullfighter asked the impresario of the Puerto Real bullring if he might see the film of his father's last bullfight. It was an understandable if unexpected request, and the impresario complied. The bullfighter studied the film. He asked that the killing be run three times, and once or twice he asked the projectionist to stop the action. Then he met Eduardo Santo Domingo again.

He did not know why Santo Domingo wanted Quintana dead, or why Santo Domingo chose him as the instrument of that death. All he could think about was the night at the Civil Guard station, and the words Quintana had spoken to his father. *After Sunday you may not have the time to do anything but run.* That, and the film of the bullfight. His father had gone in over the horns and stayed over the horns. Only then had the wind come.

Santo Domingo supplied a car and a passport. The car was a Dodge Dart rented from the ATESA office on Avenida José Antonio in Madrid. It was rented in an American name, the name on the American passport supplied by Santo Domingo.

The bullfighter drove north and spent the first night in Hendaye, buying the knife there. Even then he wasn't sure he would go through with it. It still had seemed, when he reached La Rochelle and checked into the Hotel Tour de Nesle, the rehearsal of an act he would never perform.

He drove to the Avenue Georges Clemenceau and saw Quintana's house. On the second night he saw Quintana himself. Quintana drove into the Old City and parked near the clock gate and dined at Les Flots. Soon his evening activities became predictable. He would eat at Les Flots and, sometime between nine-thirty and ten, walk along the quay to the stairs and then along the beach.

259

You'll recognize him? Santo Domingo had asked, showing the bullfighter a photograph of Jesús Quintana. He was a man about his father's age with dark hair grown down over his collar, a trimmed mustache and those chilling eyes that even in a glossy black and white photograph seemed to stare right through you. He looked rather French. I'll recognize him, he had told Santo Domingo. I'll recognize him, he thought now.

The bullfighter walked past the yacht basin and over the broad paving stones of the quay. He waited in a doorway near the restaurant. That was safe enough, anything was safe enough with the American passport. The quay was almost deserted, the French vacationers lingering over their coffee and cognac. He had rehearsed the killing several times, following Quintana to the head of the stairs that led down the beach. It took Quintana two minutes to reach the end of the quay and three minutes to cover the lighted area of the beach. Fifteen minutes later he would return to the quay.

Now the bullfighter saw him come out past the sidewalk diners in front of the restaurant. He was alone. He was always alone. He preferred his own company to the company of others. One final time the bullfighter wondered why Santo Domingo wanted him killed. He realized he did not care.

He gave Quintana a minute's headstart. Quintana had then covered half the length of the quay. The bullfighter followed him. Arms around one another's waists, a pair of lovers came by, looking neither at Quintana nor the bullfighter. Quintana had reached the stairs. He was going down.

The bullfighter waited at the top of the stairs. He could see Quintana strolling along the lighted section of the beach, close to the water.

There would be many bulls in his life and if he killed well he would take his turn of the ring, proudly smiling the smile

260

of his father and holding high the severed ear of the bull. Killing was a simple matter.

Still he waited. This was not the same.

Then he saw the film, his father hanging between the horns, waiting, waiting too long, and then he saw how the cape was lifted by the wind.

He went down the stairs quickly. If he hurried he would overtake Quintana before Quintana reached the darkness. He wanted Quintana to see him.

He removed the fisherman's knife from his pocket.

He walked quickly. He broke into a trot. The beach was deserted. He could feel the hard-packed sand underfoot.

He was very close when Quintana reached the darkness. He hoped Quintana would recognize him. It was very important that Quintana recognize him.

He stood, both feet unmoving on the sand. For a moment he could not do it.

He saw the film again, his father hanging over the horns.

He called softly: "Quintana," and Jesús Quintana turned.

"You know who I am?" the bullfighter asked.

A second passed, and another.

"Matador," said Jesús Quintana. His right hand darted quickly for his pocket.

The bullfighter let him draw the revolver, a small blackness in his hand. Then with the fisherman's knife so like a puntillo he brought the death to Jesús Quintana.